Five Days Lost

A Mylas Grey Mystery

a novel by

LUANA EHRLICH

Copyright © 2022 Luana Ehrlich

All rights reserved.

This book is a work of fiction. Names, characters, places, and incidents either are products of the author's imagination or are used fictitiously. Any resemblance to actual persons, living or dead, events, or locales is entirely coincidental.

Scripture quotations are from The Holy Bible, English Standard Version (ESV®), copyright © 2001 by Crossway, a publishing ministry of Good News Publishers. Used by permission. All rights reserved.

Visit the author's website at www.luanaehrlich.com

ISBN: 9798355370152

To James Ehrlich,
the most mysterious man I know
and the love of my life.

List of Books
by Luana Ehrlich

The Titus Ray Thriller Series:

One Step Back, the prequel to *One Night in Tehran*
One Night in Tehran, Book I
Two Days in Caracas, Book II
Three Weeks in Washington, Book III
Four Months in Cuba, Book IV
Five Years in Yemen, Book V
Two Steps Forward, Book VI
Three Steps Away, Book VII
Four Steps Missed, Book VIII
Five Steps Beyond, Book IX
One Good Time, Book X
Two Good Deeds, Book XI (Coming 2025)

The Ben Mitchell/Titus Ray Thriller Series:

Ben in Love, Book I, chronologically follows *Two Steps Forward*
Ben in Charge, Book II, chronologically follows *Three Steps Away*
Ben in Trouble, Book III, chronologically follows *Four Steps Missed*
Ben, the box set, Books I-III

The Mylas Grey Mystery Series:

A Day Ago, the prequel to *One Day Gone*
One Day Gone, Book I
Two Days Taken, Book II
Three Days Clueless, Book III
Four Days Famous, Book IV
Five Days Lost, Book V
Six Days Spent, Book VI
Seven Days Off, Book VII

The Silas McKay Suspense Series:

One Wonders, Book I
Two Believe, Book II
Three Confess, Book III
Four Doubt, Book IV
Five Alive, Book V (Coming 2025)

List of Characters
in *Five Days Lost*

Allen, Davis—Senior Senator from Missouri; head of Judiciary Committee.

Allen, Nelda—Wife of Senator Davis Allen.

Blondi, Joe—The handyman who lives above Mylas's garage.

Engel, Whitney—Owner of WEE Photography; Mylas's love interest.

Ford, Kyle—Former police detective; Associate investigator at MGI.

Grey, Curtis—Brother of Mylas; pastor of a church in Columbia, MO.

Grey, Kelvin—Father of Mylas; a private detective in Columbia, MO.

Grey, Rita—Mother of Mylas.

Hank—A member of MGI's surveillance crew.

Higbee, Carolyn—Housekeeper for Mylas.

Irving, Leslie—Associate investigator at MGI.

Lockett, Diana—Wife of Nathan.

Lockett, Nathan—Chief of Staff for Senator Allen; Mylas's best friend.

McDonald, Kendall—Receptionist at MGI.

McKinney, Theodore—Lawyer who left Mylas his estate; Also called "Mac."

Myers, Jenna—Receptionist in Senator Allen's office.

Novak, Bonnie—Financial Secretary for MGI.

Reed, Chase—Chief of Surveillance at MGI.

Rivers, Nina—Data Specialist at MGI.

Travis, Greta—Administrative Assistant at MGI.

PART ONE

Chapter 1

Friday, January 7

I woke up excited. It took me several seconds to figure out why, but once I realized the reason—actually there were two reasons—I lay in bed and thought about both of them until Babe came in the room.

Babe was my black lab.

He startled me when he trotted in the room, put his paws on my chest, and nudged me with his muzzle.

He wasn't in the habit of coming upstairs in the morning unless he and Mrs. Higbee, my housekeeper, had a disagreement while she was fixing breakfast. If that happened, he wanted my sympathy.

I scratched him behind his ears. "What's up, Babe? Have you been a bad boy today?"

He cocked his head and gave me his best doggie grin.

"You didn't steal a piece of bacon again, did you?"

Although he refused to answer my question, he had guilt written all over him—just like some witnesses I questioned back in my lawyering days.

Thus, I told him I'd be discussing his behavior with Mrs. Higbee as soon as I got dressed and went downstairs for breakfast.

In response to my warning, he went over and plopped himself down at the foot of my bed where he pretended to look ashamed.

I wasn't buying it.

I suspected he enjoyed every stolen morsel and didn't regret his actions for a minute.

Besides that, I had a feeling Mrs. Higbee's reprimand hadn't been nearly as severe as it should have been.

Mrs. Higbee was a real softie when it came to Babe.

When I adopted him from an animal shelter six years ago—not long after I inherited my former employer's law firm and estate—I did so with the expectation I'd have to convince Mrs. Higbee having a dog around the house would be a good thing.

That didn't happen.

She and Babe bonded as soon as she made his acquaintance, and it wasn't long before she was referring to him as "our" dog.

More often than not, Babe slept in Mrs. Higbee's bedroom on the first floor and only came upstairs to the master suite when she left Washington, D. C., to go visit her sister in Philadelphia.

Technically, I didn't live in Washington.

My house was located in Wesley Heights, east of the capital.

Previously, the two-story, six-bedroom residence was owned by Theodore "Mac" McKinney, who suffered a heart attack on the golf course one sunny day in May.

Although I regretted the loss of my employer—who treated me like a son—I didn't regret when Mac's will was read, and I discovered he'd named me—Mylas Grey—the sole heir of his estate. His estate included his house, stock portfolio, bank accounts, and law practice.

Even though my ambition since high school had been to become a wealthy man, and I'd gone to law school at Georgetown Law School to achieve that goal, I never imagined I'd suddenly become a multimillionaire at the age of forty with barely any effort on my part.

The irony of my sudden inheritance was that at the time Mac died, I'd come to the realization I didn't particularly like being a lawyer.

Thus, not long after Mac's passing, I sold his law practice and turned my attention to becoming a private investigator.

Naturally, that career change brought raised eyebrows from some of my lawyer friends—especially since I no longer needed to work for a living.

I didn't care.

I knew it was the right move for me.

◆ ◆ ◆ ◆

I grew up being tutored in the finer points of doing investigative work by my father, the proud owner of the Kelvin Grey Detective Agency in Columbia, Missouri, who didn't hide his disappointment when both his sons refused to follow in his footsteps and become a partner with him in his agency.

Truth be told, I didn't want to be a small-town detective because there was no money in it, whereas I was convinced if I became a lawyer in Washington, D. C., I'd be a very rich man.

My father didn't disagree with me, although he told me if I excelled at something, I wouldn't be satisfied until I found a way to use that skill set.

In fact, he told me I'd be miserable if I didn't.

Since he considered my skill set my innate investigative instincts, he didn't think I'd be happy doing anything if it didn't involve some kind of investigative work.

Both of us turned out to be right.

As I predicted, I *did* make a lot of money when I became a lawyer, but as Dad predicted, I never found any joy in it.

As soon as I realized that, I began looking for ways to use my investigative skills without becoming a detective like my father.

I finally settled on becoming a private investigator, which in my mind was nothing like being a detective.

As a private investigator, I planned to open my own agency and offer my services to high-level executives, congressional leaders, and anyone who needed someone to take care of a personal problem they couldn't or didn't want to handle for themselves.

At times, I figured this might involve ordinary detective work, but I made up my mind I wouldn't call myself a private detective.

While I was making plans to open my agency, I was surprised when I was offered a position as the chief investigator in the office of Senator Davis Allen, the head of the Senate Judiciary Committee.

The senator had his own investigative team—the R & I Group—to look into the backgrounds of the President's judicial nominees before they were presented to the Judiciary Committee.

After Nathan Lockett, the senator's chief of staff, explained the type of work I'd be doing, I immediately decided to take the job, not only because it sounded like interesting work, but also because I recognized it would yield plenty of contacts for me on Capitol Hill when I decided to leave the senator's office and start my own agency.

I finally made that decision a month ago and resigned from being Senator Allen's investigator after working on Capitol Hill for six years.

Although I planned a big official launch for Mylas Grey Investigations, I put those plans aside when Jared Daley, a famous plastic surgeon in D. C., hired me to solve his father's murder, thus becoming my first client.

Now, strangely enough, one of the reasons I was feeling excited was because after I closed the Daley case yesterday, Senator Allen called and asked me to drop by his office so he could sign the retainer agreement I'd drawn up for him with Mylas Grey Investigations.

It wasn't the retainer agreement that excited me, though.

It was the "personal matter" he said he wanted to discuss with me.

When the senator asked me about putting my agency on retainer, I suspected he had something specific in mind he wanted me to look into for him, although I couldn't begin to guess what it might be.

Now, I was about to find out.

However, the senator's personal matter wasn't the only reason I woke up feeling excited.

I had another reason. A more important reason.

Whitney Engel, a woman I met last year in Columbia, Missouri, was coming to Washington next week to see me.

Although Whitney had been here for a few days last November, our relationship had grown a lot since then.

Grown, as in I finally realized I was in love with her.

Now, I was hoping I could convince her to move to Washington so we could start planning our future together.

Truth be told, I was more excited about seeing Whitney than I was about seeing Senator Allen.

FIVE DAYS LOST: A Mylas Grey Mystery

◆ ◆ ◆ ◆

When I issued Whitney the invitation to visit me in Washington last year, I insisted she stay at my house, although I quickly assured her Mrs. Higbee would be willing to play the role of chaperone for us.

Since Whitney openly talked about her Christian faith, I didn't think she would accept my invitation if I didn't emphasize my intentions toward her were pure.

Thinking in such terms was a new concept to me. In fact, until I met Whitney, I never thought twice about inviting a woman to spend the weekend at my house.

However, all that changed a few months ago when I had an intense, eye-opening spiritual discussion with Whitney. When it ended, I had made the decision to become a Christian myself.

Although I was still learning what that decision meant for my life, as well as my thought processes, Whitney always seemed eager to answer my questions, even when I had dozens of them.

Now, as I walked in the kitchen for breakfast, I realized I wasn't the only one thinking about Whitney's upcoming visit.

Mrs. Higbee said, "When you have time, we should discuss what I need to do to get ready for Whitney's visit next week."

I sat down at the table. "I'll be able to do that on Sunday night. I should know her flight schedule by then. Will that be soon enough?"

"Oh, sure, that'll give me plenty of time to prepare the dinner menus for next week and get her room ready." As she placed a plate of bacon and eggs in front of me, along with a blueberry muffin, she asked, "Shall I put her in the Princess Room again?"

When Mrs. Higbee started working for Mac and his wife—who died several years before I met Mac—she told me she assigned each of the bedrooms a name depending on how they were decorated.

According to her, she named the first bedroom at the head of the stairs the Princess Room because it contained a large canopy bed that reminded her of a child's fairy tale, the one where a princess slept in a canopy bed and dreamed of her Prince Charming every night.

"The Princess Room sounds fine," I said. "Whitney seemed to be comfortable there."

"Do you know how long she'll be staying?"

"No, she didn't mention that," I gave Mrs. Higbee a mischievous grin, "so when I have my assistant make the reservations for her today, I may not book a return flight for her."

She chuckled. "Oh my, aren't you the naughty one?"

"Me? Are you sure you don't mean Babe?"

We both glanced over at the window where Babe had his nose resting on the windowsill staring out at the backyard.

Perhaps it was only my imagination, but I thought he looked as if he was trying hard not to look at the bacon on my plate.

"Well, since you mentioned it," Mrs. Higbee said, "Babe and I had a slight disagreement this morning when I offered him a piece of bacon, and he decided he wanted three pieces instead of just one. I doubt if he'll make that mistake again."

Babe cut his eyes over at me, but then he quickly went back to studying the backyard.

I wasn't as optimistic about Babe's self-control as Mrs. Higbee was.

♦ ♦ ♦ ♦

Before driving over to my ten o'clock appointment with Senator Allen, I went by my office to pick up the retainer agreement from Bonnie Novak, my financial secretary, and to have my administrative assistant, Greta Travis, book the plane reservations for Whitney.

Mylas Grey Investigations occupied the bottom two floors of a four-story building at the corner of L Street and 15th in Washington, D. C.

When I purchased the building a month ago, I renamed it Greystone Center.

While I changed the name primarily for publicity purposes, it also described the building's exterior, notwithstanding a strip of black marble across the front with "Greystone Center" written in raised gold lettering.

My intention was to lease out the top two floors until such time as my agency expanded, and I needed the extra room. As yet, I hadn't found a tenant for the top floors, although a few days ago, I was close to signing someone when a murder interfered with those plans.

FIVE DAYS LOST: A Mylas Grey Mystery

The good news was that I had two investigators working for me, which meant Mylas Grey Investigations was completely staffed now.

Besides me, there was Leslie Irving, who had previously been with the Bowman Detective Agency, and Kyle Ford, who was still employed with the D. C. Police as a homicide detective, but who planned to give his two-week notice today.

In addition to competent investigators, surveillance was an essential part of any investigative agency, and I was confident I'd put together a top-tier group at MGI.

Chase Reed, my surveillance supervisor—a diehard Texan—had five full-time people working for him, and when I lured him away from the Bowman Detective Agency with a higher salary, I assured him he could hire more people if he needed them.

His reply was, "I'm good for now."

Chase Reed was a man of few words.

These days, no one could run an investigative business without someone on staff who was a genius at data retrieval, who knew the hidden secrets of doing research on the internet, and who could do a little computer hacking if needed.

To that end, I risked my friendship with Nathan Lockett, Senator Allen's chief of staff, and offered the position of investigative research analyst to his data specialist, Nina Rivers, a person I'd worked with for six years as a member of the R & I Group.

Nina's ability to unearth the most obscure details about someone, as well as discover their financial data, their social media posts, and even their health issues, was truly mind-blowing.

Her skills definitely contributed to my success as Senator Allen's chief investigator, and she wasn't shy about reminding me of that.

However, her personality didn't lend itself to making rash decisions, so it took a lot of persuasion on my part to get Nina to join Mylas Grey Investigations, and she only agreed to do so last week, which meant she wasn't officially part of my staff yet, although she was already picking out her office equipment.

Unofficially, she let me know she wouldn't mind doing some research for me if I needed her help before she moved into the building in a couple of weeks.

Thus, I hadn't hesitated to use her skills on the Jared Daley case.

Now, as I entered the building and headed to Greta's office, I reminded myself to let Greta know Nina was planning to come by the building on Monday morning to see her new office.

As soon as I interviewed her, I was ready to turn over the responsibility of handling the administrative details of running MGI to Greta Travis.

Not only had Lockett recommended her, he convinced me she'd be excellent at directing, organizing, and managing all aspects of running a business, which were the attributes I needed in an assistant in order to focus on the investigative side of things.

I'd only seen two downsides to Greta's management style so far.

One was that she wasn't open to alternative suggestions if she had already made up her mind about something, and the other was that she liked to do things her own way.

So far, that hadn't caused any problems.

However, when Nina started working at MGI, it might be a different story.

Nina didn't just *like* to do things her own way; she *insisted* on doing things her own way.

Chapter 2

Once I gave Greta the assignment of getting plane reservations for Whitney, I went by Bonnie's office and picked up the paperwork for Senator Allen to sign, and then I took the elevator up to my office on the second floor.

My office suite was to the right of the elevators, and the rest of my investigative staff had their offices down the hallway to my left. The largest office, Room 215, was the surveillance crew's suite, which had a conference room, cubicles, and an office for the director, Chase Reed.

As I was unlocking my door, I saw Reed coming out of Room 215.

"Morning, Chase," I said, giving him a wave. "You look like you're headed out to a job."

"Yep," he said when he saw me. "Leslie asked me to check out an apartment building in Georgetown. It's connected to the infidelity case she's handling for Congresswoman Higgins."

"I didn't think Leslie was meeting with her until next week."

"She's not, but I had some time on my hands, and she gave me the address already, so I thought I'd go check it out."

Chase, who always wore a sports jacket to cover his gun holster, adjusted the collar over his western-style shirt, and said, "But if you've got something for me, I can change those plans."

"No, I don't have anything right now, although I have an appointment this morning that may change that. Since we closed the Daley case yesterday, I'm not working on anything right now. Next week's schedule looks pretty booked up, though."

He nodded. "Yes, it does. That's why I sent my people over to Piney Woods Park so they could learn how to use the surveillance drones you ordered. I want them to be experts before we need to use them."

"I've only seen a video of them, so I'm looking forward to seeing a live demonstration."

"They're top-of-the-line, that's for sure. Once we start using them, you may not need my crew anymore."

"Don't worry about that. Drones may be the future of investigative work, but they'll never replace a good surveillance team on the ground."

He grinned. "So I don't need to start shopping around for my Texas retirement ranch yet?"

"Definitely not. You've got plenty of time left here in Washington before you head down to Texas for your golden years."

He shook his head. "It probably won't happen anyway. I've been living here so long, my home state won't claim me anymore."

"You mean, 'once a Texan, always a Texan,' isn't really true?"

"Oh, it's true all right. If you don't believe me, just look at what I bought myself when I was down in Houston for Christmas."

He pulled his pants leg up and showed me his cowboy boots which bore the Lone Star State's flag.

"Nice."

He shrugged. "If nothing else, it's a perfect disguise. No one expects some good 'ole boy from Texas to be running surveillance on them in the nation's capital."

"Is that what makes you such a good surveillance guy?"

He shook his head as he headed over to the elevator. "Nah, it's not my boots. It's just that I'm really good at what I do."

"Modest too."

"How can I be modest? I'm from Texas."

◆ ◆ ◆ ◆

My desk phone started ringing as soon as I walked in my office, and when I answered it, I was still chuckling at Reed's comment.

"Sounds like someone's in a good mood this morning."

It was Leslie, and when I told her I'd been talking to Chase, she said, "Yeah, he can be a very funny guy sometimes."

"I'm beginning to realize that."

"It takes him awhile to warm up to people. To be truthful, even though we worked together at Bowman, I don't know Chase that well. As you've probably already noticed, he's not in the habit of revealing very much about his personal life."

"You're right. I did notice that."

We spent the next few minutes chatting about the Daley case we'd just wrapped up, and then I told her I was on my way over to deliver the retainer agreement to Senator Allen and meet with him about a personal matter.

She said, "By personal matter, do you mean you're opening an investigation for him?"

"That's possible. But not to worry. I'm aware we've already got several appointments for new cases starting next week, so if his personal matter isn't anything urgent, I'll try to put him off until Kyle gets here in a couple of weeks."

"Good idea. Next week is shaping up to be pretty busy for me."

"That goes double for me. Whitney finally accepted my invitation to visit Washington again, and when I talked to her last night, she said she was planning to come on Monday."

"Is that because she heard you got in a dicey situation with the Daley case?"

"That's what she said. She wouldn't take my word for it when I told her I was okay. She said she had to see for herself. Naturally, I didn't discourage her."

"No, I don't imagine you did." She paused a second. "I'm glad she's coming, Mylas. I'm really looking forward to meeting her. Maybe I can find a date, and the four of us can have dinner together while she's here. I saw several guys who looked interesting last night."

Leslie, who seemed to use the process of dating for entertaining herself rather than developing a relationship, was an active member of the online dating service, Elite Professionals.

"Sounds like a plan."

"I'll get to work on it. I should let you go now. It's after nine."

"Yeah. I don't want to be late for my appointment."

"I'm sure you're curious about why the senator wants to see you."

"Not really."

"Who's the funny guy now?"

◆ ◆ ◆ ◆

I was just pulling out of the parking lot at MGI when I got a call from Nathan Lockett. When I saw who it was, I found myself hoping he was about to tell me he knew I had a meeting with Senator Allen.

If he didn't, then I'd have to keep it a secret from him, and I wasn't comfortable doing that; not only because we were good friends, but also because it wasn't a good idea to keep secrets from a senator's chief of staff.

Once we greeted each other, he said, "Senator Allen just informed me he's meeting with you at ten o'clock. He wasn't forthcoming on the topic. Do you know why he wants to speak with you?"

"Only in a general sense. He said he had a personal matter he'd like to discuss. Did he ask you to be at the meeting?"

"Yes, as a matter of fact he did, but it was more like he insisted I be there. When I mentioned I was supposed to attend a budget committee meeting, he told me this meeting was more important. He didn't give me a hint as to what it was about. All he said was that he'd rather explain it to both of us at the same time."

"Do you think everything's okay with him on the home front? He and his wife aren't having difficulties, are they?"

"No, I don't think so. The senator and Nelda recently celebrated an anniversary, and when he showed me a picture of them eating at a restaurant, he got a little teary-eyed when he talked about meeting her back in his college days."

"I'm glad to hear that."

"I have a feeling whatever it is, it's the reason he wanted to put your agency on retainer."

"I was thinking the same thing. We'll know soon enough. I should be there in twenty minutes."

"Okay, see you then."

As I was about to disconnect the call, he said, "By the way, Mylas, congratulations on closing your first case. I'm amazed how soon you were able to bring things to a successful conclusion."

"Thanks, but I'm not expecting all of them to get solved so quickly."

"No, but at least the notoriety of the Daley case got you plenty of new clients just as you were about to open your agency."

"True, and according to Greta, we're still getting inquiries about our services."

"Success breeds success. Okay, I'm hanging up now. Remember, as far as the senator knows, we haven't talked."

"I won't forget. Should I also pretend we've never met?"

He chuckled. "Just think how different your life would be right now if we hadn't."

◆◆◆◆

I knew Lockett was joking, but for the next few minutes that's exactly what I did—thought about how different my life would have been if I hadn't met him.

For one thing, I would have one less friend, although we didn't become friends until several years after I went to work in the senator's office.

When Lockett first called and urged me to join Senator Allen's staff as his chief investigator, I had a feeling we'd become friends. But then, when he told me he'd be my immediate supervisor, I wasn't sure how being friends with him would work if he were in that role.

However, he said not to think of him as a supervisor. Instead, I should consider him a mentor, someone available to give instructions on how to navigate the halls of Congress, work with the federal judiciary system, and deal with congressional leaders.

After he told me that, I thought he might have heard the hesitancy in my voice, because he assured me he wouldn't be giving me advice about how to conduct investigations.

He said Mac told him I was an excellent investigator—he and Mac had been golf partners, which was the reason he decided to recommend me to the position on Senator Allen's staff.

True to his word, Lockett didn't tell me how to do my job, but when I first started working there, that didn't stop him from interrogating me about every aspect of why I did my job the way I did my job.

I figured that was because Lockett had been an Air Force intelligence officer for twenty years before joining Senator Allen's staff, and questioning people was second nature to him.

At first, I didn't push back on him—mainly because he wasn't obnoxious about it, even though I found his questions annoying.

However, one day I'd had enough—plus, I'd just had a big disagreement with the woman I was dating at the time—and I exploded at him.

"What's with the twenty questions, Nathan? I may not be doing things the way you'd do them, but I know Senator Allen thinks I'm doing a good job. Unlike you, he doesn't think I'm incompetent."

Lockett didn't say a word for maybe thirty seconds.

He just stared at me as if he couldn't believe what he was hearing.

"I'm sorry, Mylas," he finally said. "It never occurred to me that asking you questions about your methods would cause you to think I didn't consider you a competent investigator. I apologize. That wasn't my intention."

As I recall, that's when I realized Lockett reminded me of my older brother, Curtis, who had a similar way of dealing with me when I got angry or disagreed with him about something.

The difference between the two men was that Curtis's profession called for him to be tolerant, to show kindness, and demonstrate compassion for others. As the pastor of the North Point Community Church in Columbia, Missouri, that kind of attitude was expected.

Lockett, on the other hand, had every reason to put me in my place and tell me I was out of line. Instead, he apologized to me.

The moment I heard his apology, I immediately felt bad about losing my temper and stammered out an excuse.

"No. Nathan. I . . . uh . . . should be the one apologizing to you. I'm sorry. I . . . uh . . . shouldn't have lost my temper."

"I can see why you misunderstood my intentions. I was just trying to figure out how you went about getting information from people. Mac said you were a natural when it came to getting people to talk."

"I don't know about that, and with your experience gathering intelligence, I'm actually counting on learning a lot from you."

Lockett nodded and gave me a smile. "I have a feeling we'll do just fine together, even if we disagree about some things."

And that's what we did.

We learned from each other, respected our differences, and in the process, we became good friends.

It wasn't long after that encounter that I discovered Lockett and Curtis had a lot more in common than I thought they did.

Like Curtis, Lockett was a man of faith. He even went so far as to keep a Bible on his desk in full view of anyone who came to visit him.

If I ever mentioned I was having difficulty working with someone, he would offer to pray with me about the situation, and at least a couple of times a year, he would issue me an invitation to go to church with him and his wife, Diana, although I always thought of some reason to turn him down.

Not surprisingly, when I became a believer myself a few months ago, he acted as happy about my decision as my family did, and when I told him I'd like to go to church with him the following Sunday, I thought he might hug me.

However, there was still one aspect of our friendship we continued to disagree on, and it was one I had my doubts we'd ever be able to reconcile—I was an avid Kansas City Chiefs fan, and for some inexplicable reason, Lockett was a fanatic about the Washington Commanders, formerly known as the Washington Redskins.

I tried hard not to let it bother me too much.

◆ ◆ ◆ ◆

When I arrived in Senator Allen's suite, SR 335, his receptionist, Jenna Myers, gave me a big smile and told me the senator was expecting me.

Since Jenna had a tendency to gather tidbits of information about everything going on in the office and hand them out like party favors to the senator's staff in exchange for more gossip, I knew she was dying to know the purpose of my visit.

When I worked there, I used her "knowledge base" many times.

In fact, I often added to it myself.

This time, however, I told her I thought her short haircut looked nice and headed down the hallway toward the senator's office, ignoring her inquiring look.

I suspected my behavior was a dead giveaway that my meeting with Senator Allen was personal in nature. And I also figured my lack of transparency only fueled her imagination as to what the purpose of my appointment was.

In that respect, Jenna and I were in the same boat.

My imagination was also amped up.

Chapter 3

When I knocked on Senator Allen's door, it was Nathan Lockett who opened it. Even though he gave me a conspiratorial smile, his voice sounded professional and serious.

"Come in, Mylas. The senator's expecting you."

He motioned over at Senator Allen, who was standing in front of his window staring out at his incredible view of the U. S. Capitol.

The senator, whose snow-white hair and mature face made him look distinguished when he was being interviewed for the evening news, didn't look ready for prime time now. His face was haggard as he turned away from the window and greeted me.

Motioning toward the chairs in front of his desk, he said, "Go ahead and have a seat, Mylas. As you can see, I've asked Nathan to join us."

After we were all seated—the senator in his padded leather desk chair across from us—I placed the manila envelope containing the documents for the retainer agreement on the desk in front of him.

"Shall I leave this agreement with you, Senator, or would you like for me to go over it with you while I'm here?"

He waved his hand at Lockett. "Nathan, go ahead and read it. If it looks okay to you, I'll sign it right now."

I slid the envelope over to Lockett, and as he was opening it, the senator said, "I know you generated a lot of interest in your agency by solving the Daley case, Mylas, but I assume that won't prevent you from honoring the verbal agreement you made with me a few days ago to give my case your personal attention."

"You're right. There's been a lot of interest in the agency, and I've already accepted some new clients, but naturally, I'll honor our agreement and make your investigation a priority. Is this personal matter you mentioned something urgent?"

"I certainly see it that way."

Lockett handed the retainer agreement to Senator Allen. "This looks fine, Senator. I'm certainly comfortable with it."

"That's good enough for me."

The senator picked up his pen, scrawled his name above the signature line on both copies of the agreement, and handed one of the copies back to me.

"Okay, Senator," I said, as I put it back in the envelope, "I'm ready to hear about this personal matter you mentioned."

He clasped his hands together in front of him and took a deep breath. "The story I'm about to tell you will probably sound strange, maybe even unbelievable. To be honest, that's the main reason I haven't discussed it with anyone until now."

"Believe me, as a lawyer, I've heard plenty of strange stories."

"Has anyone ever told you they lost five days of their life before?"

◆ ◆ ◆ ◆

I didn't have a chance to respond before he opened the laptop in front of him and turned it around so Lockett and I could see the screen.

"This website isn't where the story begins, but it's where the story needs to start. I'm sure both of you have heard of a DNA ancestry service called DNAHeritage. Like most DNA services, you purchase a DNA testing kit from them, send it in, and a few weeks later, you're invited to view the results on their website."

The screen on the senator's laptop showed the colorful homepage of DNAHeritage where the double helix of the two-stranded DNA molecule was intertwined with faces of people in old photographs.

I assumed the senator had purchased the services of this particular testing site, because his name, Davis Vincent Allen, was at the top of the page. Directly beneath it was his ethnicity percentages, which indicated he was of Scottish Irish descent.

"Yes," Lockett replied, "Diana and I have done something similar."

"I've heard of it," I said, "but I haven't done it myself."

The senator said, "Nelda's mother loves researching her family tree, so when she bought testing kits for us and our kids a few years ago, I did the swab test and filled out the form about my side of the family. Mainly, I did it to make my wife happy."

The senator scrolled through to the next screen, which showed his DNA matches. It began with his closest shared DNA relationships—his children—and continued on to his siblings, parents, cousins, etc.

It took me a few seconds before I saw it, but when I did, I felt sure I knew why the senator called me.

Senator Allen had three children, two daughters and a son—Lizzie, Charlotte, and Thomas—all with the last name of Allen.

However, there was a fourth son listed, Jacob Robert Walker.

I didn't know he had a second son.

Evidently, Lockett was in the same boat.

He pointed toward the screen and said, "I didn't realize you had another son, Senator."

He shook his head. "Until a month ago, I didn't either."

So there it was.

◆ ◆ ◆ ◆

The senator reached over and unlocked the bottom drawer of his desk. After removing a file folder, he placed it on the desk, opened it, and took out several sheets of paper.

"Four weeks ago, I received an email from DNAHeritage notifying me I had some new DNA matches to explore."

He picked up the top sheet and laid it in front of us.

"I get emails like this about once a month, and since I'm not really into exploring my family tree, I don't pay much attention to them. Usually, the matches are distant relatives—like a third or fourth cousin—but this time, as you can see, the email said I had a close relative match. I thought that was a little odd because I'd already looked at the results from my close relative matches when I did the testing a couple of years ago."

I asked, "What does the DNAHeritage site classify as a close relative match?"

"Anything above thirty-eight percent of shared DNA, which typically includes siblings and children. Most close matches are fifty percent and of course, one hundred percent is an identical twin."

"In that case, I'm sure you checked it out immediately."

"Of course, I did. Who wouldn't?" He gestured at his laptop. "That's the screen I saw when I logged on."

I glanced over at it, and Lockett did the same.

Like me, I wondered if Lockett was imagining what Senator Allen must have felt when he saw the name Jacob Robert Walker listed alongside the names of his other kids.

"I can't begin to imagine what a shock that was," I said.

He shook his head. "No, you really can't."

He laid aside the email from DNAHeritage and placed another one in front of us.

"Within a few hours of getting that email, I received this one. It's also from the DNAHeritage site. However, this email informed me Jacob Walker had filled out the necessary forms to request my contact information, and I was being given the option of either granting his request or rejecting it."

The email had a list of choices the recipient could check to indicate how much contact information he or she wanted to grant. The choices were: email address only, email and phone number only, physical address only, or all of the above.

"Have you responded to this request yet?" I asked.

"Yes, but I only granted permission for my email address to be shared, and the email I'm using on the site isn't connected to my government email. It's more or less innocuous, the same one I use for my family and friends."

"Are you talking about dvallen@postmailink.com?" I asked.

"Yes, that's it."

"Can I assume you heard back from Mr. Jacob Walker?"

"Correct. He wrote me back right away." He held up two sheets of paper stapled together. "His response is pretty long. I'm sorry, Nathan, but I only printed off one copy."

When I took the sheets from him, I said, "Why don't I read it out loud? That way, we don't have to wait for Nathan to read it, and if either one of us has a question, we can ask you about it right away."

The senator nodded. "I'm okay with that. I've read it over so many times, I practically have it memorized by now. And yes, by all means, ask me whatever questions you like."

I figured Lockett knew the real reason why I asked permission to read the email out loud. Reading a document out loud was an excellent way to observe a person's reaction if the document contained revelations, and I was pretty sure if Senator Allen got an email from a son he never met, it contained revelations.

I noted the email was sent three weeks ago.

Although I wondered if he'd replied yet, I decided to wait until I finished reading to ask him that question.

I was guessing he had, and it was the reason he hired me.

◆ ◆ ◆ ◆

Like the senator, Jacob Robert Walker also appeared to have an innocuous email address. His was jrwflyingeagle@tootsuite.com.

"Dear Mr. Allen, My name is Jacob Walker, and when I submitted a DNA test to DNAHeritage, your name appeared as my biological father. I realize finding out I'm your son may have been as much a shock to you as it was to me. To be truthful, my mother told me my father was killed, so I wasn't hopeful I'd get a match on any of the DNA sites."

I glanced up at the senator who gave me a weak smile.

I continued reading. "My mother, Amanda Walker, was the person who created this false narrative about my father, and it wasn't until she died of a massive stroke last year that I learned the truth. When I was cleaning out her house, I came across a diary she started keeping before I was conceived. In it, she revealed she was pregnant, and although she said she knew who the father was, she said she planned to raise me as a single mom. She decided to lie and tell me my father was a pilot in the Air Force, and he was killed in a training accident. In her diary, she said she wanted me to believe my father was an intelligent man who loved his country."

I paused and asked, "Does the name Amanda Walker mean anything to you, Senator?"

He shook his head. "No, it doesn't, but once you finish reading the email, I'll tell you why I may have known her by a different name."

I flipped the sheet over to the next page, where there was another paragraph and continued reading. *"Once I read my mother's diary, I wanted to know who my real father was, and I decided the fastest way to find out was to submit a sample of my DNA to all the ancestry search websites. Unfortunately, I had no relatives to consult. My mother told me she was raised by her grandmother, who died not long after my mother graduated from high school. She claimed she didn't know who her parents were, and since I never met any aunts, uncles, or cousins when I was growing up, it was easy to believe that, although now that I know my mother lied to me all these years, I don't know what to believe. Frankly, Mr. Allen, I'm at a loss how to proceed from here. If nothing else, I'd like to open up a line of communication between us. Then, in the near future, if you're willing, perhaps we could have a face-to-face meeting. At this moment, all I'm asking is that you respond to this email. I'm looking forward to hearing from you."*

I folded the page over and asked, "Is that what you did, Senator? Did you respond to his email?"

He nodded. "Yes. I've been corresponding with Jacob by email for the past two weeks now."

Lockett said, "I wish you would have told me about this, Senator. I'm not sure I would have advised you to reply without having Nina run a background check on this guy."

"I don't believe any harm's been done, Nathan. I've found out several things about Jacob, but he still doesn't know very much about me. I've never revealed my address or anything about my family, outside of what he knows from the DNAHeritage site, and I certainly haven't told him I'm a U. S. Senator."

"That seems a little odd," I said. "Why hasn't Jacob asked you about yourself?"

"I didn't mean to imply he hasn't asked me. I've just put him off by promising to tell him all about myself once we meet in person."

"Have you set a time for that meeting yet?"

"No, I haven't responded to his last email. It's the one that he asked me where I lived, and if it would be convenient for us to get together. That's why I wanted to meet with you, Mylas. I need to know everything about Jacob Walker. I need to know what his financial situation is. I need to know what kind of person he is, and of course, I need to know if he's gonna be a problem for me in my upcoming election."

Lockett said, "I suppose you're worried your opponent might use the sudden appearance of another son to accuse you of all kinds of nefarious behavior."

"Yes, that crossed my mind. You know how ruthless George Houser can be."

I said, "I'll try to find the answers to all those questions, Senator, but first, there's something I need to ask you."

"I can guess what it is. You want to ask me about the mother of Jacob Walker, and why she didn't tell me we had a son."

"That's it. I can't investigate Jacob without knowing more about his mother."

"I understand that, but believe me, it's not that easy to talk about."

Nathan said, "We all have embarrassing things in our life, Senator."

"What happened to me isn't embarrassing. It's just strange."

"No matter how strange it is," I said, "I can't help you if you don't tell me what happened to you."

"That's really the question I want you to answer, Mylas. What happened to me?"

Chapter 4

Before Senator Allen launched into what he called his "strange story," he offered us something to drink, and although Lockett and I declined his offer, he walked over and got some bottled water out of the mini-fridge underneath his credenza.

I wondered if by making the offer he was simply stalling, or if he was using the time to decide where to begin his narrative.

I figured it might be the latter because he said, "I suppose I can't adequately explain the events that unfolded until I give you some background information."

Senator Allen said everything he was about to tell us took place in 1985 when he'd just completed his sophomore year of college and was working as a summer intern in Washington for Senator Nick Drury, the senior senator from Missouri. He was twenty years old at the time.

"When the congressional offices closed down the week of July fourth, I decided to spend a few days in New York City with some of my intern buddies. We joked about it being our patriotic duty to party in the Big Apple to celebrate our nation's birthday."

"I suppose this was before you met Nelda," Lockett said.

"Right. I didn't meet her until my junior year of college. So anyway, I told the guys I would drive my own car and meet them in New York, because Senator Drury gave me a ton of constituent correspondence to answer before he flew back to Jefferson City to celebrate Independence Day, and I wanted to get it done just so it wouldn't be hanging over my head while I was partying with my friends."

"Before this trip, had you ever been to New York City?" I asked.

"No, and what I'm about to tell you didn't take place there." He paused and rubbed his temple. "It was late by the time I left Washington on Monday, and I was already tired, so I decided I would only drive as far as Philadelphia and spend the night at a motel before driving on to New York City the following day."

The senator said he started getting hungry a little over an hour after he left Washington, so he got off the freeway in Bakerton, Maryland, and drove into town where he found a local diner.

"It was located in the town square, and the place was crowded, so when the waitress asked me if I would mind sharing a table with a nice-looking girl who was seated all by herself, I immediately agreed. After we introduced ourselves—she said her name was Shirley—we spent the rest of the meal getting acquainted with each other, although I have to admit I was the one doing most of the talking. She seemed fascinated by the fact I worked in a senator's office. She was also impressed when I told her I was attending George Washington University on an academic scholarship, and my intention was to become a lawyer. We were—"

"I'm sorry to interrupt, Senator, but if Shirley is relevant to your story, then whatever you can tell me about her would be helpful."

"I think she's relevant, but the only thing I can remember is that she lived in town and worked at a drugstore near the diner."

"Okay, at least that's something."

"When we finished eating, she said I shouldn't leave without trying the apple pie, so I ordered us both a piece and told her it was my treat. Then, I excused myself and went to the restroom. When I got back, our desserts had arrived, and she'd also ordered us some coffee. She said she didn't want me falling asleep before I made it to Philadelphia."

The senator took a long drink of water before he continued.

"I was in the restaurant another twenty minutes or so, just long enough to eat my pie and drink my coffee, but after I paid the check, and Shirley and I walked outside, I suddenly got very sleepy. In fact, I was so drowsy, I asked her if there was a motel in town, and she pointed back toward the freeway and suggested I spend the night at the Roadside Inn. She said to tell the clerk, 'Shirley sent me.' "

At this point in his story, the senator leaned back in his chair and stared up at the ceiling for several seconds. Then, he looked over at us and said, "As hard as I've tried, I can't remember anything about the motel room. The only thing I remember is falling asleep in the bed. I don't even remember getting undressed."

"Do you think you passed out?" I asked.

"No, it wasn't like that. It was more like I couldn't keep my eyes open, and I just flopped down on the bed and immediately went to sleep. It wasn't a restful sleep, though. I kept having disturbing dreams, and I'm not sure if it was in my dreams or if it was real, but there were times when I felt like I was struggling to breathe."

"What do you remember about the dreams themselves?"

"Well, the truth is, they weren't like most dreams. They were just little snippets of voices and images that didn't have any context. The most vivid thing I remember is a bright red wagon, the sort of thing little kids haul their toys around in. You know what I'm talking about?"

"I think so. My brother and I got a red wagon for Christmas one year. When I got older, I used it to deliver newspapers."

"As I recall, the wagon looked like it had never been used. I remember hearing someone say, 'Wagons should be filled with kids. They shouldn't be gathering dust.'"

"Did the voice have a face to go along with it?"

"No. I never saw anyone's face, but it was a woman's voice."

"Was there only one voice or were there several?"

"I think there was only one, but since it seemed like whoever was talking, wasn't really talking to me, then there could have been several. On the other hand, I don't remember ever saying anything."

"Why did you describe the dream as being disturbing?"

"Because although I had the sensation of movement, I couldn't feel my legs, and like I said, I had difficulty breathing, but it wasn't because I was out of breath. It was more like the air was too heavy to breathe."

"How did you feel when you woke up?"

"When I woke up, I felt like I had a hangover. My head was pounding. Truthfully, I think it was the worst headache I've ever had. All I wanted to do was take a hot shower and find some coffee."

"What time was it? Morning or afternoon?"

"It was morning. My watch said eight-fifteen. The room didn't have a coffeepot, so I took a shower, got dressed, and walked over to the office to pay my bill and find some coffee."

The senator described the Roadside Inn as one of those old-fashioned motels where guests parked their cars directly in front of their rooms, and the motel office was in a separate building with living space in the back for the manager. When guests entered the office, they summoned the manager by ringing the bell on the desk.

Senator Allen said, "I had to wait a few minutes after I rang the bell before anyone came to the office, and when an older man finally showed up, I noticed it wasn't the same person who checked me in the night before. When this guy gave me my bill, I thought he'd made a mistake. The kid who checked me in told me the room was $25 a night, but this guy presented me with a bill for $150. Naturally, I questioned the amount."

"Of course," Nathan said, "anyone would."

The senator shook his head. "He claimed I'd been in my room since Monday night, and since today was Sunday, I owed him for six nights."

Lockett said, "I bet that got your attention."

"At first, I thought he was joking, but when I realized he was serious, I began arguing with him, and that's when he grabbed a newspaper off the counter and pointed to the date. There it was, plain as could be, Sunday, July 7, 1985."

I asked, "Did you tell him you couldn't remember anything about the last five days?"

"Yes, and all he said was, 'that must have been some party.' I asked him why someone hadn't knocked on my door and inquired about cleaning the room, but he pointed out I had the sign on the doorknob that said I didn't want to be disturbed, and the night clerk told him I'd put it there as soon as I checked in."

I said, "I'm assuming that wasn't the only question you asked him. You must have had several for him."

He looked down for a moment. "Well, actually it was, but keep in mind, I was only twenty years old at the time, and I was feeling disoriented. I remember thinking all I wanted to do was get out of there, find some coffee, and get back to my apartment in Washington."

"Did you call someone?" Lockett asked. "What about the friends you were supposed to meet in New York?"

"I didn't call anyone until I got back to Washington. By that time, I decided I must have been sick. I figured I had a high fever, the flu, something like that, and I got rid of it by sleeping it off in the motel room for five days. That was the story I gave my friends about why I didn't meet them in New York. Since they seemed to think it was plausible, I just forgot about it and went on with my life."

"You couldn't have gone five days without water," I said. "Food wouldn't have mattered that much, but without fluids, you wouldn't have lasted five days, especially if you were sick."

He nodded. "Yeah, as I've thought about what happened in Bakerton, I realize I must have made it to the bathroom and drunk some water, even if I can't remember it. You can probably guess why I've been thinking about my time in Bakerton for the past month."

I said, "I imagine it's because Jacob Walker told you his date of birth, and you worked out his probable date of conception."

"That's right. He said he was born April 9, 1986. That was nine months after I spent five days I don't remember at the Roadside Inn."

"Well, Senator, you can't dispute the DNA evidence. It proves Jacob is your son, and whether you remember those five days or not, the date of his conception indicates you didn't spend that time alone."

"Yes, it would be foolish to deny Jacob is my son when the DNA clearly shows he is, but what I want you to find out, Mylas, is what happened to me during those five days. Eventually, I'll have to explain to Nelda and my other children why I have a thirty-six-year-old son I've never met. Telling them I don't remember how it happened won't be good enough. It won't satisfy Nelda, that's for sure."

Lockett gestured at the senator. "And saying you don't remember won't satisfy the press, your constituents, or your colleagues. You need an explanation that provides enough details to keep your political opponents from coming up with their own explanation."

"I'm aware of that. I know it would take Congressman Houser less than a day to come up with some sordid explanation to tarnish my reputation and accuse me of shirking my parental responsibility, even if I claimed I didn't know anything about Jacob until a month ago."

I pulled my phone out of my pocket and said, "Before I tell you how I plan to proceed, I need to be sure of my facts. Are you absolutely certain you've never told anyone about what happened to you in Bakerton until this moment?"

The senator extended his hand toward me. "I'm telling you the truth, Mylas. Today was the first time I've ever spoken about it to anyone."

"And what about Jacob? Have you told anyone about him yet?"

"No, and as soon as he wrote me, I immediately changed my settings on the DNAHeritage website. Now it's restricted access, which means anyone who wants to look at my ancestry information has to request permission from me first. If someone in my family decides to look up something on the family tree, they won't be able to see anything, which will probably send up a red flag, but I'll just have to deal with that if it happens."

"Since you did the testing two years ago, has anyone in your family shown that much interest in it?" Nathan asked.

"No, none of us have talked about our DNA results or our ancestry connections in several months, maybe even a year."

I looked up after jotting down a couple of notes on my phone. "Although I'm going to be handling your case personally, I'll need to use some people from my agency to help with the investigation, so the circle of those who know about Jacob will be getting wider in the days ahead. However, I assure you, I haven't hired anyone at Mylas Grey Investigations who isn't completely trustworthy."

"It's not you I'm worried about. It's Jacob Walker. Although he doesn't seem to have ulterior motives for contacting me, I can't be sure of that." He gave me a half-smile. "At least I can have peace of mind knowing he's not aware of my true identity."

"I'm sorry, Senator, but I have to disagree with you about that."

His eyes got big. "But why? Davis Allen isn't an unusual name. I've met several men with my name before."

"No, but Jacob might be the type of person who knows how to take what information he has and put it through a search engine to come up with additional facts. Once he gets those, he can do a deeper dive into the data. It wouldn't take him long to know exactly who you are."

"What information does he have on me?"

"He knows your full name and the names of your kids. That's enough to get him started, especially if he knows about investigative websites like *IntelManifest*, which is capable of uncovering almost anything about a person."

Lockett said, "Mylas is right. That's one of the tools Nina uses to look up information about the President's judicial nominees."

The senator shifted his weight around as if he were suddenly feeling uncomfortable. "Then there's no time to waste. You need to get started on your investigation right away."

"I agree, but first, I have some questions for you. Then, I need to ask you a favor."

"What's the favor? Let's hear it first."

"Okay. I know you're aware Nina Rivers gave her two weeks' notice so she can join Mylas Grey Investigations as my research analyst. However, she didn't want to leave your office until she's fulfilled her commitment for the full two weeks. Since her services are vital to discovering everything about Jacob Walker, as well as getting information about Amanda, the favor I'd like to ask of you is to give Nina your blessing to go ahead and start work at MGI this coming week."

He waved his hand at me dismissively. "Oh, sure. Consider it done. I'll talk to her ASAP. What are the questions you have for me?"

"You said you learned a lot about Jacob from his emails. What did you learn?"

He reached over and picked up a thumb drive from his credenza. "I made a copy of his emails for you. Everything he told me is in here."

As I took it from him, he said, "He didn't tell me much about his childhood, except that he grew up in Waterford, Maryland. And, yes, I looked it up, and it's about thirty minutes from Bakerton. He said his mother lived in Waterford until her death. Now, Jacob lives in Lanham, Maryland, outside of Washington, where he works as a Government Affairs Director at EnViron Industries."

I shook my head. "I'm not familiar with EnViron Industries."

Lockett spoke up. "It manufactures unmanned reconnaissance aircraft, better known as URAs, for our military."

"So he works with the Department of Defense," I said. "That's all the more reason for me to believe he may be aware you're a United States Senator. He probably thought of you as soon as he saw the name Davis Allen on the ancestry website."

"Psychologically speaking," Lockett said, "that would be a natural reaction, especially since he works in the Beltway."

The senator placed both hands on his desk, as I'd seen him do numerous times when he was trying to calm himself.

"What I'm most concerned about is finding the facts. That's the way I operate, Mylas. You know that. Once I have those facts, I'll be able to decide how to handle the announcement about having another son. I believe the key to finding those facts is for you to meet with Jacob, read the diary his mother wrote, and see if there's enough information in there to reconstruct what happened to me thirty-seven years ago."

"What about you, Senator? Don't you want to meet with Jacob first? I'm sure I can arrange a private meeting where you won't need to be concerned about your safety or the press getting wind of it."

"No, I prefer to do it this way. As soon as you do a background check on Jacob, then I'll contact him and agree to meet with him. When he comes to the appointment, you'll inform him of my identity, explain that I'm a public figure, and that I need to proceed with caution on this matter. Once you tell him the story of why I wasn't aware of his existence until a month ago, I can't think of any reason he wouldn't be willing to let you read his mother's diary."

"Personally, I think if he refuses to let you read it," Lockett said, "it's a good indication he has his own agenda."

I wasn't worried about Jacob allowing me to read his mother's diary; I was worried there wouldn't be enough information in it to help me solve the mystery of the senator's five missing days.

That is, if those days were truly missing.

Chapter 5

After I told the senator I'd get back to him as soon as the background check on Jacob Walker was complete, Lockett and I left the senator's office and walked across the hall to his office.

Conferring with Lockett after a meeting with the senator was a common practice when I worked for him, especially if our discussion concerned a difficult topic or the senator himself had been difficult.

I suspected Lockett enjoyed analyzing what went on in the meeting because it reminded him of a military debriefing, or maybe he thought we both needed a moment to decompress.

"Talk about an unexpected development," Lockett said, as soon as we entered his office. "Now I understand why he's been so distracted these last few weeks. I just thought it was the pressure of his upcoming reelection campaign."

He motioned me over to a club chair, but before he sat down, he strolled over to his credenza. "I need a cup of coffee. How about you?"

"Sounds good."

Lockett popped a single-serve pod in his personal coffeemaker, and while it was brewing, I asked, "Does this news affect the plans you and his campaign manager have been making for the reelection campaign?"

"Yeah, pretty much, but you never know how a personal revelation like this will affect a campaign. It usually depends on how far we can stay ahead of the rumors." He shook his head. "I really wish he would have told me about this sooner."

"You know the senator much better than I do, Nathan. Do you think he was being completely transparent with us?"

He frowned when he handed me a mug of coffee. "I suppose you're asking me that because he seemed unsure of himself when he was trying to explain what happened to him in Bakerton."

"You've got to admit Senator Allen hardly ever sounds tentative about anything. Even when the odds are against the man—like when he's about to lose a vote on the Judiciary Committee—he always sounds confident. It's one of the hallmarks of his personality."

Lockett leaned against the edge of his desk while he waited for his coffee to finish brewing. "You're right, but you're only acquainted with the senator as a fifty-seven-year-old man. I'm sure he didn't have that kind of maturity when he was twenty. I think the uncertainty you heard reflected that. When I think about my younger self, I'm mystified by my actions, and I'm sure that's true of you too."

I smiled as Lockett brought his coffee over and sat down on the sofa across from me. "Even today, I'm mystified by my actions."

"Is that your way of admitting you're sorry you agreed to investigate this situation for Senator Allen?"

"No, although I've never had to set up an investigation quite like this one before. It's not like there's a dead body with evidence I can examine that points to the killer, or there's a missing person and I can interview their friends, or a cheating husband and I can set up surveillance on him. This is completely different."

"So where do you begin?"

"Obviously, I need to begin with Jacob. But to be truthful, I doubt if he'll have the facts the senator wants, and I'll be surprised if his mother's diary gives me the full story either. However, I'm counting on gathering enough information from Jacob and her diary that when I go to Bakerton, I'll be able to uncover what happened to Senator Allen at the Roadside Inn."

"I'd be surprised if that motel even existed anymore."

I nodded. "The same could be true of the diner."

He chuckled a little as he took a sip of his coffee. "I don't envy you, Mylas. This is a toughie, plus it could take some time."

"Wait till I tell you what else is going on with me."

FIVE DAYS LOST: A Mylas Grey Mystery

◆ ◆ ◆ ◆

Since I'd already told Lockett about Whitney's plans to make a return visit to Washington, he wasn't too surprised when I told him she'd be arriving on Monday.

However, he agreed her being here when I was in the middle of running the investigation for Senator Allen could be a problem.

He said, "If you have the background check on Jacob ready by Monday, then it's possible when the senator makes the arrangements for Jacob to meet with you, it won't happen until the end of the week."

"That's what I'm hoping. That would mean I'd have the whole week to visit with Whitney without being preoccupied with the senator's case. Although if I had a whole week before I saw Jacob, and Whitney wasn't here, then I'd probably take a trip up to Bakerton while I was waiting for our appointment."

"You could still do that. Whitney might find the trip interesting."

"Are you kidding? After what happened to her the last time she came to see me, I'm not about to let her get involved in any of my cases."

Lockett shook his head. "That was such a freak thing. You had no way of knowing you were putting her in danger. I hardly think investigating the circumstances of Senator Allen's encounter with Jacob's mother thirty-seven years ago is in the same league as that psychopath coming after you last year."

"Well, let's hope not, but I'm still not going to allow Whitney to help me with this investigation."

Lockett suddenly put his cup down on the table and waved his hand at me. "Wait a second, Mylas. I just had a brilliant idea, and if I can work out the details, it could even make Whitney want to move to Washington permanently."

"That sounds too good to be true. What's your idea?"

He frowned. "No, I can't tell you just yet. I need to make some phone calls first. Then, if my brilliant idea doesn't work out, you won't be disappointed."

"It's not like I can't handle a little disappointment, Nathan. Come on. Tell me your brilliant idea."

"Not yet, but I promise I'll tell you when I see you at church on Sunday. I'll have the answers then, and if my idea is workable, then I'll need you to call Whitney right away and see if she's agreeable."

I drained my coffee mug and set it down on the table. "Since you refuse to tell me, I'm leaving."

He let out a short laugh. "I know the real reason you're leaving. You can't wait to go tell Nina she can come to work for you on Monday."

I smiled. "You've got that right. If anyone can uncover Jacob Walker's secrets, it'll be Nina Rivers."

◆ ◆ ◆ ◆

I headed back down Corridor A to the reception area, but I was glad to see Jenna was talking on the phone so I didn't have to come up with an evasive answer as to why the senator wanted to see me.

Despite that, I figured she'd find out soon enough.

The offices of the R & I Group were in Corridor C, and Nina's office was the first door on the right. The door was halfway open, and when I stepped inside, I found it empty.

It was obvious Nina had already started boxing up her things for her move to the Greystone Center, but even so, her office was still jam-packed with a bunch of office equipment, plus several computers.

Nina's love for office equipment was only surpassed by her love for her grandchildren, and even though she readily admitted she was a workaholic, she seldom missed any of their soccer games.

I attributed her desire to stay busy partly to the fact she lived alone—her husband died of a heart attack before I met her—and partly to her insatiable appetite for finding out stuff.

Facts and figures fascinated Nina more than anyone I'd ever met, and as long as I complimented her on the data and research details she dug up for me, our relationship was mostly harmonious, although she did have a tendency to offer me romantic advice, which sometimes irritated me.

"Well, this is a surprise," she said when she walked in carrying a couple of empty boxes. "Are you here to help me pack my things?"

"Sure, I can do that."

She dropped the boxes on the floor and shook her head. "Well, forget that. I'm not about to ask the famous private investigator, Mylas Grey, to engage in menial labor, not when he was all over the evening news last night after solving his first case at MGI."

I removed a box of files from one of her guest chairs and sat down. "It was only because of your expertise that I was ultimately able to put everything together."

She smiled. "Oh, I'm sure of that." She sat down behind her desk. "Seriously, Mylas, what are you doing here?"

"I had an appointment to see the senator about this." I held up the brown envelope I was carrying. "He's put Mylas Grey Investigations on retainer, and I brought him the agreement to sign."

"Well, that's—"

"He also talked to me about running an investigation for him."

Her eyes got big. "Uh . . . I'm guessing this has to be something personal. Otherwise, why wouldn't he have his own investigative team look into it?"

"It *is* personal, very personal. In fact, it's a family problem."

"Most personal problems involve families in one form or the other. In fact, all the data I've seen indicates issues with family members are the number one reason people decide to go to a counselor."

"He doesn't need a counselor for this. He needs a private investigator."

"If your intention was to make me curious, you've succeeded. Are you gonna tell me what his family problem is or do I have to guess?"

"I don't think you could guess this one, so I'm gonna tell you. But first, I want you to know Senator Allen is about to release you from your obligation to finish out your last week here. You're free to come to work at MGI on Monday."

She put her hand on her chin. "By any chance, is his generosity connected to the family matter you're investigating for him?"

"It is, and I told him if he wanted me to get the information he's requesting, I needed to have my investigative research analyst working for me full time."

She looked pleased. "Well, then, I better go find some more boxes," she paused, "but not before you tell me what's going on."

"Would you believe Senator Allen just discovered he has a son he didn't even know existed until a month ago?"

"What? Repeat what you just said." When I did, she gestured over at her computers. "Then I bet he found out because he had his DNA tested through one of those ancestry sites."

Her response surprised me. "You haven't heard about this from someone, have you?"

She must have seen the concern on my face because she quickly shook her head. "No, of course not. I was just speculating because I know that's been happening a lot lately. There's even a TV show about the unexpected results of DNA testing."

"I doubt the senator would be interested in seeing it."

"So it's true? He joined one of those ancestry sites, and that's how he found out he had another son?"

"Yes and no. That's not exactly how it happened."

I went through the senator's story about Jacob getting in touch with him and their subsequent emails, and then I showed her the thumb drive he'd made for me.

"He gave me a copy of their emails, which he says contains a lot of personal information about Jacob. I haven't read the emails yet, so I don't want to leave this thumb drive with you, but go ahead and make a copy for yourself while I tell you what else the senator told me."

After she inserted the USB drive in one of her computers, she asked, "Can I assume you want me to do a full spectrum background check on Jacob Walker?"

"Absolutely. Whatever you turn up, no matter how insignificant, I need to know it."

"Does that mean I should build a casebook on him?"

Whenever Nina did research on the President's judicial nominees, she would compile all the information she discovered, along with the supporting documentation, into what she called a casebook, an actual physical notebook, complete with color-coded tabs.

Although they were somewhat useful, I suspected Nina enjoyed seeing all the work she'd done in this tangible format, plus it gave her a chance to indulge her obsessive/compulsive side by arranging the information under topics, sub-topics, and sub-sub-topics.

"Uh . . . sure I guess you could build a casebook on him. I hadn't thought about you doing that for our clients at MGI, but I can see why that would be a good idea for some of them."

"You always told me they were very helpful when you wrote up the final report on a nominee."

"That's true. All the information in one place made it easy to get a report ready, and since this particular investigation is for the senator, he'll probably expect a report when everything's said and done."

"You're not saying you don't want me to make casebooks on the investigations you do for your other clients, are you?"

One look at Nina's face told me my answer better be no or she might reconsider joining Mylas Grey Investigations.

"No, of course not. I'm definitely not saying that."

◆ ◆ ◆ ◆

Once Nina returned the thumb drive to me, she assured me she'd get started on her research into Jacob Walker immediately, and then I told her the rest of the senator's story.

"That's amazing," she said, after I finished explaining what happened to him in Bakerton. "It sounds like he was drugged by that girl he met at the diner. Are you thinking she's Jacob's mother?"

"I see that as a possibility. She told the senator her name was Shirley, but that could actually be her real name, and Amanda Walker could be a fake name. On the other hand, maybe Shirley only set him up, and someone else, let's say Amanda, paid a visit to his motel room."

"The whole thing's really bizarre. I don't believe I've ever heard anything quite like it."

"No, neither have I. It's very puzzling."

"Personally, I think you're gonna have a hard time putting this puzzle together. There are too many missing pieces, and on top of that, it happened decades ago."

Since Nina relied on solid facts and indisputable figures, she had trouble getting her head around situations that called for creative thinking. Consequently, she wasn't all that helpful when it came to speculating about different scenarios.

Everything in her world had to be quantifiable.

"Some of those missing pieces could be in Amanda's diary," I said, "and once you take a look at Jacob's background, then the senator will arrange for me to meet him—that is, unless you come across a red flag that makes the senator change his mind and decide to meet with him himself or if you think the guy's scamming him in some way. If his story checks out, I'm anticipating one of the results of meeting Jacob will be that he gives me access to his mother's diary."

"I might be able to find out more about Amanda when I'm digging up stuff on Jacob. If you want, I could start a casebook on her too."

"Thanks, Nina, but I'd rather you concentrate on Jacob first. If his dossier is ready by Monday, then the senator will set up a time for me to meet him, and more than likely it won't be until the end of the week, which will give me several days to spend with Whitney before I have to devote myself to the senator's case full time."

"So Whitney is definitely coming next week?"

I nodded. "She arrives on Monday afternoon."

"No wonder you wanted me over at MGI as soon as possible."

"What does Whitney coming have to do with you being at MGI?"

She gave me a mischievous grin. "I'm sure you want to impress your girlfriend with all the people on your staff, not to mention your beautiful facilities."

I let out a short laugh. "Actually, I think Whitney might like it better if I had a two-room office in a basement. She claims she's a small-town girl, and according to her, my life in Washington intimidates her."

"Anything unfamiliar can be intimidating." She looked around the room for a few seconds. "I'm feeling a little intimidated just because I'm leaving this place and going to a different job."

Suddenly, I realized I hadn't thought about the emotions Nina might be having by giving up a secure job she'd held for over a decade and taking a position at a new business like Mylas Grey Investigations.

"I'm sorry I haven't thought about how difficult this change must be for you. I should have been more sensitive about your feelings."

She gave me a half-smile and shook her head. "Oh, don't be silly. I don't expect you to understand. Guys are notorious for ignoring the obvious, especially when it comes to women."

"True, but is there anything I can do to make it easier for you?"

She waved me off. "No, don't give it another thought. As long as I have my office set up the way I want it, I'll be fine. You *did* say I had carte blanche when it comes to the computers and other office equipment I want, didn't you?"

Before I could answer, she said, "If I were you, I'd say yes, because I've already ordered a bunch of stuff."

I pretended to be shocked at this news, and then I nodded and said, "Yes, that's exactly what I said, and I told Greta the same thing."

"She's your administrative assistant?"

"And office manager."

"I've met Leslie, and you've told me how good Chase Reed is, but you haven't had much to say about Greta."

"Uh . . . Greta is very efficient. She runs a tight ship, and . . . uh . . ."

I stalled for a couple of seconds as I tried to come up with Greta's positive attributes without saying anything negative about her.

"And . . . uh . . . uh . . . she's passionate about her two miniature schnauzers. She told me they've won several dog shows."

"She used to work for Senator Matten, didn't she?"

"That's right. Did you ever meet her?"

"No, but one of his legislative assistants told me she's well-organized and knows how to get things done. He also mentioned she likes to do things her own way."

"Well, that's true of all of us, isn't it?"

"Don't look at me. I wouldn't know anything about that."

Chapter 6

As soon as I got back to my office at the Greystone Center, I inserted the thumb drive in my laptop and read the emails Jacob Walker and Senator Allen had been sending to each other.

The senator did a masterful job of keeping attention focused on Jacob and away from himself, and he primarily did it by asking Jacob a ton of questions. Since he was a former prosecutor, as well as a politician, that technique didn't surprise me.

What surprised me was how forthcoming Jacob was with his answers. He even provided details the senator hadn't asked him.

In reality, his answers sounded like they were from someone who was eager to talk about himself, but as I thought about it, I realized that was probably true, especially since Jacob was answering questions from a father he never knew.

The senator asked, *"Did you attend college in Maryland?"*

Jacob said, *"I went to the University of Virginia in Charlottesville. It was easy to make that decision because they offered me an academic scholarship, but I was also impressed with their Political Science Department. I've been interested in government and politics ever since I was in high school, and by my senior year, I knew I wanted to be a political science major. That's what my degree is in—Political Science—but I also have a double major in Communication."*

Since Jacob told the senator the position he held at EnViron was Government Affairs Director, I figured he had a degree in government, or at the very least, some previous experience in a legislative office.

As I read through the emails, I couldn't help but wonder how the senator felt when he found out he had a son who shared his interest in politics. I had to believe that discovery created some powerful emotions in him, especially since the senator's other son, Thomas, had never shown any interest in his father's political career.

When the senator wrote Jacob back, he asked, *"Was government your only interest in high school?"*

"No, I also played basketball, a sport I still love today. Waterford North—where I went to high school—made it all the way to the state basketball tournament my senior year. My teammates and I had been friends since elementary school, and I'm still friends with most of them today. They helped me get through the tough times in my life."

"So you grew up in Waterford. Did you ever live anywhere else?"

"No, not until I went away to college. I was born at Waterford Memorial Hospital, and even though my mother told me she grew up in Waterford, I found out she lied to me. In her diary, she said she was living in Bakerton when I was conceived. Naturally, I'm interested in how you met my mother in Bakerton. Is that your hometown?"

"I'll tell you all about myself when we meet in person, but for now, would you mind telling me a little more about the circumstances of how you grew up? Like, what kind of house did you live in? Could your mother afford to take you on vacations? What was your economic situation?"

"My mother worked at the AxonTeague Pharmaceutical Company, Waterford's major employer. Almost everyone in town had at least one family member employed at AXT. She worked in the manufacturing sector on an assembly line, but later, when I was in high school, she became a supervisor. So, yeah, she made a decent living for us, and although I knew I wasn't rich, I never thought of myself as poor."

When the senator wrote back and asked several other questions about Jacob's childhood, along with a couple of questions about Amanda's background, Jacob evidently decided to take a page out of the senator's playbook, and instead of responding, he said he'd answer those questions when they met in person.

"I'm open to meeting you anywhere in the U.S., or at least in the lower forty-eight," Jacob said, *"but I'd need at least a week to make the travel arrangements and request some time off from work."*

The senator wrote back. *"I'll see what I can do and get back to you in a few days."*

Jacob said he was looking forward to hearing from him again, and that was their last email.

As I removed the thumb drive from my computer, I had to agree with the senator—Jacob gave him a lot of information about himself.

Now, I couldn't wait to see what Nina found out about him.

◆ ◆ ◆ ◆

Even though I promised Senator Allen I'd be the chief investigator on his case, I slipped the thumb drive in my pocket and walked down the hall to Leslie's office so I could brief her on the case.

I did this primarily because I'd made a commitment to my staff to keep them updated about every investigation going on at MGI.

I instituted this policy so everyone would feel they were part of a team, but from a personal standpoint, I wanted my investigators to be aware of what I was working on in the event I needed their assistance, or in a worst case scenario, that something happened to me.

As I walked past a partially furnished office on my right—which Greta had already assigned to Kyle Ford—I made a mental note to tell him about this policy when he eventually came to work at MGI.

That couldn't be soon enough for me, especially if we continued to be inundated with inquiries about the agency.

The thought of turning down a client because I didn't have sufficient staff didn't sit well with me, primarily because it made me wonder if I made the right decision by opening the agency early in order to take on the Jared Daley case.

After reminding myself I had prayed about that decision, I pushed those doubts aside and tapped on Leslie's door a couple of times.

When I heard her say, "It's open," and I stepped inside, I suddenly realized I hadn't been in her office since she finished moving in.

Even though I'd hired Inez Flora, a commercial interior designer, to help Greta decorate the place, I later found out Greta instructed Inez to follow the same color scheme throughout the offices; namely, charcoal, ivory, light gray, and dark purple.

Uniformity was a big deal to Greta, so I figured she wasn't happy when Leslie told me she'd added a few personal touches of her own—namely, a pink elephant—to her office décor.

"I've come to see your pink elephant," I said when I walked in.

Leslie, who was seated behind her desk, laughed and pointed over at a corner of the room. "There it is. You can't miss it."

She was right.

A gigantic pink elephant—maybe half the size of a newborn elephant—was prominently displayed in a corner of the room between a pair of gray draperies and a large potted plant.

"I like it," I said. "It definitely says, 'This is Leslie's office.'"

Leslie pushed a wisp of her short blond hair away from her eyes. "I agree, but I think Greta wanted all the offices to say, 'These are Greta's offices,' plus, she thought my pink elephant clashed with the purple chairs in the room and that painting over there."

Across from Leslie's desk was a seating area with two purple chairs and a light gray sofa. Mounted on the wall above the sofa was an oil painting consisting of two large colored splotches of purple and charcoal paint and nothing else.

I sat down in the guest chair in front of her desk. "I have no idea what kind of personal items Kyle will bring with him when he moves in. When I showed him his office, he said he was afraid he'd mess the place up when he got here. He said he might just work out of his car like he usually did."

She shook her head. "Whenever I'm around Kyle, I get the impression he's someone who likes nice things. I bet his comment was just his way of telling you he was looking forward to working for a first-class agency."

"I'm just sorry I didn't know about his interest in leaving the police department sooner. If I'd known that, he'd already be working here and be available to help with all our new clients."

"It sounds like you weren't able to put Senator Allen's personal matter on the back burner. Did it turn out to be something urgent?"

"Yes, it definitely did."

I quickly filled her in on the senator's shocking news, and then I handed her the USB drive with Jacob's emails on it.

"Here's a copy of the emails between Jacob and the senator. If you don't have time to look at them right now, don't worry about it. Nina's putting together a dossier on him, and I guarantee you she'll find a lot more information about him than these emails reveal."

"But you've already read them?"

"Yeah, I've read them. I wanted to get a feel for Jacob's personality before the senator made arrangements for me to meet him in person."

"So what was your impression of him after reading the emails?"

I shrugged. "Jacob sounds like an authentic guy whose world was turned upside down when he found out his mother lied to him about his father. Since he talked about his friends getting him through some tough times in high school, I'm wondering if he had issues with his mother when he was growing up. Of course, that happens to a lot of teenage boys, but the fact that he looked to his friends to help him, instead of a family member, might indicate that."

"Perhaps by the time he got to be a teenager, he realized some things she told him weren't adding up."

"That could be it. He's obviously a very smart man, but he also sounds angry and frustrated in these emails, especially at his mother."

"That's understandable. I can't imagine how angry I'd feel if I discovered everything my mother told me about my father was a lie, and since Jacob's mother isn't around to answer his questions, I'm sure that must add another layer of frustration."

"I'm curious to see how he reacts when he learns his father is a senator, but not just any senator, a powerful one at that."

"Are you absolutely certain he doesn't know that already?"

"No, I'm not sure about that at all."

"Then, I'd proceed with caution if I were you."

"That's my plan."

◆ ◆ ◆ ◆

As I was driving home at the end of the day, I started thinking about how Jacob Walker grew up, and it made me realize how fortunate I was to have grown up in a home where both my parents were not just present, but they willingly made sacrifices for their sons.

Suddenly, as I remembered a scene from my childhood, I surprised myself by getting a little emotional. I suppose it surprised me because it was hardly an earthshaking event.

In fact, it wasn't an event at all.

What I remembered was an ordinary day in my life.

It was a scene from my junior high days. My dad was sitting in the bleachers on a cold windy day watching me play football—a totally inconsequential football game—but there he was, cheering me on as if I were playing in the Super Bowl.

Since he'd just come from work, he was still in his suit and tie.

My brother Curtis was sitting right there beside him, although he wasn't paying much attention to the game.

He was mostly interested in what the cheerleaders were doing—or wearing.

My mother wasn't in the bleachers with them because she always insisted on having her own folding chair next to the stands, closer to the action, so I'd be able to hear her shouting instructions at me.

Although I'd just spoken to Dad after he saw me on the evening news a couple of nights ago, I suddenly felt the need to hear his voice again, and I realized I had the perfect excuse to call him.

He answered my call after only one ring.

"Hi, Mylas. What's going on? Don't tell me you're calling to let me know you'll be on the news again tonight."

"Let's hope not. My preference is to fade into obscurity and stay there. Being famous for four days was enough to last me a lifetime, or maybe even longer."

He laughed. "I hear you. My face is so familiar around town that whenever I show up at somebody's office asking questions, they think I'm there to investigate them."

"Maybe you need to hire more people for your agency and let them do the legwork."

"I can't believe what I'm hearing. Is my son really telling me how to run *my* agency when I've been doing it for decades, and he just opened his own detective agency less than a week ago?"

"No, Dad, it's Mylas Grey *Investigations*. I'm a private *investigator*, not a private detective."

"Oh, that's right. I stand corrected. Well, how's everything going with the agency now that it's up and running? Has that free publicity paid off? Have you gotten any new clients yet?"

"Oh, you bet. More than I anticipated. I was actually calling to get your advice about my newest case. Do you have time for me to run something by you now?"

"You know I've always got time for you, Son. What kind of case is it? Another murder investigation?"

"No, it's not another murder investigation, but I think you'll find it just as intriguing."

To say Dad was fascinated when he heard the details of how Senator Allen discovered he had another son would be an understatement. Then, when he described how difficult it would be for me to investigate something that happened years ago, I thought he sounded jealous I was getting to do it.

Since he often told me how much he enjoyed investigating cold cases when he was with the Columbia Police Department, I figured his envy stemmed from the years he'd spent doing that.

"I'm sure you realize it won't be that easy investigating something that happened that long ago, Mylas. The way you approach the investigation will have to be entirely different, especially if you don't have any witnesses to interview or evidence to examine."

"That's what I wanted to ask you. I vaguely remember you told me about a cold case you worked on that involved an incident in a grocery store, but the store had been demolished several years before you got the case. I'll be surprised if the same thing hasn't happened to the Roadside Inn or that diner in Bakerton. Do you have any suggestions about how I can recreate what happened during those five days Senator Allen lost when he was in Bakerton?"

"You must be talking about Fulsom's Grocery and Produce on Third and Elm. It was torn down to build the new post office. Hmmm. Let me see if I can remember the details of that case."

He was quiet for a moment. "As I recall, a little girl was kidnapped from that store and never found, but when some new evidence came to light several years later, my lieutenant had me reopen the case. Of course, that meant I needed to locate the owner."

"Yeah, that's the one. How were you able to find him?"

"The way I located him was by asking the people who owned the nearby businesses a lot of questions. From what they told me, I pieced together what happened to him when he sold the place. I figured out he moved to Dalton City, where he used to go hunting every fall."

"So that's it? Your advice is to ask the people in Bakerton a lot of questions about the Roadside Inn and the woman in the diner?"

"Yeah, pretty much. You said it's a small town, so it shouldn't be that hard to find people who lived there when Senator Allen spent the night—or I guess several nights—there."

"I hope you're right. That's what the senator wants to know—if the woman in the diner is connected to those days he spent in the motel room where Jacob Walker was conceived. He also—"

"Wait a second, Mylas. You're not automatically assuming the woman he met in the diner is Jacob's mother, are you? That's something you need to watch out for in cold cases—making assumptions."

"No, I wasn't making that assumption. I'm not sure she's even connected to what happened at the motel."

"Good. That's exactly how you should think about it. And here's something else about cold cases. Don't be afraid to expose someone's buried secrets, or go down an unknown road, or question a person's motives for wanting to dig up the past. I realize all these may not apply to Senator's Allen's situation, but it's something to consider."

"I appreciate your insights. Well, Dad, I've just pulled in my driveway, so I better say goodbye. Thanks for your help."

"Before you go, Mylas, tell me what's happening with you and Whitney. You know I'm only asking because your mother will want to know if you mentioned her in this phone call."

I laughed a little. "You can tell Mom everything's fine between us, and Whitney's flying to Washington next week to see me."

"You know that news will make her day."

"Remind her it's just a visit. We're still getting to know each other."

"Do you really think it'll do any good for me to say that?"

"Probably not."

PART TWO

Chapter 7

Sunday, January 9

As I was driving over to Grace Fellowship Church on Sunday morning—located in the Ashton Heights section of Washington—I received a text from Nina.

"Making good progress on putting together the dossier on Jacob's background. It should be ready by tomorrow morning, but I might be able to send it to you tonight."

I waited until I pulled in the church parking lot before texting her back. *"Great news, Nina. As usual, you've exceeded my expectations."*

I paused before hitting the send button while I asked myself if I was laying the praise on a little too thick, but knowing Nina, I decided it was just the right amount.

Once I sent the text, I grabbed my Bible out of the passenger seat and headed toward the church lobby. When I was about halfway across the parking lot, I saw Lockett and his wife, Diana, getting out of their SUV, so I walked over and joined them.

Diana gave me a quick wave. "Hi, Mylas. What's this I hear about you convincing Whitney to make a return visit to Washington?"

"I'm glad to say it didn't take too much convincing. Maybe her last visit wasn't as scary as I thought it was."

She smiled. "Or maybe she's willing to overlook that experience because she can't wait to see you again."

Lockett shook his head. "My wife, the matchmaker."

"Me?" she said, giving his arm a squeeze. "What about the arrangements you've made to give Whitney an incentive to move to Washington?"

"What arrangements would those be?" I asked, as we entered the lobby. "I've been waiting all weekend to hear this brilliant idea of yours."

Lockett motioned down the hall toward a coffee bar called Brewed Blessings where people gathered before the morning worship service. "We've got a few minutes before the service starts. Let's go grab some coffee, and I'll tell you all about it."

When we got there, Diana offered to get our coffees while Lockett and I found an empty table. Once we were seated, he pulled a flyer out of his pocket and handed it to me. "Have you seen this?"

I studied it a minute.

The heading said, "Proposed Children's Building for Grace Fellowship Church." Along with a description, there was an architectural rendition of the structure, including drawings of children entering a two-story building from a playground at the side.

I nodded. "I saw it a few Sundays ago when one of the ministers handed out this flyer. If I recall, he said there'd be another announcement about the cost once the fundraising committee brought their report."

"Good. So you know what I'm talking about. Well, I'm one of the members of the fundraising committee, and we decided to develop a brochure as a means of getting people to contribute to the building campaign. Someone suggested we personalize the brochure by using photographs of the kids who go to Grace Fellowship, so we agreed to hire a professional photographer to take pictures for the publicity."

"Uh-oh. I think I know where this is going."

"Hold on. Don't get ahead of me. As you've obviously guessed, my idea was to hire Whitney to be the photographer, and when I polled the committee, they signed off on it immediately. In fact, they were happy I'd already found someone. So what do you think, Mylas? Would Whitney be interested in doing it?"

"I'll be glad to ask her. You know she loves photographing kids."

Whitney owned a professional photography business called WEE Photography. The name was based on her initials—Whitney Eloise Engel—but it also described her specialty, which was taking pictures of babies and small children.

She started her business after her husband died of pancreatic cancer shortly after their tenth anniversary, and I suspected her decision to start her photography business helped ease the pain of his passing and deal with her feelings about not having any children of her own—she suffered two miscarriages during their marriage.

"When you talk to her about it," Lockett said, as Diana arrived with our coffees, "tell her one of the church secretaries will make all the appointments with the parents of the kids. That's not something she'll need to worry about."

After thanking Diana for the coffee, I smiled and said, "I'll give Whitney a call after church. I suspect she'll be surprised to learn I've arranged for her to work while she's in Washington."

Diana shook her head. "I'm sure that's true. She's probably anticipating spending all her time with you."

"Oh, it won't take her more than a day or two to take the pictures," Lockett said, gesturing at Diana, "and since I know Mylas has an investigation he needs to be working on, having this photography job will mean Whitney won't be bored while she's here."

Diana gave her husband a skeptical look. "I thought you said hiring her to take the pictures was a way to get her to move here."

"Yeah," I said, "how does that fit into this scheme of yours?"

"The beauty of hiring Whitney as the photographer for the brochure is that she'll get to meet a lot of the parents here at Grace Fellowship, and those contacts could possibly lead to her being asked to do individual photography sessions for the kids or their families, which I figure might encourage her to make the decision to move to Washington." He took a sip of coffee. "Do you see how that works?"

"Yeah, I see how it works," I said. "To be honest with you, I haven't talked to Whitney about the possibility of moving to D. C. and bringing her photography business with her."

"Well, don't you think it's about time you did?" Diana asked.

"You won't get any argument from me."

Lockett said, "Personally, I think this photography assignment is the perfect opportunity for you to introduce the topic. If you really want her to move here, then you should convince her to take this job."

After we emptied our cups and headed toward the worship center, I started thinking about Lockett's statement.

He'd brought up a good point.

Did I want to convince Whitney to take this job?

Was that really a good idea?

◆ ◆ ◆ ◆

Although the pastor's sermon usually kept my attention, this Sunday my thoughts kept drifting between the Jacob Walker case and Whitney's visit.

That didn't mean I wasn't listening to what the pastor had to say about Proverbs 3:5-6, the scripture he was using as the basis for his sermon. As I understood it, he was urging us to trust God to know what's best for us even when we don't understand what's going on.

He also said if we would acknowledge God's sovereignty in our lives, he would show us which road to take when we came to a crossroads and had to make a decision about which way to go.

With that in mind, I decided I needed to trust God to show Whitney whether or not to accept the photography assignment for the church brochure. I wouldn't try to influence her one way or the other. I would just be the messenger.

Having made that decision, I grabbed some fast-food on my way home from church and gave Whitney a call when I got to my study.

She said she'd just gotten home from church herself, and then she told me she was planning to spend the rest of the afternoon packing.

"I can't tell you how much I'm looking forward to seeing you tomorrow. What's the weather like? It's not snowing there, is it?"

"No, it's cold, but there's no snow in the forecast. Actually, I think it's supposed to warm up while you're here."

"Really? Then I may need to rethink the clothes I'm bringing."

"This may sound like an odd question, Whitney, but were you planning on bringing your camera with you?"

"Uh . . . sure. I don't usually go anywhere without at least one of my cameras. Why? Is there some reason I shouldn't bring a camera?"

"No, it's just the opposite. Would you believe Nathan has a photography job for you while you're here? I think he's afraid you'll get bored if I have to work during your visit."

She laughed. "Boredom has never been a problem for me. I always have plenty of books to read on my tablet, and I'm never without my sketchpad. Like I've told you before, I'm not expecting you to be my tour guide on this visit. I know you must have plenty of things to do after just opening your agency."

"Being the boss *does* have its perks, so I'll make sure I have some free time. What would you like me to tell Nathan about the job?"

"I'm not sure. What kind of photography assignment is it?"

"It involves children, so it's definitely in your field of expertise."

I spent the next few minutes telling her about the brochure, and the concept the fundraising committee had for personalizing it by including photos of the kids who went to Grace Fellowship Church.

"I love that idea," she said. "I can see how personalizing it would be an attention-getter, plus an incentive to give to the campaign."

"He wanted me to mention that one of the church secretaries will be responsible for setting up the appointments with the parents of the kids. You won't have to do anything but show up and take pictures."

She chuckled. "Well, there's a little more to a photography session than that, but I have to say it sounds like a fun assignment. What do you think? Should I agree to do it?"

"I'm fine with whatever you decide. And don't worry about transportation to the church, or the kids' houses, or wherever you need to be. I'll get Joe to drive you to any location. You remember Joe, don't you? He's my handyman. Or, if you'd rather not have him chauffeur you around, you can drive yourself. We can work out those details when you get here."

"It sounds like fun. I think I'll do it." Suddenly, she laughed. "I can't believe I just said yes."

"You can always change your mind."

"No. I have a really good feeling about this. I'm sticking with it."

"I'll give Nathan a call and let him know."

"Be sure and tell him I said thank you for considering me."

"I will, and if you don't mind, I'll give him your phone number, and the two of you can work out the rest of the arrangements yourself."

"No, I don't mind. That's probably the best way to do it. Speaking of arrangements, thank you for getting everything worked out about my plane ticket. To be truthful, I was looking for an email from you about my flight schedule, and when someone named Greta sent me an email Friday afternoon, I thought it was spam. I almost didn't open it, but just before I deleted it, I remembered that your assistant's name is Greta."

"Oh, I'm sorry. I should have told you I was having Greta make your reservations. I asked her to make sure your flight arrived in the afternoon since Mrs. Higbee wants to fix dinner for you. Greta said your plane gets in at four-fifteen. I hope that's a good time for you."

"Yes, it's perfect. I have to admit, Mylas, I'm not used to having someone I've never met make plans for me."

For a moment, I thought Whitney might be irritated with me because I hadn't made the arrangements myself, but then she said, "Thank you for paying for my ticket, Mylas. I just hope my visit won't be too hard on Mrs. Higbee. I know the last time I was there she really outdid herself."

"Are you kidding? She can't wait for you to get here. She's almost as excited about it as I am—not quite, but close."

"Please tell her not to go to a lot of trouble for me."

"I'll share a little secret with you. Mrs. Higbee seldom listens to me." Whitney laughed.

Tomorrow couldn't get here soon enough for me.

◆ ◆ ◆ ◆

For the next couple of hours, I sat in front of my computer learning everything I could about Bakerton, Maryland.

Even though I figured Nina would give me the pertinent statistics when I was ready to visit the place, I went ahead and studied the aerial views, read the town's history, and viewed the dozen or so photographs on their website.

The end result of my research was that when I finished, I had a pretty good idea of how big the town was and how it was laid out.

Like most small towns in the area, Bakerton had a town square with a courthouse in the middle and various businesses—from law offices to retail shops to banks—on the streets surrounding it.

Branching out from the town square was a residential area with dozens of older homes—some with a historic designation—while a few miles beyond the town square were a couple of subdivisions with newer homes. Near the freeway was a modern shopping center, along with a few gas stations and some restaurants.

There was no Roadside Inn listed on the website as part of the town's accommodations, although there were three motels in Bakerton, all of them right off the freeway and all of them connected to national motel chains.

As I studied a city map, I jotted down a couple of questions on my phone to ask Senator Allen what he remembered about the diner, and just as I finished, a text popped up from Nina.

"Are you available to talk now?"

Instead of texting her back, I called her.

"Hey, what's up?" I asked. "Don't tell me you're working on the Jacob Walker case. I didn't mean for you to work on it all weekend."

"Oh, don't give me that. You knew I wouldn't quit until I got done. What about you? I bet you're in front of your computer right now."

"Guilty as charged. I've been immersing myself in the culture of Bakerton, Maryland."

"Anything interesting pop up?"

"Not unless you consider the Bakerton Historical Museum, the Art and Crafts Depot downtown, or the Sutter Grist Mill interesting. Those seem to be the town's main attractions."

"Well, if you want, when I get my office set up next week, I'll see what else I can find out about Bakerton, but in the meantime, I wanted to let you know I finished the dossier on Jacob. I don't have his casebook prepared yet, but I can get that done in a few days."

"That's great, Nina. Why don't I pick up the physical copy of the dossier from you tomorrow morning when you come to the office? I plan to be there by eight o'clock so I can introduce you to everyone."

"Okay, that works for me. I'll email you a copy of the dossier for your records when we get off the phone."

"Do you mind hitting the highlights for me now? What's the bottom line?"

"The bottom line is Jacob appears to be exactly who he says he is. Everything he told the senator about growing up in Waterford is authenticated by what I found out about him. Like he told the senator, he lives in Lanham now, which is about thirty minutes from D. C."

After Nina gave me the details of Jacob's childhood—the names of his friends, the broken arm he had in seventh grade, his grade point average in high school, the kind of car he drove in college—she reiterated there wasn't any discrepancy between what she found out about him, and what he told the senator about himself.

"Most of the details I described were available in either his yearbooks or his school records, but nowadays, people are always posting things on social media about what happened to them in high school. That's where I discovered what kind of car he drove, and a bunch of other things you'll find out about him in the dossier."

"Does Jacob use social media a lot?"

"No, not really, but one of his basketball buddies from high school does. He has dozens of pictures on his account, and he comments about them all the time, tags everyone in the photographs, and makes them available to anyone who wants to see them."

"Not into privacy, is he?"

"No, but I'm not complaining."

"Can I assume everything checked out about Jacob's mother working at AXT in Waterford?"

"Yes, and I didn't have any problem getting into their archived personnel records and finding an employee named Amanda Louise Walker, who began working at AXT thirty-seven years ago. Jacob wouldn't have even been born then. She was employed at AXT until she retired three years ago."

When Nina didn't say anything for a moment, I felt my pulse quicken. If she got quiet, that usually indicated she'd found something she figured I'd be interested in, but she wanted me to dig for it.

I got out my shovel.

Chapter 8

The first thing I did was question Nina about Amanda's employment at AxonTeague Pharmaceutical, and whether she worked on the assembly line at the drug company like Jacob mentioned in his emails to Senator Allen.

"Yes, that's where she worked for ten years, same job, same responsibilities. When Jacob started high school, she became a supervisor for that same assembly line unit, and then before she retired, she was promoted to division manager."

"Sounds like she was a good employee."

"Yeah, that's what it sounds like, and that's how it appears on the surface."

"Do I hear a note of skepticism there?"

"Well, I thought ten years seemed like a long time for someone to work on an assembly line without moving up the ladder, so I took a look at the work records of some of the other employees, and sure enough, most of them received pay increases and were assigned jobs with more responsibility after just a couple of years."

"Why wasn't that true of Amanda?"

"That's what I wanted to find out. I figured it was either a disciplinary problem, health issue, or poor work ethic, and to find out, I . . . uh . . . well . . . uh . . . let's just say I did some exploring and worked my magic."

When Nina "worked her magic," as she called it, I knew I shouldn't ask too many questions, so all I said was, "So which one was it?"

"It turned out to be a health problem. At least, that's what I suspected after reading her evaluation reports for those ten years."

"Really? Are you telling me you saw . . . Oh, forget I said that. Just tell me what kind of health problems you think she had."

"I don't know that yet. In her annual evaluations, there are notes about time off for doctor visits and absences due to medical concerns, but whatever she was dealing with is never spelled out in those evaluations. There's a reference to the medications she was taking, but those medications are never named."

"Since she was eventually promoted, did something change?"

"I believe so. The year before she was promoted, her evaluation referred to her improvement, commended her attentiveness to detail, and noted her lack of absences. It also included a recommendation that she be considered for a promotion."

"And what about when she became a supervisor? Did her evaluations mention any health issues?"

"No. She seems to have had smooth sailing after those early years, and she received excellent evaluations as a supervisor."

"Naturally, I'm curious about the medications she was taking."

"So am I, but I haven't been able to find out anything . . . at least not yet, but I'm still working on it."

◆ ◆ ◆ ◆

I told Nina it wasn't necessary to spend any more time digging into Amanda's past. I figured I'd get those answers when I met with Jacob in a few days.

"Right now," I said, "I'm more interested in what you found out about Jacob's present situation. You said he lives in Lanham, Maryland. Give me a synopsis of his living arrangements, family life, finances, anything of interest I might need to pay attention to."

"Okay. When I send you the summary sheet after we get off the phone, I'll include more details of what I'm about to tell you, and of course, I'll have the documentation in the casebook later, but the synopsis of Jacob's present situation is that he's thirty-six years old, single, never been married, and owns a condo in Lanham."

"New or old condo?"

"New. It's not one of the older, downtown condos everyone's paying top dollar for these days. He bought this one five years ago after renting an apartment in the same area. He drives a Honda SUV, has a checking account at a bank near his condo, a retirement fund where he works, and his credit rating is average for his age group."

"So there aren't any red flags popping up for you about the guy? Is that what I'm hearing?"

"That's what you're hearing. Keep in mind I'm only looking at the data behind the man. He could be a complete jerk or a perfect gentleman, but the facts and figures I have here don't tell me which one he is. Sorry, but I can't give you any insight into his personality."

"Not even from reading his emails?"

"I couldn't tell that much about him from his emails. Could you?"

"Yeah, I picked up a few things. I thought he came across as a nice guy, someone who wants to connect with his father, maybe get to experience the family he never had, but I also sensed some anger and frustration in some of his answers."

She let out a short laugh. "Your insight into Jacob's personality is completely based on feelings and not on observable facts."

"I can't deny that, but within a few days I'll have firsthand, observable facts to back up those feelings."

"Or disprove them."

"That too."

◆ ◆ ◆ ◆

When I was on Senator Allen's staff as head of his investigative team, I followed office protocol when I needed to meet with the senator.

That protocol consisted of contacting his chief of staff, that is, Nathan Lockett, and requesting an appointment with the senator.

Since I no longer had that kind of relationship with the senator, I figured it was acceptable for me to contact the senator directly without going through Lockett.

However, as I sat at my desk, with my finger poised over Senator Allen's personal cell phone number, I hesitated.

Would the senator view our relationship differently now?

Probably not.

Like most long-time congressional leaders on Capitol Hill, once Senator Allen put on the mantle of power, he discovered the accessories that went with it—deference, awe, admiration, and reverence—were almost as prized as the garment itself.

After thinking about it a little more, I decided it would please the senator, and probably be advantageous to me, if I kept the protocol of our relationship intact.

With that in mind, I punched in Lockett's number instead.

Lockett immediately assumed I was calling to let him know about Whitney and whether she was willing to take on the photography assignment, so I covered that topic first.

Once I told him when Whitney would be arriving, and I shared her contact information with him, I went over the basics of what Nina found out about Jacob Walker.

"This report makes me feel a little better about the situation," he said. "At least, Jacob doesn't sound like he's some complete nut job."

"No, there's no indication of that."

"As soon as you go over these details with the senator, I'm sure he'll want to make arrangements for you to meet with Jacob. The senator's schedule is clear in the morning, so if you're available, I'll go ahead and make the appointment for you."

Lockett's quick offer to schedule an appointment with the senator confirmed I'd made the right decision about not contacting him directly, so after giving myself a mental pat on the back, I said, "That works for me, Nathan. Just shoot me a text with the time."

"Will do."

As I was about to disconnect the call, I heard Lockett say, "Oh, wait a second, Mylas. I need to give you a heads up about a derogatory article that ran in the *St. Louis Post-Dispatch* concerning Senator Allen. He'll probably be upset when you meet with him tomorrow, and I don't want you to think it has anything to do with you or the situation with Jacob. His bad mood will strictly be because of this article. He's stewing over it big time."

"You mean it ran in today's paper, the Sunday edition?"

"Unfortunately, yes."

"Well, that's a bummer."

Although politicians hated to have negative stories written about them, no matter when they were published, articles that ran in the Sunday edition of a newspaper tended to have a greater impact on the voters.

There was disagreement about what was behind this.

Some thought it was because more people tended to read newspapers on Sunday, while others figured it was because articles appearing in a Sunday edition were usually written by top-tier journalists and more people paid attention to them for that reason.

Lockett said, "Yes, the fact that the article ran today is part of the reason he's upset about it, but that's not the only reason. The article itself is what's disturbing him. It's extremely critical of the senator in a personal way, accusing him of spending too much time in Washington and thus being out of touch with the people of Missouri. The journalist who wrote the story also intimated Senator Allen was spending countless hours on the golf course and was seldom at the Capitol. She even quoted an unnamed source who claimed there was evidence the senator misused campaign funds for personal use."

"This sounds like the beginning of a smear campaign by George Houser. Didn't he use this same tactic when he was running for his House seat two years ago?"

"Yes, and Houser also ran a dirty campaign when he was a candidate for a state office. The thing is, it usually works for him."

"I can see why the senator might be upset by the article. Thanks for the warning, Nathan. I won't take his attitude personally when I see him tomorrow."

After he promised to send me a text with my appointment time, Lockett said goodbye and while I waited to hear back from him, I opened my internet browser to see if I could find the article he mentioned in the online edition of the *St. Louis Post-Dispatch*.

It was there all right, and after reading it, I understood why it concerned Lockett and angered the senator. Not only was there nothing redeeming about the article, it was filled with innuendos and information I knew to be incorrect.

But, as soon as I reached the end of the piece and saw the name and picture of the journalist who wrote it, I knew why.

It was written by Fiona Burkhart, a Washington-based journalist known for her willingness to write about gossip and scandals, as long as the person feeding her information reciprocated by giving her an exclusive story or arranging an interview with a well-placed government official.

In this case, I figured she got her half-truths and skewed facts from George Houser, the senator's presumed opponent in the upcoming fall election. Or, since she made no secret of the fact she disagreed with the senator's policy on most issues, perhaps Ms. Burkhart decided to go after Senator Allen herself without any outside influence.

I was acquainted with Ms. Burkhart.

We met a few months after I became the senator's chief investigator for the R & I Group, when I was vetting Judge Casey Alcorn, one of the President's nominees for the Fifth Circuit Court of Appeals, and Lockett saw an article she'd written about the judge.

Since I was investigating Judge Alcorn, Lockett wanted me to take her out to dinner and see if I could find out where she got her information.

Although Ms. Burkhart was pleasant enough, even flirted with me a little, she refused to tell me anything about her source.

Then, as we were leaving the restaurant, she turned to me and said, "I've heard the rumors about you being an excellent investigator, Mylas, but don't make the mistake of thinking Senator Allen is the only person on Capitol Hill who hires investigators to make their job easier."

At the time, I didn't know if she was referring to legislators or journalists, but after reading some scathing articles she wrote that presented government officials in a less than flattering light, I realized she probably meant that journalists also hired investigators.

I came to this conclusion after noticing there were certain aspects of her articles—detailed accusations, chronological timelines, and eyewitness accounts—that bore all the hallmarks of a good investigator, someone who'd done some heavy-duty legwork, and I didn't believe that investigator was Fiona.

When I asked Nina about it, she had no idea what private detective Ms. Burkhart might be using. "To be truthful, Mylas, I'm not that interested in finding out either."

"I can't believe what I'm hearing, Nina. When I joined Senator Allen's staff, you told me you loved ferreting out information and scouring the internet for obscure facts. Why aren't you interested in knowing which investigator Ms. Burkhart uses for her reporting?"

"Because Fiona Burkhart isn't a reporter. She's a gossip columnist who speculates about people's lives. Facts aren't important to her. What she writes about is pure fantasy. Why should I waste my professional skills on her?"

At that point, I dropped the subject, and since I'd never had an occasion to bring it up again, I forgot about it.

Now, even though I was curious about where Ms. Burkhart got her information for the article she wrote in the *St. Louis Post-Dispatch* about Senator Allen, I failed to see how it had any bearing on the Jacob Walker case, so I shut down my browser and clicked on my email, intending to look at the summary sheet Nina sent me.

But then, when I glanced down at my watch, I realized it was time for my standing appointment with Mrs. Higbee, the one we had every Sunday evening to go over her weekly household schedule.

The one where she informed me what she would be doing.

The one where I pretended to be in charge.

◆ ◆ ◆ ◆

Mrs. Higbee and I always met around the kitchen table. It was the only time we sat at the table together when it wasn't formally laid out with placemats, place settings, and platters of food.

Not that there wasn't food available.

There was always food available if there were at least two people in Mrs. Higbee's kitchen. However, on Sunday evenings, the food was served buffet style on the kitchen counter, which meant we each took a plate, filled it with the selections we wanted, and brought our plates over to the kitchen table where Mrs. Higbee had her calendar, her long to-do list, her grocery list, and a gigantic notepad.

Tonight, the buffet consisted of all the ingredients for a ham and cheese sandwich, plus a bowl of potato salad, a plate of veggies—including a spicy dip to disguise the taste of the celery and carrot sticks—some baked beans, and fudge brownies.

Occasionally, Joe Blondi, my handyman and groundskeeper who lived in the apartment above my detached garage, joined us for the Sunday evening buffet. But Joe—a wrongly accused ex-convict who came to work for Mac after he got him released from prison—wasn't a person who enjoyed people, so he didn't eat with us that often.

Besides people, Joe made no secret of the fact he didn't enjoy Babe's company, so I was surprised when I walked in the kitchen and asked Mrs. Higbee why I didn't see Babe around.

"You don't see Babe because Joe took him for a walk. They've been gone for almost ten minutes, and since Joe can't last for more than twenty minutes, I'm sure they'll be back soon."

"I have a hard time believing it was Joe's idea to take Babe for a walk. Did you ask him to do it?"

She brought her plate over to the table where I was already seated. "Yes, I did," she said, nodding her head. "Every time I went by your study this afternoon, I heard you on the phone, so I didn't think you'd have time to walk Babe tonight."

"My phone calls are done for the day, but you're right, I'll be busy this evening going over a dossier for an appointment I have tomorrow morning."

"But you're picking Whitney up from the airport, aren't you? You're not sending Joe after her?"

"No, of course not. I'll be there when her plane lands."

"That's good. What about the rest of your week? Do you know when you'll be eating here and when you'll be eating out?"

Although I assured Mrs. Higbee we'd be having dinner at the house tomorrow night, I wasn't able to give her much of a schedule beyond that. To explain why, I told her about the photography sessions Whitney would be doing for the church's fundraising brochure.

Her reaction to hearing this was predictable. "Hmmm. I wonder if I should bake her some cookies to take to the kids? I bet they would do anything she wanted them to do if she brought them cookies."

I suggested she ask Whitney that question, and even though she said she would, I saw her write down several items on her grocery list.

By the time our planning session was over, the two of us agreed that Whitney and I would have at least three dinners at my house during the week. I figured this would be a sufficient amount for Mrs. Higbee to show off her culinary skills, especially since I pointed out she would also be fixing us breakfast every morning.

Although it wasn't technically part of the meal planning session, once we had the schedule, she informed me she'd purchased a new duvet for the bed in the Princess Room, along with matching pillows for the chaise lounge.

"That's fine, Mrs. Higbee, but Whitney specifically asked me to tell you not to go to a lot of trouble for her."

She waved her hand at me dismissively. "Oh, that's just because she's a sweet girl, and she's not used to having someone take care of things for her. It probably makes her feel uncomfortable."

"You're right. That's pretty much what she told me."

Mrs. Higbee reached over and took my empty plate, stacking it on top of hers. "You were the same way when you first moved in here after Mac passed away. If you remember, it took you a few weeks to let me do your laundry, not to mention make your bed for you."

"I'd forgotten that." I gave her a smile. "Thanks for reminding me."

She gave me a smile back. "My pleasure."

I shrugged. "I admit it didn't take me long to get accustomed to a different lifestyle. I adapted pretty quickly."

She bobbed her head up and down a couple of times as she removed the plates from the table. "And I'm sure Whitney would do the same . . . if she really wanted to have a different lifestyle."

I started to ask her if there was some reason why Whitney wouldn't want to have household help or a higher standard of living, but Babe rushed into the kitchen at that moment—with Joe trailing behind him trying to grab his leash—so I never got the chance.

Or, maybe I wasn't that interested in hearing the answer.

Chapter 9

Monday, January 10

When I arrived at the Greystone Center a couple of minutes before eight o'clock on Monday morning, Nina's SUV was already parked at the side of the building.

Nina wasn't in her vehicle, but when I entered the building through the employee entrance and heard laughter coming from the break room—just around the corner from the back door—I recognized her low chuckle immediately.

Identifying Greta's laughter took me a few seconds longer—perhaps that's because I wasn't expecting to hear the two of them yukking it up together.

I headed for the coffee machine when I walked in. "Good morning. I see the two of you have already met each other." I nodded in Nina's direction. "I'm sorry I'm late, Nina. I was hoping to get here before you arrived so I could introduce you to everyone."

She shook her head. "I was too excited to sleep, so I went ahead and drove over here thinking I'd have to wait in the parking lot until eight before someone showed up, but when I arrived at seven-thirty, I saw a light on inside, and when I knocked on the door, Greta let me in."

"I'm always here by seven-twenty," Greta said. "When I worked on Capitol Hill, that's when congressional staffers arrived, so I'm used to it. Besides, I suspected Nina might show up early today."

After pouring myself some coffee, I glanced over at Nina. "Have you been upstairs to see your office yet?"

She nodded. "I took some boxes up there as soon as Greta let me in. I couldn't believe what a nice office it is. It's a perfect size."

"You can thank Greta for the decorating job."

Nina smiled. "Yes, she told me she chose the colors."

Greta shook her head at Nina. "I just hope all that office equipment you ordered will fit in that space. The delivery guy brought in so many boxes on Friday, he had to make three trips."

"Oh, there's plenty of room. I'm sure everything will fit once I get the boxes unpacked. I just need to get it all arranged."

"I don't mind helping you with that," Greta said. "The interior designer Mylas hired said I had an eye for that sort of thing."

Nina took a sip of her coffee before she responded. "Thanks for the offer, Greta, and I might take you up on that later on, but I need to get everything unboxed first."

Greta gave Nina a half-smile as she walked over to the sink and started rinsing out her empty coffee mug. "Sure, just let me know."

A few seconds later, as she was leaving the room, Greta gestured at some photographs on the table next to Nina's purse.

"Thanks for sharing your cute pictures with me," she said. "We'll have to get our babies together for a play date soon. I bet they'll enjoy being with each other almost as much as we'll enjoy watching them."

When Greta left, I walked over and glanced down the hallway to make sure she entered her office before I sat down next to Nina.

"What babies was Greta talking about? Your grandkids aren't babies anymore."

She reached over and picked up the photographs. As soon as she showed them to me, I decided I shouldn't have been concerned about her ability to get along with Greta.

Nina's "babies" were two dogs, which I didn't think looked all that different from the pictures I'd seen in Greta's office of her two miniature schnauzers, although Greta's dogs were groomed a little differently, plus they were wearing blue ribbons around their necks.

"When you walked in," Nina said, "Greta was just telling me about being at a dog show this weekend, and I was showing her these pictures of the two dogs I recently adopted, Giga and Mega.

"Cute names."

"Thanks. I thought so. Their full names are Gigabyte and Megabyte. When I rescued them at the animal shelter, I was told they were part schnauzer, and Greta said she agreed."

When I heard that, I wondered if Greta was laughing *with* Nina when I walked in or *at* Nina, or rather at Giga and Mega, who obviously weren't blue ribbon winners.

I didn't mention that to Nina.

◆ ◆ ◆ ◆

By the time we finished our coffee, a couple of the surveillance team members arrived, and once I introduced them to Nina, we took the elevator up to the second floor.

As we got off, I pointed down the hall to my right. "My office suite is down here, but I'm sure Greta told you that when she was showing you around."

"She didn't really show me around. She just took me to my office." She gave me a crooked smile. "After she left though, I did a little snooping on my own."

"Why does that not surprise me?"

She shrugged. "What can I say?"

"I'd invite you to see my office now, but I really need to get the dossier on Jacob Walker from you. I have a ten o'clock appointment to go over it with Senator Allen this morning."

"I can come see your office another time. If you follow me down to my office, I'll grab the dossier for you." As we began heading down the hallway, she asked, "Do you have any questions for me about the dossier? I assume you read it last night."

"Oh, yeah, I read it. I *did* have one question. Did you come across anything that indicated how Jacob got his job at EnViron Industries? There are usually so many applicants for a government affairs position, a person can't get an interview unless they know someone."

She opened her office door. "I'm sorry, Mylas. I don't have that information right now. It's not something I'd ordinarily find in his personnel record, but if I had to guess, I'd say his previous job could be the reason he got this one."

I paused in the doorway and looked around.

Greta wasn't exaggerating.

There were so many boxes in Nina's office—most of them I identified as office equipment—I had a hard time believing she'd be able to fit everything inside once she got them unpacked.

I said, "When you say Jacob's previous job, are you talking about the position he took at the Federal Communications Commission when he graduated from college? That's the only one I remember seeing on the summary sheet."

"Yes, that's it."

She walked over to her desk and removed a brown envelope from a leather attaché case. "Jacob was the Assistant Coordinator for Public Affairs at the FCC. I'm guessing the title of that position was enough to get him an interview at EnViron Industries."

After pulling some papers out of the envelope, she came around the side of her desk and handed me a sheet with several photographs on it. "Of course, being a good-looking guy probably didn't hurt anything either." She tapped her fingernail on a photo. "What do you think?"

It was the first time I'd seen a photograph of Jacob, and I was taken aback by it. "I'm sure you're right. He . . . uh . . . uh . . ."

"Bears an uncanny resemblance to Senator Allen? Is that what you're thinking?"

"Yeah. That's it. Of course, I don't know if that's because I'm looking for it or if he really does favor him."

"Trust me. He favors him. His eyes are exactly the same shape, and he has the same high forehead. If you go to the next sheet, you'll see a photograph of Amanda. I downloaded it from her personnel file at AXT, and you can tell Jacob has his mother's nose. Overall though, he looks like a younger version of Senator Allen. There's no denying it."

"No, there's no denying it. I've seen several pictures of the senator before his hair turned white, and he had dark-brown hair just like Jacob does in these photographs."

"All these pictures were taken within the last five years, except for this one of him in his high school basketball uniform. I pulled three of these pictures from social media, but the rest of them I downloaded from the EnViron website."

I pointed to a photograph that showed Jacob sitting with a young lady at what appeared to be some kind of awards banquet. "You wouldn't know if this woman is his date or just one of his EnViron colleagues who happened to be sitting with him, would you?"

She tilted her head and gave me her you've-got-to-be-kidding-me look. "What a foolish question. Of course I do. I found a group picture of her with her department co-workers at EnViron. I even know her name. It's Felicia Grassley."

"But you don't know if she's both a colleague *and* his date for the awards banquet?"

"No. How could I know that?"

I smiled at her.

Her blue eyes widened. "Are you implying you have that information? I thought you didn't know anything about Jacob. Why did you have me doing all this research if—"

"Wait a second, Nina. Hear me out. I know absolutely nothing about the man except what you and the senator told me. Despite that, I'm guessing Felicia was his date for the evening, and I'm basing that on his body language in this photograph."

I pointed at Jacob in the photo. "See how he's leaning in toward her? And then look at the placement of their hands on the table. They're right next to each other. If you enlarged this photograph, you'd probably be able to see their hands are actually touching."

"So you're saying they're in a relationship?"

"I'm not positive about it, but I'm seeing it as a possibility."

She took the sheet from me and gave it a closer look. "I can't tell if you're right or not, but I could do some more research to see if there's any evidence they're in a relationship." She paused and looked back at her desk. "But first, I need to get some things put away here."

"No, forget about doing more research." I gestured at the brown envelope. "Once I show Senator Allen the dossier and hear how he wants to proceed, I'll get back with you this afternoon about what else I need on Jacob, or anyone else associated with this case."

Nina returned the photographs to the envelope and handed it to me. "But I thought you were picking Whitney up from the airport this afternoon. You're not having her take a taxi to your place, are you?"

I shook my head as I headed for the door. "No, I wouldn't ask her to do that. I'm picking her up myself."

"That's good. Be sure and tell her I said hi, and that I'm looking forward to seeing her again."

"Will do."

On my way back down to my office, I asked myself why both my housekeeper and Nina questioned me about my plans to be at the airport to meet Whitney. Even if I *had* asked Whitney if she would mind taking a taxi, I didn't think that would be such a big deal.

I felt certain Whitney could handle it. After all, she was a forty-five-year-old businesswoman. Why wouldn't she be able to find her way around Washington? In fact, I felt certain most of my female acquaintances would be offended if I implied they weren't capable of navigating the city.

Since I was walking past Leslie Irving's office at that moment, I realized she was a perfect example of what I was thinking, although I immediately decided putting Leslie in the same category as Whitney wasn't a good comparison.

The two women were nothing alike.

Leslie was more assertive than Whitney, more of a risk-taker, more self-assured, and much more outspoken.

As if to validate my point, I heard Leslie talking on her phone as she came around the corner from the elevators.

"Well, those are just the breaks," she was saying to her caller. "Tell him he needs to suck it up and get on with his life."

Leslie smiled and gave me a brief nod as we passed each other.

Ordinarily, I wouldn't have thought anything about her brash tone, but today it reminded me I'd gotten used to being around women in Washington who were constantly under pressure to defend their turf, assert their power, and demand respect.

If they chose not to do so, they weren't around very long.

By the time I entered my office and sat down at my desk, I thought I understood why Nina and Mrs. Higbee were so concerned about my attitude toward Whitney.

They were afraid I might not be aware Whitney wasn't used to the rarefied air of Washington.

They must have sensed her uneasiness about living in Washington when they met Whitney during her last visit, and they didn't think I was aware of it or thought it was that important.

That realization gave me pause.

Why would they have that impression of me?

Sure, I had a tendency to get absorbed in a case or preoccupied with certain aspects of an investigation, but I was in love with Whitney, so wouldn't that mean I was tuned in to her emotions and what she was thinking?

Evidently, Mrs. Higbee and Nina didn't think so.

They were wrong about that. I was sure of it.

♦ ♦ ♦ ♦

When I arrived at Senator Allen's office suite, I discovered Jenna had taken the day off, and Toni McCaffrey, Lockett's secretary, was taking her place at the receptionist's desk.

Unlike Jenna, she didn't seem the least bit curious when I told her I had an appointment with the senator.

"Yes, he's expecting you," she said, waving her hand toward Corridor A. "Just go knock on his door."

As I approached the senator's door, Lockett was coming out of his office across the hall, and once we greeted each other, I tapped on the senator's door a couple of times.

His "come in" sounded more like a growl than a welcoming invitation, and when I glanced over at Lockett, he raised his eyebrows at me before I turned the knob, and we walked inside.

The senator was seated on his leather couch surrounded by a stack of newspapers, and from what I could tell, they were all newspapers from Missouri. The one he was reading was the *Jefferson City News Tribune*, but he laid it aside as we walked over.

Extending his palm toward Lockett, he said, "Can you believe every single newspaper in the whole state decided to run that article about me? Why would they bother? It's all a bunch of lies."

Lockett didn't have time to respond before the senator gestured at me and said, "I hope you have some good news for me, Mylas."

"I believe so."

After Lockett and I sat down in the wing-back chairs across from the sofa, I opened the envelope containing Jacob's dossier and handed him the summary sheet, along with the photographs and the extra page Nina had included on Amanda.

The summary sheet was on top of the photographs, and he began reading it first. Since I didn't have another summary sheet for Lockett, I gave him the full dossier, and he immediately began thumbing through it.

"Nothing I'm seeing here contradicts anything Jacob told me about himself," the senator said. "Of course, there's a lot in here he didn't tell me, like where he banks and what kind of car he drives, etc., but I wouldn't expect him to tell me that. Naturally, I'm really glad to know he's never been in trouble with the law, and he doesn't have a criminal record. I'd really have a hard time if—"

Suddenly, Senator Allen froze as he flipped over to the photographs.

It was hard to tell if he was even breathing.

Lockett, who was still reading from the data sheets, looked up and asked, "What's wrong, Senator?"

He turned the page around for Lockett to see.

"This is my son. This is Jacob."

Lockett studied the photographs for a few seconds, and then he nodded. "Yes, Senator. He looks like your son, all right."

The senator appeared to get teary-eyed for a moment, but then he turned the page and saw the next photograph, the one of Amanda Walker from her AXT personnel file.

After taking a deep breath, he asked, "Is this Jacob's mother?"

"Yes," I said, nodding my head, "that's Amanda Walker."

He shook his head. "Well, when I met this woman at the diner in Bakerton, she told me her name was Shirley."

Chapter 10

After the senator made this statement, I asked him if he was absolutely certain the woman in the picture was the same young lady he ate dinner with in Bakerton thirty-seven years ago.

He bristled at my question. "Of course I am, Mylas. I realize it was a long time ago, but as you know, I have an excellent memory. And besides that, we sat across from each other for over an hour. If I say this is a picture of Shirley, you can be certain it is."

I had no idea if the senator's testy reaction was because I seldom challenged him, or because Ms. Burkhart's article had already put him in a bad mood, but since his observation made his case less complicated for me, I didn't care which one it was.

"This is actually very good news, Senator," I said. "It means the focus of my investigation will be on Amanda. Even if there were other people involved in what happened to you in that motel room, she was obviously present, so that's where I'll begin."

His hand shook a little as he looked down at the photograph again.

"I just wish I could recall something besides the confusing memories of my dreams. I can't tell you how frustrating that is."

"I realize it—"

Suddenly, as I was speaking, the senator tossed the papers aside, got up from the sofa, and walked over to his desk.

"—must be difficult for you, Senator, but if—"

"I'm sending Jacob an email," he said, sitting down at his computer. "I want to meet him somewhere right away, this week if possible."

"Okay, that's fine, but—"

"No, don't try to talk me out of it, Mylas. This matter needs to be settled sooner rather than later."

As he was typing on his computer, I looked over at Lockett to see what his response was to the senator's sudden decision.

He gave me a shrug.

I suppose, like me, he didn't see any reason for him not to email Jacob, although I admit I would have preferred for us to discuss it first.

"I wasn't going to talk you out of it, Senator," I said. "I was just wondering whether you meant you were planning to meet Jacob in person, or you wanted me to go in your place like we talked about the other day."

The senator sighed and sat back in his chair. "There, it's done. I told Jacob I was in the Washington area, and I was ready to meet him whenever he's available. My only request was that we meet at a restaurant of my choosing."

Being in charge of where to meet someone or hold a meeting was a tactic the power players on Capitol Hill often used. They did it primarily to make sure everyone knew who was in charge, but in this case, I wasn't sure if that was the senator's motive.

After Senator Allen came over and sat down on the sofa again, he motioned at me. "To answer your question, Mylas, yes, I still want you to go in my place, but I'm not going to tell Jacob that's what I'm doing. Otherwise, he might not show up."

Lockett said, "I'm glad to hear you're sticking to that plan, Senator. I wouldn't advise you to meet him in a public place until you've made an announcement about your relationship. Wherever you go, there's always a reporter hanging around taking pictures of you, and . . . well . . . with the family resemblance, someone might start asking questions before you had the answers."

"I'm curious why you wanted to choose the location," I said. "Was it out of habit or something else?"

The senator smiled at my question. "I suppose by 'habit' you're referring to the . . . uh . . . tradition in this town that the . . . uh . . . person with the most clout gets to choose where to meet. Is that what you mean?"

"That's a very diplomatic way of putting it, but, yes, that's what I was asking."

"The answer is no. That's not the reason I wanted to choose the location. I decided to suggest we meet at a restaurant because I think he'd expect me to do that. That's what most people would do if they were meeting a complete stranger and didn't have any background information on them. They'd meet in a public place. I believe the best place for me, or rather for you, to meet him is at Romanos."

"Oh yes, Romanos," Lockett said, nodding his head. "That's perfect." He looked over at me. "Are you okay with that, Mylas? I'm sure you're familiar with their facilities, aren't you?"

I nodded. "If you're referring to their private rooms away from the main dining area, then yes, I'm familiar with them. During my lawyering days, I went there with Mac when we needed to meet a client who didn't want to be seen at our offices."

"So you understand why I'm going to suggest that restaurant?" the senator asked. "Even though it's a public place, you'll be able to meet with Jacob privately in one of their club rooms. As soon as I hear from him, I'll have Nathan make a reservation at Romanos in my name so you and Jacob can talk freely without fear of being overheard."

"That's good because it's difficult to predict what kind of reaction he'll have when he realizes you lied to him and sent me in your place instead of meeting him yourself like you said you would. I'd rather be alone with him when I tell him about your reason for doing that."

The senator frowned. "I'm not exactly lying to Jacob. I'm really looking forward to meeting him, but because of my position, I need to take precautions."

"I'm sure when Mylas explains it to him, he'll understand why you didn't come yourself," Lockett said, "but whether Jacob does or not, that's the way it has to be."

The senator said, "That brings up something I wanted to talk to you about, Mylas. I haven't decided whether you should tell him you're a private investigator whom I've hired to look into his claims of being my son, or whether you should tell him you're a friend of mine, or even someone on my staff. What do you think?"

"I know exactly what I plan to tell him, Senator."

He stiffened a little. "Uh, okay. What is it?"

"The truth."

I paused to let that sink in.

"With all due respect, Senator, unless you give me permission to do that, I can't accept this case."

The senator leaned back against the couch and stared at me. "Well then, Mylas, you should tell him the truth. Like I said, I was undecided about it, but it sounds like you have a very strong opinion about it."

"It's the right thing to do. You don't want to begin a relationship with your son under false pretenses, plus I've never regretted being honest with someone. On the other hand, I can't count the number of times I've regretted not telling the truth."

"I agree with Mylas," Lockett said. "Jacob has been lied to by his mother all his life, and since he's trying to figure out what the truth is, the more open and honest with him you are, the more likely he is to help you figure out what happened in Bakerton."

"Yes, I see your point," the senator said, "and I hope you're right."

I said, "When you get a reply back from Jacob, would you mind asking him to bring Amanda's diary to the restaurant with him? Even though you won't be there, maybe I can convince him to give it to me. If not, then perhaps he'll at least allow me to look through it."

"I was already planning to do that, and I was also going to let you know you have my permission to tell him everything that happened to me—or at least everything I remember from the time I walked in that diner to when I checked out of the Roadside Inn five days later. It might not help him deal with his anger issues after learning his mother lied to him about me, but it's possible there's something in my story that will trigger a memory of what Amanda told him."

When the senator mentioned the diner, I was about to ask him what he recalled about where it was located, but before I could do that, his computer dinged.

"It sounds like I have a new email," he said, walking over to his desk. "I wonder if Jacob has sent me a reply already."

Seconds later, he said, "Yes, it's from Jacob."

◆ ◆ ◆ ◆

The Senator was quiet for a minute as he read through Jacob's email. When he finished, he read it out loud to us.

"Thanks for getting back to me, Davis. I agree it's time for us to meet in person. I understand this will be strange for both of us, and I assure you, I don't have any problem with you choosing where you want to meet me. Any restaurant in the D. C. area is fine with me. Would it fit your schedule to meet at noon on Wednesday? Unfortunately, I have an appointment I can't break tomorrow, but I want us to get together as soon as possible, so just name the restaurant, and I'll be there."

The senator looked up from his computer. "What do you think, Mylas? Should I tell him Romanos at noon on Wednesday?"

Although I would have preferred not to meet with Jacob so soon after Whitney got to Washington, there were only two activities on our schedule for the week.

First, I planned to show her around the Greystone Center tomorrow, and then sometime during the week, she was scheduled to take pictures for the church's fundraising brochure.

Even if she wasn't tied up with a photography session on Wednesday, I figured she'd understand if I told her I had a lunch appointment.

With that in mind, I nodded and said, "That works for me."

Lockett asked, "When I make the reservation, do you want me to just use your last name, Senator, or would you prefer I use your full name and title?"

The senator, who was already typing his reply to Jacob, said, "Just use Allen like you always do without my title. There's less chance one of Romanos' waiters will alert the media if you do that. I'm telling Jacob the reservation will be in the name of Allen at Romanos at noon, and I'm asking him to bring his mother's diary with him."

Once the senator sent his email and returned to the sofa, I said, "Unless something changes after I meet with Jacob, I plan to drive up to Bakerton and see if I can locate someone who either knew Shirley, or rather Amanda, or who knows someone who knew her back then. I've already been doing some preliminary research on the town, but I was wondering if you remember where that diner was located relative to the courthouse?"

He looked off in the distance a moment and thought about my question. "When I exited the freeway, I was on the main road that led into Bakerton. I don't remember what the name of it was."

"The name of that road is Kingston Highway," I said. "About five miles down that road is Main Street, and once you turn left on Main Street, you're two blocks away from the town square."

"I remember there were a couple of fast-food places to eat on Kingston Highway, but I wanted to find a restaurant where I could sit down and have a real meal. Since there wasn't a place near the freeway, I figured there was probably something in town, so I drove down Main Street looking for one. When Main Street ended at the square, I had to turn and—"

"I'm sorry for interrupting, Senator, but when you say you had to turn, which way did you turn? I'm asking because last night when I was reading the history of Bakerton, I noticed they changed the traffic pattern in the downtown area ten years ago, and now it's no longer a one-way street around the square."

"Oh, I see. Well, I know I was facing the front of the courthouse, and as I remember it, I turned right. When I did, that's when I saw the Black Bear Diner. It got my attention because there was a wooden carving of a life-size black bear outside the building."

"Okay, so it was the Black Bear Diner, and it was to your right as you made the turn to go around the square. With that kind of description, I shouldn't have any trouble asking questions about it."

"After Jacob contacted me through the ancestry website," the senator said, "I did a search for the Roadside Inn and the Black Bear Diner on the internet, but I didn't come up with anything."

"No, I didn't either," I said. "I suspect they're no longer in business, but in a small town, there's always someone around who can answer questions, so I'm not too worried about that. You mentioned Amanda told you she worked at a drugstore near the diner. I noticed there's a nationwide chain pharmacy located on the west side of the square, so that could be where she worked. Do you recall if she said the drugstore was on the square?"

He shook his head. "No, I couldn't say for sure. I really wasn't paying attention to what she said about herself."

"I understand."

"I'm embarrassed to admit she was able to keep me talking non-stop about myself the whole time we were eating together. She seemed enthralled by anything I told her about my personal life, no matter how insignificant it sounded to me."

"I'm sure that was flattering, and who knows, maybe that was her intention."

"I just wish I'd been more mature so I could have recognized what she was doing."

"You said she was an attractive girl, but do you recall having any other impression of her?"

"Any other impression? Well, I thought she was a small-town girl who was very excited to meet someone who worked on Capitol Hill. To be honest, I probably made it sound like I was running the place, even though I was only an intern."

"And was there anything else about her appearance that got your attention? Like for instance, did she seem healthy to you?"

He looked puzzled. "I'm not sure I know what you mean, Mylas."

"I mean did she seem like someone who was in good health? Or, to put it a different way, did she look sick to you?"

Lockett spoke up. "That's a strange question, Mylas. I'm betting you have a specific reason for asking it, don't you?"

"Yes, I do," I said, gesturing at the papers the senator put aside when he got up to write the email to Jacob. "If you look at the last page of the documents I gave you, then you'll see Nina has some information about Amanda's work history at AxonTeague. In it, she describes some documents she came across that seem to indicate Amanda was on some type of medication."

"That's surprising," the senator said, picking up the documents and turning to the last page. "Jacob didn't mention anything to me about his mother being sick."

Once he read through the paragraph where Nina had written a brief synopsis of what she gleaned from Amanda's yearly evaluations, he said, "To answer your question, I don't remember thinking Shirley, or rather Amanda, looked sick at all. In fact, the state of her health never entered my mind."

"Okay, that's what I wanted to know."

Lockett looked up from reading Nina's documents and said, "If I were you, Mylas, I'd bring up the question of Amanda's health with Jacob. If there's anyone who would know about the medications she was taking—except for her doctors, of course—I expect it would be her son."

"I plan to do that, but once Jacob realizes I'm not Davis Allen, I'm not sure he'll be open to answering any questions about his mother's health, or perhaps anything else for that matter."

The senator spread his hands out toward me. "In the event Jacob doesn't understand why I couldn't meet him in person, then you have my permission to call me, and I'll talk to him over the phone. Perhaps a word from me will reassure him of my intentions."

"What are your intentions, Senator?"

He stared at me without saying anything for several seconds. "My intentions? I thought I had made them perfectly clear. As soon as you find out the circumstances of Jacob's conception, then my press secretary and I will come up with a formal announcement about Jacob being my son. I'll keep the explanation simple and refer to ancestry services like DNAHeritage that made the discovery possible. Hopefully, that'll be the end of it."

"I wasn't asking about your intentions regarding your reputation. I was asking about your intentions regarding Jacob."

"Uh . . . okay. I guess I thought that was obvious. He's my own flesh and blood. He carries my genes. I'll claim him as my son."

"And that's to be expected, but from what I could tell in his emails, he sounds eager to connect with you as soon as possible. Even more than just connect. I believe he's looking forward to having a close relationship with you, a father/son relationship."

The senator slowly nodded his head. "I agree with that, but it sounds like you think I should do something about it right away."

"You're right, I do. When I meet with Jacob on Wednesday, I'd like to be able to tell him about the plans you've made to get together with him in person, even before my investigation is complete. I believe doing that will convince him of your good intentions more than having a conversation with him over the phone."

"I agree, Senator," Lockett said, "and once Mylas gives us his assessment of Jacob, I don't have a problem making arrangements for you to have a private meeting with him." He held up the dossier. "As far as I can tell, there's nothing in his background that poses a security risk to you."

The senator took another look at the page containing the photographs of Jacob. "Yes, Nathan, go ahead and find a place that's suitable for me to spend some time with him. Just make sure it's private and inaccessible to the media."

Lockett nodded. "I'll get to work on it this afternoon so Mylas can tell Jacob of the arrangements on Wednesday."

The senator took a deep breath. "I'm sure both of you realize my life's about to change forever."

"Yes," I said, "and so is Jacob's."

Chapter 11

Lockett and I didn't have a chance to talk after we left our meeting with Senator Allen. He said he needed to get to a lunch engagement, and I told him I needed to get back to the office and talk with Nina before I left for the airport to pick up Whitney.

When I headed out of the Russell Senate Office Building and over to the parking garage where my Audi was parked, I was thinking about the instructions I planned to give Nina about locating the owners of the Black Bear Diner and the Roadside Inn.

If I hadn't been concentrating on that, I might have spotted the journalist, Fiona Burkhart, coming around the corner of the building and been able to avoid her by crossing the street before she saw me.

However, by the time I saw her, there was nothing to do but keep on walking and hope she didn't remember me.

No such luck.

"Well, if it isn't Mylas Grey," she said, stopping on the sidewalk in front of me, "the famous private detective whose face I keep seeing on the evening news every night."

"Hi, Ms. Burkhart. It's nice to see you again." I gave her a smile. "Since I know you're the type of journalist who loves to get her facts straight, I'm not a private detective. I'm a private investigator, and the only reason you were seeing me on the news was that I was trying to catch a killer. I figured all that publicity helped me do that. Generally, I try to stay out of the media spotlight as much as possible."

"Methinks one doth protest too much."

When I heard her paraphrase the line from Shakespeare, I suddenly remembered she wasn't averse to showing off her English Literature degree from Princeton, something she managed to refer to several times during the meal we had together several years ago.

I ignored her comment.

"How are things with you, Ms. Burkhart? It's been awhile since I've seen you, but I know you've been keeping yourself busy."

"Why so formal, Mylas? I thought we agreed to be on a first-name basis when we had lunch together a few years back."

"Yes, I remember that now. My mistake, Fiona."

After slinging her large handbag over her shoulder, she flipped her hand toward me. "But to answer your question, everything's going great. As you may have noticed, my articles are being run in all the major newspapers now, and just recently, I received an offer from a cable news network to become an on-air contributor. As you've experienced yourself, that's gonna help my career immensely."

After telling her congratulations, I took a step to the side, hoping she'd get the hint I considered our conversation was over, and it was time to move on—literally move on down the sidewalk—especially since we'd covered all the social niceties.

However, she didn't budge.

Instead, she gestured toward the Russell Building and said, "Were you here drumming up business for Mylas Grey Investigations or were you paying a condolence call on your former boss Senator Allen?"

I shook my head. "There's no reason for me to do either one of those. My phone's been ringing off the hook with new clients, and when I spoke with Senator Allen just now, I didn't see any evidence he needed my condolences . . ."

I hesitated, wondering if I should go any further, but my emotions got the best of me, so I did ". . . despite the article you wrote about him in the *Post-Dispatch* yesterday."

"Forgive me, Mylas, but I don't believe you. Oh, I'm sure your recent notoriety has brought you some new clients, but I suspect the senator was so upset about my article that he hired you to find evidence to refute the claims I made about him." She paused as if she expected me to respond. When I didn't, she said, "I'm right, aren't I?"

"Even if you were, Fiona, I wouldn't divulge information about a client. I'm sure you know that."

She grinned at me. "Of course I know that, but as far as I'm concerned, your presence here today is proof your agency has taken him on as a client."

"If my coming to see my former boss is your idea of proof, then that explains a lot about the veracity of the article you wrote about him."

She let out a short laugh. "You sound a lot like a lawyer defending his client, but since you used to be one, I guess that's to be expected. I'm not surprised the senator hired you, Mylas, but could I give you some advice about investigating the evidence against him?"

"I'm always open to advice, Fiona."

"And that's one of the reasons I find you so charming, Mylas, but what I don't find charming are legislators who think they can come to Washington and do whatever they please without having to follow the laws they were sworn to uphold."

"Believe it or not, I don't disagree with you, but you're mistaken if you think Senator Allen is one of those legislators."

"Time will tell, Mylas, which brings me to my advice."

"I'm listening."

"If you want to prove me wrong about the senator, then I'd advise you to lay aside your preconceived ideas and begin your search for answers in less obvious places."

"I'd say that's pretty good advice about any investigation, and I promise you I'll keep it in mind."

She reached inside her handbag and pulled out a business card. "Here's my number in case you misplaced it."

As I slipped her card inside my jacket, she said, "You're welcome to call me anytime, Mylas, and it doesn't have to be about Senator Allen. I'm sure we have some mutual interests we can always discuss."

I smiled. "I don't doubt that for a minute."

This time when I took a step forward, I gave her a brief wave and kept on walking.

She waved back. "It was nice running into you, Mylas."

The feeling wasn't mutual.

♦ ♦ ♦ ♦

When I arrived at the Greystone Center, I was surprised to find Detective Kyle Ford's vehicle in the parking lot.

Although I didn't think there was much chance of it, I was hoping he'd changed his mind about giving his two-week notice at the D. C. Police Department and was ready to come to work at MGI today.

When I walked through the lobby and greeted my receptionist, Kendall McDonald, she said, "Oh, by the way, Mr. Grey, the new investigator you hired is upstairs looking at his office. He told me he wanted to check something out."

"Thanks, Kendall. I'll go say hi to him. He's not supposed to be here for another two weeks, but I was hoping he'd changed his mind. We could use his help with some of our new clients."

"Yes, and we're still getting lots of phone calls, although not as many as last week." She motioned at an eBook reading device on her desk. "Last week, I barely had time to read my textbook."

When I interviewed Kendall for the receptionist job, she told me she was working on her master's degree in criminal justice—although with her youthful looks, I had a hard time believing she was already a college graduate—and when I asked her if she thought she'd be able to get some of her reading assignments done if she became my receptionist, she admitted that's what she was thinking.

Her honest answer impressed me, and when I hired her, I told her I didn't mind if she studied on the job as long as we weren't busy.

"So you're saying you wish things would slow down?" I asked her.

"Oh no, not really. I mean . . . I know you need clients, Mr. Grey, so it's fine if I don't have time to study while I'm at work."

"That's good to know, Kendall."

As I started to walk away, I looked back at her and said, "I've told you it's okay to call me Mylas, haven't I?"

"Yes, but I don't think I could do that. It just doesn't seem respectful. I hope you understand."

"Oh sure, I understand."

What I understood was that Kendall was taught to show respect for older people by not addressing them by their first name.

I was taught the same thing.

At the time, I didn't think I'd ever be one.

◆ ◆ ◆ ◆

I found Ford in his office talking to Leslie. Actually, he wasn't talking to her. They were both laughing. I presumed it was something Ford said since Leslie was laughing the loudest.

Ford, a broad-shouldered African American in his early fifties, was the detective who showed up at the crime scene on my last case, and when he learned I was looking for another investigator for my new agency, he told me he was thinking about retiring from the DCPD, and he wondered if I'd be willing to interview him for the position.

Although I hadn't thought about hiring a former police detective, I realized he might be a good fit for the agency, plus when I asked Leslie about him, she told me she considered him a first-class detective after working with him on a homicide investigation when she was at the Bowman Agency.

What sealed the deal for me was when he showed up after I got myself in a tight spot with the Jared Daley case. Once that happened, I told him he aced his interview, and I hired him on the spot.

"Hey, Kyle. It's good to see you," I said, as I walked in his office. "Does this mean you're moving in today?"

"I wish I were. After I told my lieutenant I was leaving in two weeks, he put me on desk duty. I may die of boredom before I walk out of there."

"Once you get here, I guarantee you won't be bored," Leslie said. "This infidelity case I'm working on has so many moving parts to it, it's keeping me up at night, and I have appointments with two new clients at the end of the week."

"I wish you were here to help me with the case I'm working on," I said. "I think I told you Senator Allen put our agency on retainer, and now he has me looking into a personal matter for him that goes back thirty-seven years." I glanced down at my watch. "I wish I had time to give you the details, but I need to go talk to Nina before I head to the airport to pick up someone."

"I'd really like to help you out," Ford said, looking around the room, "but I just came by to get an idea of what kind of personal items I should bring with me when I officially move in."

When Ford noticed Leslie giving me a smile, he said, "Did I miss something? Am I not allowed to bring any personal items with me?"

"Oh, you can bring any personal items you want," I said, "but you need to keep in mind we have an art critic on staff, and she'll let you know if she doesn't think your office decorations meet her standards."

"What are her standards?"

"I'm not exactly sure, except I know a pink elephant doesn't fall within her guidelines."

I headed out the door. "I'll let Leslie explain that to you."

◆ ◆ ◆ ◆

After leaving Ford's office, I dropped in on Nina—who'd made a lot of progress with her unpacking—and once I told her about my conversation with the senator, she said she'd start doing research on the Black Bear Diner and the Roadside Inn right away.

What seemed to excite her more than anything was when I told her Senator Allen recognized Amanda as the woman in the diner who said her name was Shirley.

"The data on fake names show people do it for illegal activities," she said. "Most career criminals use some kind of alias. Of course, nowadays, it's not unusual for people to use fake names on their social media accounts, but back then, there wasn't any such thing, so at least we know that can't be the reason she was calling herself Shirley."

"It could have been a spur-of-the-moment thing. Maybe Amanda pulled the name out of the air when the waitress asked her if she would mind sharing a table with a stranger."

"I suppose so, but that's just pure conjecture on your part. You don't have any basis for thinking that."

"No, but I've seen pictures of Senator Allen when he was serving as a summer intern for Senator Drury, and he was definitely a handsome young man, so maybe he intimidated her, and she thought Shirley sounded like a lot more interesting name than Amanda did."

"I'll see if I can find out if the CVM Pharmacy on the square in Bakerton is the same drugstore where Amanda told him she worked, and if it is, then there could be some employment records that indicate what name she was using. Depending on what I find, I could even locate where she was living in Bakerton."

"I'll check with you later about that. I'm bringing Whitney by the office tomorrow, so we can talk about it then."

"Before you go, I'd like to run something by you."

"Okay, go ahead."

Nina walked around and sat down behind her desk where there were two wide-screen monitors. After moving her mouse around, she said, "While I was unpacking, I was thinking about Jacob working at the FCC and his present position at EnViron, and it occurred to me he could have met Senator Allen at some point in the last ten years or so. I know both of those positions require spending time on Capitol Hill talking to lawmakers."

"Yes, that's possible, and that's why I told Senator Allen when Jacob looked on the ancestry website and saw the name Davis Vincent Allen listed under his DNA results, he may have connected the name with the senator."

"True, so that means he could already suspect he's related to Senator Allen before you show up at the restaurant."

"Right, and in a way, that may not be a bad thing. Maybe he'll understand why the senator hired me to check him out first."

Nina swiveled one of her monitors around and said, "When I was thinking about this, I got in the pictorial archives of the Senate Committee on Commerce that oversees the FCC and came across this picture from six years ago when the senators on that committee were holding a hearing. Look who I discovered sitting on the third row behind the FCC commissioner."

I bent down and studied the image, and when I did, I immediately recognized Jacob, although he looked younger than his picture on the EnViron website. On the other side of the room was a dais where a row of senators was seated, and Senator Allen was among them.

I said, "That's Jacob all right, and it looks like he's staring straight at Senator Allen."

"That was also my impression, but since there are six other senators seated beside him and Jacob is all the way across the room from him, I wouldn't swear to that in a court of law."

I motioned at her with my open palm. "So tell me, Nina. Are you showing me this picture for informational purposes only, or are you hinting at some kind of pre-planned conspiracy on Jacob's part?"

"For informational purposes only. I don't have any basis for speculating about what Jacob knows or doesn't know, but you've always told me when you interview someone, you like to have as many details as possible before you sit down across from them. You said that's why you ran surveillance on people before interviewing them."

I nodded. "That was true when I was interviewing judges, but since your background check on Jacob has been so thorough, I wasn't planning on running surveillance on Jacob in this case."

"Of course, my research has been thorough. That's why you hired me, and why you're paying me the big bucks."

I made a point of walking over to her credenza and looking at all the equipment she'd unpacked: a digital scanner, a hard disk cloning device, two laptops, a spectrograph—used for analyzing voices—and what appeared to be a dedicated computer I figured she was setting up to run facial recognition software.

When I finished scrutinizing everything, I said, "It's also why I shelled out the money for this collection of what I assume are the necessary tools of your trade."

"Your assumption is correct. I'm anticipating I'll need everything there . . ." she paused and gave me an impish grin, " . . . plus a few more things as well."

"As long as you continue to give me answers when I ask questions, I'll write checks for whatever you think you need."

"You may wish you hadn't said that."

"I doubt it, but I can't say the same for Greta."

"Oh, I think I can handle Greta."

I didn't doubt her.

Chapter 12

As I was driving to the airport to pick up Whitney, I kept mulling over my conversation with Nina. Something about it bothered me, but I couldn't pinpoint what it was.

I finally realized it was something I told her after seeing the photograph of Jacob in the same room with Senator Allen at the FCC Senate Hearing several years ago.

Nina said she showed me the image because she knew I wanted information about someone before I interviewed them. She also mentioned I usually ran surveillance on them, and I told her I didn't think it was necessary to put Jacob under surveillance because her background check on him had been so thorough.

Now, I questioned if I was making a mistake not doing it with Jacob.

Before I had lunch with him on Wednesday, would I be more comfortable knowing his activities from the previous day? Would I feel less apprehensive about meeting him if I could identify the people around him and observe his overall demeanor?

I decided the answer was definitely yes, but what I couldn't decide was whether to call Chase Reed and run a full-scale twenty-four-hour watch on Jacob before our Wednesday lunch.

Would that be overkill?

Was there any need to focus on Jacob when the scope of my investigation was what happened to the senator in Bakerton?

By the time I arrived at the airport, I hadn't made up my mind about what to do, so I didn't make the call to Reed.

I knew the reason I couldn't decide.

I had something more important on my mind—rather someone.

◆ ◆ ◆ ◆

The airline app on my phone indicated Whitney's flight was on time, and since I told her I'd meet her in the baggage claim area, that's where I headed once I parked my car in the short-term lot.

As I waited to cross the street before entering the terminal building, I found myself checking the security around me.

My actions were mostly out of habit.

Being situationally aware was second nature to me, something my father taught Curtis and me from an early age—along with how to handle a gun, defend ourselves in a fight, and tail someone without being noticed.

Now though, in the process of checking out my environment, I suddenly felt my gut churn—a feeling I often had when someone was watching me. I immediately tried to spot the person, but either they were very good at blending into the crowd or they had entered the terminal already.

I told myself I was surrounded by at least three dozen people, so it wouldn't be unusual for someone to take notice of me for one reason or another.

Perhaps they saw me on the evening news last week.

Once I entered the terminal, I couldn't completely shake the feeling I was being observed, so while I waited for Whitney to come down the escalator, I positioned myself against one of the back walls—where there was a colorful mural of abstract art—and scanned the faces of anyone who didn't appear to belong in the baggage claim area.

I was looking for someone who wasn't intent on locating their luggage, or who wasn't chatting with a passenger from their flight, or who wasn't discussing something with a traveling companion while waiting for their luggage to arrive.

I finally narrowed my search down to two men, both of whom were alone and appeared to be occupied with their cell phones, especially when I happened to look in their direction.

After observing each of them for several minutes, I decided I was wrong, and they weren't interested in me. I also realized I wasn't getting the same vibe of being watched since entering the building as when I was standing outside. That realization caused me to ask myself if I'd misread the situation entirely.

Was I just being paranoid?

Having neurotic thoughts wasn't really a problem for me, but I didn't have time to delve any further into my psyche because Whitney was suddenly standing in front of me.

"Hey there, stranger," she said. "Long time no see."

"It's been *way* too long," I said, putting my arms around her slender waist and giving her a quick kiss on the cheek.

She looked over at the baggage carousel. "When I walked up, you seemed to be very interested in someone over there, or were you just people-watching?"

"Mostly people-watching. It's a hazard of the trade, but right now, all I'm interested in is you. How was your flight?"

As Whitney began describing her seatmate, I gave my full attention to what she was saying, although I admit I was also admiring how attractive she looked in her brown leather jacket and blue jeans.

The first time I saw Whitney, I remember thinking her turned-up nose and beautiful smile were her best features. Now, though, I realized they only emphasized her incredible hazel-colored eyes.

After she told me she was completely worn out after listening to the non-stop conversation of the passenger next to her, I said, "You may think you look exhausted, but you look gorgeous to me."

She touched the lapel of my suit coat. "You're pretty handsome yourself, Mr. Private Investigator. Look at you all dressed up in your pin-stripe suit. Have you been seeing clients today?"

"Actually, I've just seen one client today. That was Senator Allen, and since he seldom wears anything but a suit, I dressed accordingly."

"Senator Allen is your client now?" she asked, glancing over at the carousel where the suitcases were starting to arrive. "That seems a little odd."

"It is a little odd."

"If it's allowed, I'd love to hear about it."

"It's allowed if you promise not to call your friends in the media and give them the story."

"I don't have any friends in the media."

"Consider yourself fortunate."

◆ ◆ ◆ ◆

Once Whitney and I left the airport and were on our way to my house, I kept my eye on the rearview mirror just to make sure I wasn't being followed.

After we'd gone several miles, and I couldn't spot any vehicle with a discernible pattern of surveillance, I decided my earlier impression was just some fluky thing and nothing to be concerned about.

Although I briefly considered mentioning the incident to Whitney, I discarded that thought almost immediately, especially when she brought up her last visit to Washington.

"Several of my friends at church yesterday asked me if I felt okay about coming to Washington after what happened to me the last time I was here, but I told them I wasn't nearly as anxious about that as I was about doing a good job photographing the kids for the church's fundraising brochure."

I reached over and squeezed her hand. "You'll do a great job, Whitney. I have no doubt about that. Did you and Nathan decide when you'll be doing the photo shoot?"

"The church secretary was setting up the appointments for Wednesday and Thursday. I'll work with the younger kids in the morning and the older ones in the afternoon after they get home from school. I'm supposed to call the church office tomorrow to find out the appointment times. You don't have any trips or sightseeing excursions planned for those days, do you?"

"No, since you told me not to make any plans for us to do any sightseeing, I followed your instructions."

"What about showing me your new office?"

"Oh sure, I still plan to do that. We'll go over there tomorrow, and I'll give you an exclusive tour of the Greystone Center and introduce you to everyone. Of course, you've already met Nina."

"But didn't you say she wouldn't be at work for two more weeks?"

"Her plans changed when Senator Allen became my client, but I'll tell you about that at dinner. Right now," I said, pulling up in the circle drive in front of my house, "I'm sure Mrs. Higbee will want your full attention the moment we walk through the front door."

My prediction turned out to be true, and after Whitney gave her a warm greeting, along with a hug, the two ladies went upstairs with Babe trailing behind them.

As I was getting Whitney's suitcase out of the trunk of my car, Joe came around the side of the garage and offered to take it upstairs for me. I was about to tell him I'd do it myself when my phone vibrated, and as soon as I saw Lockett's name on the screen, I let Joe take care of Whitney's luggage, and I went in my study to take his call.

After I answered my phone, Lockett asked, "Are you alone or should I call you back?"

"I'm alone in my study. As soon as I brought Whitney to the house, Mrs. Higbee took charge of her, which means I may not see her again until it's time for dinner. What's up?"

"I wanted to let you know about the arrangements I've made for Senator Allen to meet with Jacob in private. My plan was agreeable to the senator, so you can go ahead and tell Jacob about it when you meet with him on Wednesday."

"That was fast work, Nathan. What's the plan?"

"Diana and I will be having a small dinner party at our house on Friday night, and the senator and Jacob will be among our invited guests. Having dinner at my house shouldn't draw the attention of anyone in the media, so once the meal's over, Senator Allen and Jacob will adjourn to my study where they can spend some time alone."

"I assume Diana approved of this plan."

He chuckled. "I wouldn't be telling you about it otherwise. And by the way, she wanted me to give you and Whitney an invitation to join us for dinner. That is, as long as you haven't made other plans."

"I've tried to keep our schedule this week open-ended, so I'm pretty sure we can make it, but I may need to reassess that if things don't go well with Jacob."

"I get that, and the same goes for the dinner party."

"Before you get off the phone, Nathan, I wanted to give you a heads up about something that happened when I was leaving the Russell Building this morning. I had already planned to tell you about it tomorrow, but I can do it now, if you like."

He chuckled. "I won't be able to sleep tonight if you don't tell me about it now."

After I described my encounter with Fiona Burkhart, Nathan seemed more frustrated than amused by her assumption that Senator Allen hired me to dispute the allegations she had made against him.

"It's hard for me to understand why people take that woman seriously when she gets things so wrong," he said.

"I suppose it's because she occasionally uncovers the truth about a corrupt politician or stumbles across a Cabinet official who's cheating on their spouse, or finds a staff member with secrets to tell."

"Yeah, but you've got to admit those instances are pretty rare."

"True, but I just wanted to let you know I ran into her in case she tries to get in touch with you. If she happens to mention anything about the senator hiring me, you know it has nothing to do with the Jacob Walker case. She's operating under the assumption I'm helping Senator Allen defend his reputation."

"Gotcha. I'll keep it in mind. I suppose you didn't deny it."

"I didn't deny it and I didn't verify it."

"Sounds like the Mylas Grey way of doing things, all right."

"Yep. That's my philosophy. Keep 'em guessing."

◆ ◆ ◆ ◆

Mrs. Higbee had laid out two elaborate place settings for Whitney and me in the formal dining room, and once she questioned us for a few minutes—did we want ice in our water, were the homemade rolls still warm, would Whitney like a different kind of dressing for her salad—she finally left us alone.

She also banished Babe from the dining room, although I wasn't sure how she managed it, except I suspected bribery was involved.

After she left, I said a short blessing over our food, and then Whitney reached over and laid her hand on top of mine.

"I'm really excited to be here with you, Mylas, but I don't mind telling you, I'm still overwhelmed by your gorgeous house, not to mention your housekeeper and . . . uh . . . all of this."

She motioned over at a china cabinet in the oversized dining room that ran the length of one wall and was filled with expensive china, crystal, and glassware that Mac had accumulated for himself.

"You're not alone," I said, passing Whitney a platter piled high with Mrs. Higbee's perfectly cooked beef tenderloin. "I get overwhelmed by Mrs. Higbee all the time, and believe it or not, I'm still pretty amazed by this place."

Whitney smiled as she placed a slice of meat on her plate. "Actually, I was thinking about how comfortable you seem in this environment. I wonder if you realize how intimidated the average person would feel talking to a senator or some of the other people in your circle of friends, whereas you seem to be at ease with them."

"You're right. I'm not intimidated by them, but I'm sure that's because my father taught me whenever I'm dealing with a celebrity, a high-ranking official, a wealthy businessman, or any famous person, I should focus on what makes them a person, not on what makes them famous. If I do that, he said we'd both enjoy each other's company."

She nodded. "Your dad is such a down-to-earth guy. So do you remember how you applied that when you met Senator Allen for the first time?"

I had to think about her question a minute. "When Nathan took me into his office to meet him, I noticed some photographs of his wife and kids on his desk. In one of them he was tossing a football to his son, so even before Nathan did his formal introduction of me, I pointed over to it and said something like, 'That's a great picture, Senator Allen. My dad and I used to toss the football back and forth to each other all the time. It's one of my fondest memories when I was growing up.'"

"Was Nathan surprised you didn't give him a chance to introduce the senator to you before you started talking to him?"

"Yes, I believe he was, and I'm sure he was upset with me. On the other hand, my comment seemed to please Senator Allen, and he went on to brag about his son's football abilities just like any proud father would. He even asked me some questions about my own father."

"I try to do something similar if people get tensed up when I'm photographing them," she said, taking a drink of her iced tea, "so I can see how making that connection with Senator Allen about his son would make a conversation with him less intimidating."

"It's ironic that we're talking about Senator Allen's son because the case I'm investigating for the senator is actually about his son."

"Is he in some kind of trouble?"

"No, I'm not investigating the son I saw in the photograph. This is a different son, and until a few weeks ago, Senator Allen didn't know he even existed. He found out through a DNA ancestry website."

Whitney looked shocked. "You're kidding."

"No, I'm not kidding. It's quite a story."

She laughed. "Enough with the suspense. Tell me the story."

I spent the rest of the meal describing Jacob Walker's initial email to Senator Allen, what the senator remembered about his stopover in Bakerton, and the revelations Jacob made about his mother in his emails to the senator.

When I finished, she said, "I can just imagine the shock Senator Allen felt when he got the email, and then to realize Jacob had to have been conceived during those five days he spent in Bakerton must have been mind-blowing. I suppose I can understand why a young twenty-year-old college intern would think he was just sick, and that's why he couldn't remember anything about the days he spent in that motel room, but I'm not sure I would have just let it go like that."

"I've thought the same thing, but everyone's different."

"So what happens next? Have you started your investigation yet?"

"Yes, or rather Nina's been doing some preliminary research for it. I told the senator I needed her to come to work for me right away so she could start looking into Jacob's background before the senator agreed to meet with him. In the process of doing that, she discovered several things about Amanda, including a picture of her, and this morning, the senator identified Amanda as the woman in the diner who told him her name was Shirley."

"But the senator doesn't remember her coming to his motel room?"

"No, he insists he doesn't remember anything once he got to the room, except that he was so sleepy he immediately went to bed."

"Maybe he'll get some answers from Amanda's diary once he and Jacob get together. Has the senator made plans to do that yet?"

"He told Jacob he'd meet him at the restaurant on Wednesday."

"So father and son will be introduced to each other for the first time on Wednesday. That's sure to be an emotional time for them."

"No, that's not gonna happen. Senator Allen won't be meeting Jacob on Wednesday. He's sending me in his place."

She frowned. "But why would he do that?"

"For several reasons. First, the senator is well-known and easily recognizable, so when he goes to a restaurant in this town it always draws a lot of attention. As you can imagine, that atmosphere doesn't lend itself to the type of encounter these two men need to have for their first meeting. On the other hand, if the man Jacob knows as Davis Allen suggested they meet in a secluded place, that request would surely make Jacob suspicious about his intentions. And naturally, he's not about to tell Jacob in an email that Davis Allen, the father he discovered through a DNA sample, is *the* Senator Allen."

Whitney wiped her mouth with her napkin and laid it down beside her plate before she responded. "That doesn't seem right to me, Mylas. I'm sure Jacob is really looking forward to meeting his father for the first time, and now he's about to be very disappointed."

"I felt the same way, and that's why I plan to try and soften that disappointment by telling him the senator has made arrangements to meet him at a private residence this Friday night."

"The senator's inviting him to his house?"

"No, Nathan and Diana are giving a dinner party at *their* house, and that's where the senator will meet Jacob. By the way, we're also invited to that dinner party."

Her eyes got big. "To a dinner party with Senator Allen?"

"Yes, but I haven't accepted Nathan's invitation yet. I'll only tell him we're coming if it's okay with you."

She nodded. "Oh yes, I'm fine with it. It sounds like an interesting evening."

Her quick answer surprised me.

Maybe the thought of living in Washington wasn't as distasteful to her as I thought it was.

PART THREE

Chapter 13

Tuesday, January 11

After stuffing ourselves with Mrs. Higbee's pancake breakfast—she insisted we have both blueberry and pecan—Whitney and I headed over to the Greystone Center.

As I made the exit off the freeway onto L Street where my building was located, I commented on the unusually warm weather we were having in Washington, a statement that prompted Whitney to suddenly put her hand to her forehead and say, "Oh dear, I forgot to give you the wool scarf your mother sent you. It's still in my suitcase."

"My mother sent me a wool scarf?"

"Yes, when I saw her at church on Sunday, she gave me a gift bag from Bergman's and showed me what was inside. She said you used to have a scarf just like it when you were younger."

"Is it red?"

She nodded. "Yes, it's solid red. It looks like it would keep you really warm, too warm today, that's for sure."

I nodded. "It might keep me warm, but it isn't something I'd wear in my line of work. Wearing a bright red scarf would only draw attention to me. I'm surprised my mother forgot that. I'm sure Dad has never worn a red scarf."

"She said she gave you one like it when you went off to law school at Georgetown. That's probably what she's remembering."

"Yes, she's right. She did give me a red scarf, but I wasn't worried about being noticed then. Actually, I wanted to be noticed," I looked over at her and smiled, "preferably by the opposite sex."

"And I'm sure you were," she said, returning my smile. "That reminds me of something I wanted to ask you about Senator Allen's story. When he described going into the Black Bear Diner in Bakerton, did he tell you whether it was his suggestion to share the table with Amanda, or did Amanda take the initiative and make the offer?"

I thought for a moment. "I believe he said it was the waitress who asked him if he would mind sharing a table with someone."

"Umm. Okay then," she brushed the air with her hand, "you can forget the theory I came up with that Amanda was at the diner looking for an opportunity to meet some nice-looking guy that night."

As I pulled in the parking lot at the Greystone Center, I let out a short laugh. "You've been working on theories about my case?"

"I guess you could say that. One of these days you can return the favor and help me with a photo shoot."

"Okay, it's a deal."

We sealed our deal with a kiss.

◆ ◆ ◆ ◆

Whitney made no secret of the fact she was impressed with my office building. She oohed and aahed over the décor, the colors, the reception area, everything.

She seemed equally delighted to meet Greta, Kendall, and my bookkeeper, Bonnie, and I was surprised by how much I enjoyed watching them interact with her.

However, it wasn't until we got on the elevator to go up to the second floor that I realized I'd been looking forward to introducing Whitney to my staff and showing her around the place ever since my realtor showed me the building.

I figured I was anxious to share it with her because she'd been so enthusiastic about my launching Mylas Grey Investigations when I mentioned it to her last Thanksgiving, despite the fact I knew she'd prefer that I move back to Columbia and take over my dad's PI agency.

As I thought about how encouraging she'd been and how often she told me she was praying for me as I made decisions about everything from my MGI logo to the people I needed to hire, I found myself getting a little choked up about it.

"You've gotten awfully quiet," she said, as we stepped off the elevator. "Is everything okay?"

"To be truthful, I was thinking about how supportive you've been throughout this whole process of getting my agency up and running. Even though I've invested a ton of money in this building, not to mention the personnel, I'm convinced your prayers have made the difference in how smoothly things have gone for me."

"I don't have any doubt you've said a few prayers yourself."

I nodded as I motioned for her to follow me down the hallway to my office. "You're right, and maybe it doesn't surprise you, but when I thought about doing this, I didn't imagine I'd be praying for everyone on my staff to get along with each other. That's the sort of problem that didn't occur to me when I decided to start my own agency."

She laughed. "That's not a problem for us self-employed people."

Once I ushered Whitney into my office, I invited her to take a look around while I checked my email and phone messages.

She immediately walked over and examined the painting on the wall in my seating area, a painting I assumed the interior designer had chosen because the colors in it were mostly gray, purple, and ivory.

"Well, what do you think?" I asked, as I hung up the phone. "Does that painting meet with your approval?"

"Yes, it's very appropriate for this space, and if I'm not mistaken, this artist is one of the up-and-coming contemporary painters in the art world today. I'm sure you paid a lot for this painting, but I believe it should retain its value for many years to come."

As she continued looking around my office, I opened my email and found a short note from Nina. *"I've discovered a few more things about Jacob Walker that could be relevant. Stop by and see me when you get a chance."*

When I told Whitney I needed to go down to Nina's office and talk with her about the Jacob Walker case, I asked her if she'd like to come with me.

She nodded enthusiastically. "Oh, sure. I've been looking forward to seeing her again. I remember she expressed an interest in photography when you introduced us last year, although it wasn't really a conversation about photography. It was more about how to take action shots of her grandson's soccer games."

"That sounds like a conversation Nina would have, all right."

Before we arrived at Nina's office, I stopped off at Room 215, the surveillance crew's suite, and spoke to Hank, who was seated at the conference table working on a piece of equipment.

It appeared to be a listening device, the kind used to remotely monitor conversations in a room.

After introducing Hank to Whitney, I asked him if Reed was around. "Yeah, he's in the building," he said, nodding his head, "but he went down to Leslie's office. They're discussing the surveillance we ran on her client's husband last night."

"Okay, thanks. I'll catch up with him there."

Once we left Hank, Whitney asked, "Were you planning to use your surveillance people to keep an eye on Jacob Walker?"

"Maybe. I've thought about having Chase—he's my main surveillance guy—take a look at Jacob's movements today just to see if he's doing anything unusual before he meets with the senator tomorrow. That's probably unnecessary, but I keep thinking about it."

"What would he be looking for? What's something unusual?"

"He'd check to make sure Jacob wasn't moving out of his apartment, packing his car for a trip, or making a purchase at a gun store before he showed up at the restaurant to meet the senator."

"Oh, wow. Are you saying Jacob could be planning to harm the senator and get out of town? You really think that's a possibility?"

"Only a small possibility. He gave no indication in his emails he was even aware the senator is his father, so that's why I said it probably isn't necessary to run any surveillance on him, but I'd still like to know if Jacob is going to work and keeping to his routine today."

"Where is he employed?"

I stopped in front of Nina's door and knocked a couple of times. "EnViron Industries in Lanham, Maryland. That's about thirty minutes north of here. It's also where he lives."

Whitney looked over at me. "If it would make you feel better about meeting Jacob, I don't mind driving to Lanham this afternoon."

"Uh . . . okay. I'll think about that."

◆ ◆ ◆ ◆

Nina seemed delighted to see Whitney, and she looked especially pleased when Whitney told her how relieved I was to have her working at Mylas Grey Investigations.

"Mylas said he knew his PI agency would be a success if he could convince you to come to work here," Whitney said, "so I was thrilled when he told me you decided to say yes and help him out."

"He's a pretty smart guy," Nina said, cutting her eyes over at me. "I knew he'd eventually figure out he couldn't do this without me."

"Okay, Ladies, let's move on," I said, gesturing at Nina. "What kind of new information do you have on Jacob? Don't tell me you've discovered he's a serial killer."

When I saw Nina glance over at Whitney, I said, "I've already told Whitney all about Jacob, so she knows what's going on."

"No, as far as I can tell, Jacob isn't a serial killer, but since you're always on the lookout for red flags, I thought I'd alert you to a couple."

She handed me a sheet of paper with some numbers on it.

"As you can see, Jacob is a month behind on his car payments, plus he has a substantial credit card balance, and he's only paying the minimum on it."

"Uh-huh. I can see that."

"I'm sure you agree he could use an infusion of cash."

"I hear what you're saying, Nina, but in his emails to the senator, he's never dropped any hints about money or mentioned his personal finances. However, he seems like an intelligent guy, so I don't suppose he'd bring it up to the senator right away."

"No, if his game is to milk the senator for money, he'd keep quiet about his finances until much later."

I glanced over at Whitney, who was standing off to the side listening to us. If I was reading her facial expression correctly, she was disturbed by our conversation.

I asked, "How do you feel about it, Whitney? Do you think Jacob's debt means he's out to get money from Senator Allen?"

She winced. "To be honest, that seems a little cynical to me. Of course, I haven't read his emails, but from what I understand, when Jacob submitted his DNA to the ancestry services, he was just doing it to find his father. It's hard for me to believe he was also scheming to get money out of him at the same time."

Nina said. "You could be right, Whitney. I'm sure Mylas and I have become overly pessimistic about people in the last few years. That's what happens when you spend all your time investigating some of America's most outstanding citizens, and you discover most of them have an overabundance of skeletons in their closets. It's easy to forget that not everyone has ulterior motives."

I nodded and gave Nina back the report on Jacob's finances. "There's really no way to know how relevant this stuff is until I meet with him tomorrow, but thanks for getting me this information. You know I can never have too many details on a subject. Don't hesitate to let me know if you find out anything else about him."

"Sure thing." She laid the paper down and came around the side of her desk. "So what kind of plans do the two of you have for the rest of the day? Anything fun?"

Whitney looked at me and grinned. "Since I knew I was coming to visit Mylas at a time when he needed to work, I made him promise not to make any plans for us."

"I don't know how much fun this will be," I said, "but Whitney said she didn't mind if we drove over to Lanham this afternoon and took a look around. Doing so will give me an opportunity to see Jacob's condo and check out EnViron Industries. It's possible I might even be able to see him in person before I meet with him tomorrow."

Nina leaned in toward Whitney, partially covered her mouth with her hand, and pretended to share a secret with her. "If you didn't know already, Mylas has a tendency to get a little fanatical about his preparation for meeting someone he's investigating."

Whitney whispered back, "I'm beginning to realize that."

◆ ◆ ◆ ◆

As we were coming out of Nina's office, I saw Reed and Leslie standing in her doorway, and when I stopped and introduced Whitney to them, Leslie invited her in to see her office.

Once we stepped inside, the two ladies engaged in a few minutes of social chitchat about Whitney's flight, the unusually warm weather, and yes, the pink elephant in the room.

Meanwhile, I stood there silently and observed them.

Leslie, the taller of the two, was inclined to choose flashy accessories, dress in the latest fashion trends, and wear colors that complemented her platinum blond hair. Today, she had on a black pantsuit with a zebra-print blouse, several silver chains around her neck, a pair of large hoop earrings, and black, three-inch heels.

Whitney, about an inch shorter, was wearing a tailored white blouse over a pair of dark brown pants. Her only accessories were a pair of gold earrings in the shape of teardrops and a printed silk scarf around her neck—the yellow and orange colors in the scarf accented her medium-length brown hair.

When Leslie invited us to have a seat on the couch, I said, "We shouldn't take up any more of your time, Leslie. I know you have several appointments on the calendar today, so we better be going."

Whitney smiled and said, "It was nice meeting you, Leslie."

"Same here." Leslie gestured at me. "FYI, Mylas. I'll update you later on my infidelity case, and of course, I'm anxious to hear what's happening with Jacob Walker."

"Sure, I was going to send you an email later, but I can give you the bottom line now. Nina was able to locate a picture of Jacob's mother, and Senator Allen identified her as the woman he met in the diner at Bakerton; so I'll be meeting Jacob tomorrow for lunch at Romanos, although he thinks he's meeting his father. That's it in a nutshell."

She smiled. "That should be an interesting lunch."

"I'll be surprised if it isn't. This afternoon, Whitney and I are driving over to Lanham to see what I can find out about Jacob before I meet with him tomorrow. It could be a wasted trip, but I'd feel better if I could lay eyes on him before he shows up at the restaurant."

"I hear you. If nothing else, you need to make sure the Jacob Walker in Lanham is the same Jacob Walker at the restaurant tomorrow."

I nodded. "My thoughts exactly."

As we headed toward the door, Leslie said, "Wait a second, Mylas. Before you go, do you and Whitney have any plans for dinner tonight? I know we talked about the possibility of me finding a date and the four of us getting together for dinner, so would tonight work for you?"

I glanced over at Whitney, who didn't look opposed to the idea—although she didn't look overly enthusiastic either—but after she smiled and said, "That's fine with me," I nodded at Leslie and said, "I told Mrs. Higbee we'd be eating out tonight, so yeah, that should work for us. Do you already have a date for the evening?"

"No, but I was thinking about asking Kyle Ford to have dinner with me. When he was here yesterday, we talked about getting together. If he's available, he'll be my date, but if not, I'll grab someone online."

After Leslie offered to make us reservations and text me later about where to meet her and her unknown date, Whitney and I walked back down to my office. Once I closed the door, I said, "I'm sorry, Whitney. I forgot to mention Leslie wanted us to have dinner together. Are you okay with that?"

"Uh . . . yeah, I guess so."

"If you don't—"

"No. It's not a problem. I'm fine with it." She looked a little nervous as she adjusted the scarf around her neck. "I admit when you talked about Leslie, I never pictured her as some tall fashion model with an effervescent personality. That was a big surprise to me. She's very nice, though, and I'm sure she's a good investigator and an asset to your agency."

I walked over and put my arm around her. "Do you mind telling me how you pictured Leslie?"

She looked up at me and smiled. "As less attractive, less self-confident, and less impressive. If I sound a little jealous, it's only because I am."

I pulled her closer to me. "You've got it all wrong. Whitney. She's the one who should be jealous of you. You're not only gorgeous on the outside, you're also gorgeous on the inside. You have a quiet inner strength that radiates beauty, and I find it just as appealing—in fact, more so—than how beautiful you are on the outside."

"Okay, now you've made me blush."

"And that just proves my point. I doubt if Leslie can remember the last time she blushed."

A few minutes later, after Whitney grabbed her jacket and we were about to leave the office, she asked, "Were you surprised when Leslie told you she was planning to invite your new investigator to go out to dinner with her? If she's interested in him in a romantic sense, there could be some future disruptions to those employee relationships you were talking about. How do you feel about them getting together?"

"I agree with your assessment, but Kyle has a good head on his shoulders, and so does Leslie, so I'm sure they're both aware of the pitfalls. Actually, I'm glad she's asking Kyle out tonight. That way you'll be able to give me your opinion about how well they'll be able to work together.

"Shall I also give you my opinion about how long it'll be before their romantic relationship affects your agency?"

I smiled. "Yes, please do, but I'm more interested in short-term events right now, so let's grab some lunch and head over to Lanham. Once I know what Jacob's up to, then I'll think about what's going on with Kyle and Leslie."

"Of course, there might not be anything going on with them."

"And the same could be true of Jacob."

"I'm not sure you believe that."

She was right.

Chapter 14

I took Whitney to The Lockerbie for lunch. I chose it because it was close to the expressway we'd be taking to Lanham, and also because the restaurant's décor featured local artists.

After ordering lunch, Whitney discussed the artwork with me, and when she did so, she brought up her father, which made me think it was okay for me to ask her some questions about him.

She often talked about her mother, a retired nurse who lived in St. Louis, and her married sister, who also lived in St. Louis, but she seldom mentioned anything about her father, a high school art teacher who died of a heart attack when Whitney was just a teenager.

Even so, once I began asking her questions about what she remembered about her father, she didn't seem to mind talking about him, and she continued doing so after we left the restaurant and headed up the expressway toward Lanham.

I was fascinated by her memories of him because they were from a child's point of view. What she recalled were the bedtime stories he told her, their play dates at a local park, and their Saturday visits to art galleries in St. Louis.

A few minutes after she began telling me about the way her father insisted on viewing a painting, I realized a vehicle was following us.

It was a late-model silver Toyota Corolla.

It got my attention when I got stuck behind a semi-truck and the Corolla had the opportunity to pass me, but it appeared to deliberately reduce its rate of speed in order to stay behind my Audi.

At least, that's what I thought was going on.

I had to be sure, though.

I decided not to mention my suspicions to Whitney—primarily because of what happened the last time she visited me—so I asked her to explain what her father taught her and her sister about viewing a painting, and then when I could safely do so, I moved into the next lane and accelerated.

Whitney said, "My dad told us we should first look at what he called the form of the painting—that is, the type of paint used, the scale, the name of the artist, those sorts of things—and then he said once we did that we should move on to the content of the painting."

The Toyota Corolla did the same.

It also moved into the next lane and accelerated.

"The content had to do with the feel of the painting," she said. "He asked us questions like, is it dramatic or subtle? What are your feelings as you study it? Do you feel happy? Sad? Disturbed? Angry?"

Whitney looked over at me as if she expected me to respond.

"Hmmm," I said, hoping I hadn't missed a question. "That's very interesting."

She chuckled. "Are you sure you're interested?"

"Of course I'm interested. How do you think the early art training you got from your father affected your desire to be a photographer?"

As soon as I saw the exit sign for Lanham, I reduced my speed and flipped on my right-turn indicator.

It appeared the Corolla's destination was also Lanham.

The Corolla's right-turn signal started blinking.

Now, as Whitney began telling me how she felt sure her interest in the medium of photography came out of her father's early art training, I was forced to make a decision.

Should I take evasive action and lose the Corolla before I headed over to EnViron Industries, or should I wait and see if the Corolla intended to follow us to our destination?

As I tried to make up my mind—while keeping my ears tuned to what Whitney was saying—several other questions popped up.

Namely, who was in the Corolla?

Why were they following us?

Were they connected to Jacob in some way?

Could the person tailing us be tied to another case? Last week, I made an appointment with the wife of a Pentagon official who claimed her husband was following her. Was that what was going on here?

I made my decision.

I decided to follow my original plan and drive over to EnViron Industries. If the Corolla followed us there, then perhaps I could see who was inside the vehicle once we got to the parking lot.

At the very least, I should be able to get a license plate number.

Once I did that, Nina could work her magic.

◆ ◆ ◆ ◆

The building that housed EnViron Industries was a three-story concrete structure trimmed in silver with blue-tinted windows and professional landscaping.

The concrete and steel sign facing the highway identified the building as the administrative offices of EnViron Industries. It didn't indicate where their manufacturing facilities were located, but since Nina said this was the address where Jacob had his office, I wasn't concerned about that.

I was more concerned about what the Corolla would do when I pulled in the parking lot at the side of the building.

I had my answer before I even found a parking space.

The vehicle drove on down the highway.

I figured since the lot wasn't that full, the Corolla's driver thought it was too risky to follow me inside and decided to drive past it.

That was a wise decision.

It also told me something about the person behind the wheel.

It told me whoever was following me had surveillance experience and figured I would have noticed the Corolla, especially if the driver stayed inside his vehicle instead of entering the building.

"Are we going inside?" Whitney asked, once I parked the Audi in the last row facing the building.

"No. There's no need to do that. The only reason I came by here was to see if I could spot Jacob's SUV. I'd like to know if he's at work today."

I took my phone off my dashboard holder and scrolled through the notes I'd made after reading Nina's dossier. "Jacob's car is a white Honda SUV. The license plate number is 8DE7621."

Whitney and I looked around the parking lot where there were several white cars and plenty of SUVs.

However, I didn't see a white Honda SUV.

What I did see was a silver Toyota Corolla in the parking lot of the building adjacent to EnViron Industries. The car was parked facing forward, which meant the driver was in a position to look directly into the lot where my Audi was parked.

"Would you mind opening the glove box and handing me that pair of binoculars?" I asked.

After Whitney gave the binoculars to me, she said, "Do you see Jacob's car? I don't see it anywhere."

I focused the glasses on the Corolla and memorized the front license plate number. "No, I don't see his SUV in the lot. If you're wondering if that concerns me, the answer is yes."

I gave the binoculars back to her and typed the Corolla's license plate number on a note-taking app on my phone.

Next to the number, I wrote, "dark-haired male, Caucasian, around forty, clean-shaven," a generic description to be sure, but there was nothing distinctive about the guy's features.

No moles. No tats. No facial hair. No scars.

I tried to look on the bright side, though. At least now I had a general description of the person following me.

"Yes, I can see you're concerned," Whitney said. "What do you think it means?"

"It could mean any number of things. Whenever I try to figure out why someone is acting a certain way, I do my best to put myself in their shoes, which means I'm asking myself what I would be doing the day before I was supposed to go to a restaurant and meet my father for the first time."

"And the answer is?"

I clicked on a different app on my phone—a telephoto camera—and pointed my phone at Generic Man. Even if the picture wasn't that good, I knew Nina would enjoy the challenge of identifying him.

"Let's see," I said, after taking a few pictures. "If I was a time-management nerd, and I didn't know how long it would take me to get to Romanos or exactly where the restaurant was located, I'd probably make a dry run there today. Jacob told Senator Allen he had an appointment today, so maybe that's what he's doing."

I took a quick look at the photos I'd taken. They were a little out of focus but still identifiable. The biggest problem was that Generic Man appeared to be looking in the direction of where I was parked.

Did he know I was shooting pictures of him?

Not likely, but possible.

It was time to leave.

"That sounds reasonable," Whitney said. "I sometimes scout out the location of where I'm meeting someone for a photo shoot before I have to be there."

She gestured at my phone. "Do you mind telling me why you're taking pictures? You know I would take some for you if you wanted."

I thought of several things I could tell her—like I needed them for the case file—but that was a lie.

Lying to Whitney bothered me, even though I was used to lying to people, both as a lawyer and as an investigator.

I put my phone back on my dashboard and turned on the ignition. "I'll explain what I was doing in a few minutes, but first, let's go check out Jacob's condo and see if his SUV is there."

"Uh . . . okay, sure."

I wondered if the note of uncertainty I heard in her voice meant she thought I was keeping something from her.

I suspected it did.

◆ ◆ ◆ ◆

I was planning to tell Whitney the truth, but before I did that, I wanted to be sure Generic Man didn't follow us over to Jacob's condo.

To do that, I turned east out of the parking lot, even though Jacob's condo was due west of the EnViron building.

At the next stoplight, as I was checking my rearview mirror, Whitney asked, "How far is Jacob's condo from his work?"

"About five miles."

A few seconds later, I spotted the Corolla three car lengths behind me, so when the light turned green, I whipped over to the far right-hand lane and immediately took the next right-hand turn.

This sudden maneuver surprised Whitney, who put her hand on the dashboard to steady herself.

"I'm sorry," I said. "I should have turned left out of the parking lot. Jacob's condo is back this way."

She smiled but didn't say anything.

After going south for a couple of blocks, I turned down a side street and made my way back to the highway.

Once I headed west, I never saw the Generic Man in his Toyota Corolla again.

A few minutes later, we arrived at the Lakeside Gardens Condominiums, a development of approximately three dozen two-story condos located across from a man-made lake—presumably, the reason for the name.

Each condo looked a little different due to the type of building materials used—some were red brick, some were white stone, some had siding on them—and as soon as I parked in a visitor parking space at the entrance to the complex, I also noticed each of the condos had a garage, which was a big disappointment to me.

Whitney asked. "Which one is Jacob's?"

"He's in C4." I gestured off to my right at a row of seven condos with a sign indicating it was Building C. "I believe that gray one in the middle with the red shutters is his."

"These condos all have garages. How will you tell if he's home or not?"

"I was just thinking about that."

I took one last look in my rearview mirror to make sure there was no sign of the Corolla, and then I turned and faced Whitney. "I'm not sure how to tell you this, Whitney, so I'm just gonna say it."

She bit down on her lip. "That sounds a little ominous."

I reached out and touched her arm. "No, Whitney, everything's fine. We're perfectly safe. You're perfectly safe. We're not in any danger."

"So what's going on?"

"Someone's been following us ever since we left the restaurant."

Whitney immediately turned around and looked out the back window. "Really? Who's following us?"

"They're not following us now. I lost them when I made that turn at the intersection. I'm pretty sure I know what you're thinking, but this isn't a repeat of what happened when you were here before."

"How can you be sure?"

"Because that's not what it feels like to me. That's probably not very reassuring to you, but you'll just have to trust me on this. My intuition says the guy was only running surveillance on me."

"You know it was a guy?"

I nodded. "That's why I was taking pictures on my phone. He was parked in the parking lot next to the EnViron Industries building."

"Why would he be running surveillance on you?" She looked over at Jacob's condo. "Is it because of Jacob?"

"That doesn't seem likely. Only the senator and a few people at my agency know I'm investigating him. I think there's a better chance it's someone who's connected to a case I accepted last week, or perhaps someone who saw me on the news and decided to follow me for the sheer excitement of it. I really don't think there's anything to worry about."

"Okay, I won't worry about it, especially since you don't seem that concerned."

"You're right, although I *am* curious about why the—"

I stopped in midsentence when a white Honda SUV entered the complex and pulled in the driveway of C4.

Chapter 15

Whitney looked over to see what I was staring at, and seconds later, when we saw a man emerge from the vehicle, she reached down in the floorboard and unlatched her leather photography bag.

"Is that Jacob?" she asked, attaching a telephoto lens to her camera. "Would you like me to take some pictures of him?"

I glanced down at the photograph Nina had sent me of Jacob from the EnViron's website. "That's him, all right. Sure, go ahead. Nina can never have too many pictures in her files."

When Jacob opened the back door of his SUV, I figured there was either a passenger with him or a dog in the backseat.

Instead, he removed a garment bag from a department store, along with a couple of shopping bags.

"Now you know why he wasn't at work today," Whitney said. "He decided to skip work and go shopping."

As she continued using the repeat mode on her camera to shoot images of Jacob as he was walking toward his front door, she added, "I bet he bought himself some new clothes to wear tomorrow. He probably wants to look his best when he meets his father."

"That would be my guess too."

Once Jacob went inside, Whitney placed her camera in her lap. "So what's next? Is there another location in Lanham you want to check out?"

"Not really, but if you don't mind, I'd like to stick around here a few more minutes and see if he comes out of his house again."

"What makes you think he might do that?"

"Well, first of all, he didn't put his car in the garage."

She looked around at the other condos. "There aren't that many cars parked in the driveways around here. Is there a reason for that?"

"Some condominium complexes require owners to park their car in the garage unless they plan to leave in a couple of hours. Nina said these are new condos, so I'd be surprised if this condominium association doesn't have some sort of regulation like that."

"What's the other reason you think he might be leaving soon?"

"As far as I could tell, he didn't lock his car. Of course, he had his hands full, so maybe he couldn't manage it, but if he—"

"You could be right," she said, picking up her camera and pointing it at the front door again. "He's coming out again."

As soon as Jacob got inside his SUV, I turned the key in the ignition and glanced over at Whitney. "Are you okay with me following him? I'd like to know what's on his schedule now."

"Oh, yeah. I'm fine with it. I'd like to know too."

I listened for any hesitancy in her voice.

I didn't hear any.

She sounded confident.

Maybe even a little excited.

◆ ◆ ◆ ◆

There was no indication Jacob suspected he was being followed. The quick glances I saw him take in his rearview mirror appeared to be nothing more than safe driving procedures, and he never executed a single maneuver to check for a tail.

Like most law-abiding people, I doubt if he even considered the possibility someone might be running surveillance on him.

In reality, if I'd given it more thought, I probably could have predicted what his next move would be, especially after I saw the shopping bags and realized he was getting ready for tomorrow.

But, in my defense, I was a little distracted by having Whitney with me, and I figured that was the reason I failed to consider where he could be going.

In fact, when I saw him drive in the parking lot of a strip mall not far from his condo, I thought he might be meeting someone.

I even told Whitney to get her camera ready.

But Jacob wasn't meeting anyone.

He was at the shopping center to get a haircut.

As soon as we saw him get out of his car and walk inside the Quick Cuts Salon, I told Whitney I'd seen enough, and moments later, we were headed back down I-95 to Washington.

"Well, what do you think?" Whitney asked, as I made the turn into my gated community. "Was this a useful trip or not?"

"Very useful. There was nothing about Jacob's actions I considered suspicious, so that gives me a lot of confidence he's exactly who he says he is. And, in the short time I was able to observe him, he didn't seem nervous or uptight, which is another good sign."

"But what about the guy who was following us? Aren't you worried about him?"

"No, not at the moment, but I reserve the right to change my mind if Nina's able to come up with an ID for him. Meanwhile, when we see Leslie tonight, I'd like to get her opinion about what happened today. And if Kyle's her date, I might discuss it with him too. That is, as long as it's okay with you."

"I'm fine with it." She reached over and squeezed my arm. "And thank you for being honest with me today, Mylas. I know you're concerned about me, but when I prayed about coming back to Washington again, the Lord told me everything would be okay, so no matter what happens, that's the house I'm living in."

I let out a short laugh. "That's the house you're living in?"

She smiled. "That's a phrase I adopted not long after Mark died. It was something a sweet old lady from my church said to me when she dropped by the house to bring me a casserole. I'm sure she could tell I was feeling overwhelmed by Mark's death and what my future held, so she asked me, 'what kind of house are you gonna live in now that your husband's gone?'"

Whitney stopped talking for a moment when she noticed I was getting a text, but I waved her off. "It's from Leslie, but I'll read it later. Go ahead. I want to hear the rest of your story."

"Well, just to clarify, I was living in the same house I'm in right now, the one on Sandusky Drive, so I told her I planned to stay right where I was. That's when she said, 'No, I'm not talking about this house. I'm talking about the house in here.' At that point, she placed her hand on her heart and reminded me about the parable Jesus told of building a house on solid rock, and she said it was up to me to decide what kind of materials I was going to use for my heart house."

I nodded. "Did she have some suggestions for you?"

She shook her head. "No, she said that was up to me, although she said she wouldn't advise building my house with 'what could have been' or 'why did this happen to me?' She said those houses weren't fit to live in. Instead, she told me to 'find yourself some promises from Scripture. Build your house on them, and you'll have a house built on solid rock.'"

"It's obvious you've done that."

"I haven't always succeeded, but I've tried. So today, while I'm here with you, I'm living in the house of God's assurance that I'm supposed to be here, and he's working everything out for my good."

"I'm living there too, Whitney, and if you ask me, besides bringing you a casserole, the lady also brought you some good advice."

"Yes, but in reality, her advice was a lot better than her casserole."

◆ ◆ ◆ ◆

As soon as I pulled in front of my house, I read the text from Leslie and then told Whitney what she said.

"Leslie made reservations for the four of us at the Golden Door. That's an upscale restaurant on 8th Street. She said she and Kyle would meet us there at seven."

"Okay, so Kyle's coming. That's good. I'm anxious to meet him."

Since it was nearly five o'clock, Whitney went upstairs to her room to get ready, while I retreated to my study to send an email to Nina.

After explaining why I was sending her the Toyota's license tag number and the images of Generic Man, I told her I would check with her in the morning before I went to my lunch appointment to see if she was able to get an ID on him or his car.

Once I checked my afternoon emails and replied to the urgent ones, I asked Babe—who'd been nuzzling my hand and dropping his tennis ball at my side from the moment I walked in the door—if he'd like to go play ball for a few minutes.

His response was to grab the ball and head out of the study.

I followed him into the kitchen—where I said hello to Mrs. Higbee, who was sitting at the kitchen counter working a crossword puzzle.

From there, Babe raced into the laundry room and jumped around until I opened the door to the backyard.

I gave Babe a good workout for the next fifteen minutes, and I probably would have exercised him a few minutes longer if Senator Allen hadn't called me.

When I saw his name on my screen, I deliberately threw the ball out toward the wooded area beyond the swimming pool, and then I went over and sat down on one of the patio benches to take the call.

"Hi, Senator. This is Mylas speaking."

"Hi, Mylas. I hope I haven't caught you at a bad time. I thought about getting Nathan to give you a call, but I decided I wanted to speak to you personally before you met with Jacob tomorrow."

"Have you heard from Jacob since you made the appointment with him?"

"Yes, I got another email from him this morning, but nothing's changed. He just sent me a short note saying he was looking forward to meeting at Romanos tomorrow."

I debated whether I should tell the senator I'd made a trip up to Lanham, and I'd spent a couple of hours running surveillance on Jacob, but before I could say anything, he said, "I'm calling you for a couple of reasons, Mylas. First, I've decided I definitely want you to call me while you're at the restaurant with Jacob so he can hear my voice and I can give him my personal assurance I'm looking forward to seeing him in person."

"Sure, I can do that, and for what it's worth, I think it's a good idea."

He was quiet for a moment or two and then he cleared his throat and said, "The second reason I'm calling is to let you know I've been giving a lot of thought to the dreams I had about the red wagon when I was in that motel room."

"Did you remember something else about them?"

"No, not exactly but I've been wondering if what I interpreted as dreams might actually be what I experienced while I was under the influence of the drugs I was given."

"So you think you actually saw a red wagon in the motel room?"

"Maybe, but remember I told you I had the sensation of movement, so now I've been asking myself if it's possible I wasn't in that motel room for every one of those five days. Maybe I was taken somewhere in a vehicle, and that's where I saw the red wagon."

Babe finally succeeded in finding the ball, so as I was listening to the senator, I picked the ball up from where Babe had dropped it at my feet and pitched it over to a clump of bushes where I figured he'd have a hard time finding it.

"When you say you had the sensation of movement, can you describe what that felt like? Was it up and down? Was it a gliding motion? Did you feel as if you were being carried?"

"Uh . . . let me think about that a second."

Babe had worked himself up into a frenzy trying to locate the ball, and at one point, he looked back at me like he thought I might have only pretended to throw the ball—something I'd done before.

I waved him back toward the bushes.

He continued searching.

"I think the best way I can describe it is that it was sorta like being on a raft in a swimming pool or the sensation of floating along in a boat. I know that's not very helpful, but it's the best I can do."

"Every piece you can add to the puzzle is helpful, so don't hesitate to let me know if you remember anything else."

"I just wish I hadn't been so dismissive of what happened to me, and I'd gone searching for answers right then and there."

"That's okay, Senator. I'll get you the answers you want."

Babe's persistence paid off, and he finally located the ball.

When he dropped it at my feet, he gave me a triumphant look, and I rewarded him by scratching him behind his ears.

"That's why I hired you, Mylas. If nothing else, I know you'll keep at it until you find what you're looking for."

Yep. Me and Babe both.

FIVE DAYS LOST: A Mylas Grey Mystery

◆ ◆ ◆ ◆

When Whitney and I arrived at the Golden Door restaurant at precisely seven, Leslie and Ford had already been seated at a table.

The restaurant required a jacket but no tie, and as I anticipated, Ford was wearing a suit *and* a tie, so I'd done the same.

Leslie and Whitney were in dresses.

Leslie was in a short, sleeveless red dress, and Whitney was wearing a shiny, off-white dress with long sleeves.

Both ladies complimented each other on how they looked.

Ford and I shook hands and made no reference to our apparel.

After I introduced Whitney to Ford, Leslie proceeded to act as the hostess of our party of four and suggested we order pan-fried calamari with hot cherry tomatoes for an appetizer. In addition, she had some recommendations for previous entrées she'd eaten at the restaurant, but when it came time for each of us to order an entrée, I noticed none of us followed her suggestions.

As a police detective, Ford was used to grilling people, and that was more or less the technique he used on Whitney when he asked her questions about why she was in the photography business. However, she seemed to take his interrogation in stride and didn't mind it.

While they were talking, Leslie leaned over toward me and asked, "Did you learn anything about Jacob from your trip to Lanham today?"

"A little. I found out he likes to be well-prepared."

"So you actually saw him?"

In the middle of telling Leslie about seeing Jacob arrive at his condo with some shopping bags, I noticed Ford had finished his conversation with Whitney and was listening to my account of our surveillance.

When I finished, he asked, "Is this the case you mentioned yesterday? The one you're working on for Senator Allen?"

"Yeah, and it's a strange one. Do you wanna hear more about it?"

"You bet, except don't expect me to take notes while I'm eating."

Like Leslie, Ford was an avid notetaker, although instead of using a cell phone or a tablet, he used the old-fashioned method of taking notes on a notepad he carried in his pocket.

I shook my head. "No notes will be required."

While we were enjoying our appetizers—which turned out to be very good—I gave Ford a brief overview of the Jacob Walker case and how it related to Senator Allen.

However, it wasn't until the waiter left with our entrée orders that I brought up what I really wanted to discuss with Ford and Leslie.

"I had something a little unexpected happen today when Whitney and I drove over to Lanham, and if you don't mind, I'd like to get both your opinions on it."

They each joked about how they were always willing to give their opinions, so I said, "A guy in a late model Toyota followed us from Washington all the way to the EnViron Industries headquarters building in Lanham, and while Whitney and I were sitting in the EnViron's parking lot, I was able to get a picture of him. He was in a parking spot at the next building over from us, so the image is a little out of focus, but I'd like to know if either of you recognize him."

I showed Leslie the picture of Generic Man first, but after she stared at him for a few seconds, she shook her head. "No, I've never seen him before."

When I gave Ford my phone, he took one look at the picture and immediately handed my phone back to me.

"Oh yeah, I know this guy," he said, "but I can't imagine why he was following you."

I grinned. "You've officially made my day, Kyle. So who is he and what can you tell me about him?"

"His name is Lewis Bond, and he's a PI."

"Really? I haven't heard of him. Does he have his own agency?"

"Nah. Or at least he didn't when I talked to him. At that time, he was working for the agency run by Trudy Phelps, but keep in mind that was several years ago."

"You mean the one with the billboards around town that say, 'Phelps can Help?'"

Ford grinned. "That's the one."

Leslie asked, "Have you considered the possibility Bond's surveillance of you doesn't have anything to do with Jacob Walker, and maybe it's related to another case?"

"Yeah, that occurred to me."

"It could even be related to your recent notoriety or to a case you haven't started working on yet."

As Leslie was making these suggestions, I was tempted to text Nina and have her start doing research on Lewis Bond, but when I looked across the table at Whitney, I suddenly realized she was being left out of the conversation, so I put my phone away and said, "Okay, that's enough shop talk for tonight. I'll figure out what's going on with Lewis Bond tomorrow."

Perhaps Leslie sensed the same thing, because she gestured at Whitney and said, "I know Mylas will be tied up at noon tomorrow, so why don't the two of us have lunch together?"

After Whitney thanked her for her invitation, she explained about the photography job she had with Grace Fellowship Church, and why she couldn't do that, and when the ladies moved on to another subject, Ford gestured at me and said, "Just so you know, Lewis Bond isn't a very nice guy. If he shows up again, I'd think twice about confronting him, especially if you're alone."

"Thanks for the tip. Right now, all I'm interested in is who he's working for and why he was following me."

I paused a second.

"You think maybe Phelps can help with that?"

Ford laughed.

Another reason I liked the guy.

He laughed at my jokes, such as they were.

Chapter 16

Wednesday, January 12

The spectacle that greeted me when I came out of my study on Wednesday morning to tell Whitney goodbye before she left for her photography assignment was unlike any I'd ever seen at my house before.

As she came downstairs carrying two camera bags, my handyman Joe, who was sitting in the foyer waiting for her, immediately sprang to his feet, displaying an exuberance I'd never seen in him before.

Granted, yesterday he seemed pleased when I asked him to be Whitney's driver for her photography shoot, but I admit I was a little surprised when I let Babe out in the backyard before breakfast and saw Joe polishing the Mercedes—one of the cars I inherited from Mac.

And, I was equally amazed when I saw him sitting on the bench in the foyer wearing a dark blue blazer with a pair of freshly laundered khakis. The only thing lacking in his attire was a chauffeur's hat, although I couldn't say for sure he didn't have one in the Mercedes.

Unfortunately, as soon as Joe jumped to his feet, Babe got all excited and let out several loud barks while running around in circles.

Meanwhile, Mrs. Higbee came out of the kitchen carrying a plastic container full of cookies, which she immediately handed to Joe while scolding him because he wasn't helping Whitney with her equipment.

As this chaos was going on around her, Whitney stopped at the bottom of the stairs and looked over at me.

I shrugged. "Nothing like a little chaos to start your day."

Mrs. Higbee said, "Whitney, I'm sending these cookies with you so you can give the kids a treat after you finish taking their pictures."

Joe took Whitney's camera equipment, plus the cookies, and motioned her toward the front door. "I'll be waiting for you outside by the car whenever you're ready, Ms. Engel."

Whitney thanked him, and then after she told Mrs. Higbee how much she appreciated her thoughtfulness, I steered her into the study so I could be alone with her for a few minutes.

Once I shut the door, I put my arms around her, gave her a hug, and said, "I hope you enjoy your day, Whitney. I know the kids are gonna love you."

She tilted her head toward me and smiled. "I've never had a problem with the kids. It's the adults who give me fits."

After cupping her face in my hands and giving her a lingering kiss, I said, "I think I may have a solution to your problem."

"Is that right?"

"Forget about rewarding the kids. Tell the adults if they cooperate, they can have one of Mrs. Higbee's cookies."

◆ ◆ ◆ ◆

When I arrived at my office, I contacted Nina and let her know I was available to speak with her about Lewis Bond, and she said she'd be down to my office in five minutes.

While I was waiting on her, I got a text from Chase Reed, *"When are you leaving for Romanos? I've decided not to give the assignment to someone else. I'll be watching your back today."*

Last night, after Whitney and I told each other good night, and she went up to her room, I called Reed and told him about being followed to Lanham. "Well, shoot," he said. "What's that about?"

"I'd be surprised if it has anything to do with the case I'm working on for Senator Allen, but since I have a lunch meeting at Romanos tomorrow with someone who's connected to the case, I'd like for you to assign one of your people to watch my back."

"Is that all you want them to do, just let you know if someone's on your tail again?"

"Yeah, that's it. No... on second thought... if it looks like someone's about to follow me inside the restaurant, I don't want that to happen, so a diversion would be in order."

He said he'd assign someone to take care of it and get back to me.

Now, according to the text he'd just sent me, he'd given himself the assignment.

I texted him back. *"I'm leaving for Romanos at eleven-fifteen. If a situation comes up, you can always text me. It won't be a problem."*

Nina arrived in my office two minutes later.

When she stopped in the doorway and looked around the room, I realized she hadn't been in my office yet, so I gave her a moment to take it all in.

She nodded. "I'll say this. It's a lot nicer than your office in the Russell Building, but I'm guessing it was your interior decorator who chose those off-white chairs around your conference table. What was she thinking? Doesn't she realize those chairs will have to be cleaned twice as often as dark-colored chairs?"

"I'm sure that never crossed her mind, but go ahead and take a seat in one. I think you'll find it's very comfortable, plus you can adjust it according to your height."

Nina, who was barely five feet tall, moved the lever on her chair so her feet were touching the ground. "You're right, this is nice, and yeah, they're very comfortable. Of course, that just means people will sit around the table and talk to you long after the meeting's already over."

"I'm the boss," I said, taking the chair across from her. "I'll just tell them they have to leave."

"Well, I won't be staying long enough for you to tell *me* to leave," she said, opening the laptop she'd brought with her. "I don't have that much to tell you about Lewis Bond, but that could change after the search program on one of my computers finishes running."

"I may not need that much biographical information on him. All I'm interested in right now is the name of the guy's employer so I can find out why he was following me."

"Well then, I can tell you he definitely works for Trudy Phelps. He's one of her detectives, and the Toyota is registered to her agency."

"He's one of her detectives? He doesn't just run surveillance?"

"No. I was able to verify he has his own PI license, plus I came across a newspaper article about a court case that took place five years ago that identified him as a private detective. He was listed as one of the witnesses testifying against the defendant."

"Well, spare me the details. I don't have time to hear them right now. What about the Phelps agency? What kind of clients does Trudy Phelps handle?"

"As far as I can tell, she's got a two-tiered system. She handles family matters, small business stuff, and does walk-ins, probably from her billboard advertising, and then she has what she calls her executive services. She may handle those cases herself since I noticed the testimonials she has on her website are mostly from professional people, and they mention her specifically."

"Is there any possibility you could find out the names of the clients she has right now?"

Nina folded her hands together in front of her. "Now, Mylas, what kind of question is that? Of course there's a possibility."

"That's music to my ears, Nina."

She snapped the lid shut on her laptop and pushed her chair away from the table. "I'll let you know when I've finished the song."

◆◆◆◆

I left the Greystone Building at eleven-fifteen and headed over to the Georgetown area where Romanos was located.

It took me thirty minutes to get there.

Because the traffic was heavy, I had a hard time deciding if I was being followed or not. At one point, I thought I spotted the Toyota Corolla, but then, I didn't see it again. However, I figured if Bond *was* following me, he wasn't driving the same vehicle he drove yesterday.

Switching out vehicles was standard operating procedure at a PI agency, especially if there were other vehicles available.

Naturally, Reed knew that, so I decided to put Bond out of my mind and concentrate on what was about to happen when I met Jacob.

After observing the guy's calm demeanor yesterday, I was hopeful he wouldn't have a meltdown when he found out I wasn't the senator.

In addition to that, I was counting on the luxurious ambience of Romanos to be the perfect backdrop for an agreeable meeting. If Senator Allen had suggested Jacob meet him at a chain restaurant in a less affluent part of town, I probably wouldn't have been as optimistic.

Romanos was a five-star restaurant specializing in Italian food, so the exterior of the building had a Mediterranean look to it—red-tile roof, white stucco exterior, black metalwork over the windows. That same theme could be seen in the restaurant's landscaping with a large gurgling fountain in the middle of a flowerbed at the entrance.

Since it was winter, there weren't any flowers in the beds, but the restaurant's landscaping service had done a good job of covering the bare spots with plenty of year-round foliage, which made the absence of flowers less noticeable.

Before going inside, I paused on the sidewalk to see if Reed had sent me a text about being followed to the restaurant.

I'd done the same thing earlier after parking my car, but at that time, there hadn't been any texts from Reed. However, I knew if I checked one more time, I'd be able to put it out of my mind.

Still no texts.

At least, that's what I thought.

Then, as I was about to slip my phone back in my jacket, I felt it vibrate. Reed's text said, *"You were tailed by a blue Ford pickup. He started following you a block from the Greystone, and now he's parked in the lot across the street from Romanos. I'm keeping my eye on him."*

I acknowledged the message and resisted the temptation to take a quick look at the parking lot across the street.

A few seconds later, I walked inside Romanos and told the hostess I had a reservation.

I gave my name as Mr. Allen.

◆ ◆ ◆ ◆

It was eleven forty-five when the hostess led me past the main dining area and down a long wide hallway. The restaurant's private rooms were located on both sides of the hallway, and each dining room had its own separate door.

Having been there before, I knew some of the rooms were suitable for parties of twenty, while others were designed for more intimate gatherings. I assumed Nathan had reserved one of the smaller rooms for this occasion.

The interior of the restaurant was decorated in the style of an Italian villa—as were the private rooms—and since most Italian villas had names as well as numbers to identify their location, each of the private rooms at Romanos was identified by a name.

As the hostess escorted me down the hallway, she explained Romanos' private dining rooms were named for famous Italian poets—something I remembered when I was there before—and the dining room reserved for my party was named Villa de Carducci.

"In case you're not aware," she said, "Giosuè Carducci is Italy's national poet."

At the moment, I had no interest in Italian poets, so when she paused to take a breath, I said, "Could you tell me if the other member of my party has arrived yet?"

She pursed her lips. "No, Mr. Allen, you're the first to arrive."

A few seconds later, she stopped outside a private room with a colorful ceramic nameplate on the door that said Villa de Carducci.

After ushering me inside, she swept her hand around the room and said, "Do you find this room suitable?"

Once I assured her the room was more than adequate, she strolled over to a serving buffet where there was a crystal carafe full of ice water, and while she was filling a water goblet, I walked over and sat down at the four-person table.

The rectangular table was covered in a white linen tablecloth and the table was arranged with two place settings directly across from each other on the table's long side. Immediately after placing the ice water in front of me, the hostess announced our waiter would be Simon, and then she left the room, quietly closing the door behind her.

Five minutes later, at exactly noon, the hostess opened the door and entered the room again.

Directly behind her was Jacob Walker.

His face lit up the moment he saw me.

FIVE DAYS LOST: A Mylas Grey Mystery

◆ ◆ ◆ ◆

I'd been assuming the second Jacob laid eyes on me he'd immediately know I wasn't Davis Allen.

That seemed like a logical assumption because I knew I couldn't possibly look old enough to be the father of a thirty-six-year-old man.

I couldn't, could I?

Nah, not a chance.

In addition to that, I agreed with Lockett there was a good chance Jacob already knew his father was Senator Allen.

Or at least, he suspected it.

Evidently, though, judging by the expression on his face, Jacob didn't have a clue I wasn't Davis Allen.

As the hostess left the room, Jacob approached the table and offered me his hand.

I rose to my feet.

"I can't thank you enough for coming to meet me," he said, giving me a wide-mouth smile. "I'm not sure what I should call you. Is it okay if I call you Davis?"

"I'm sorry to tell you this, Jacob, but I'm not Davis Allen. My name is Mylas Grey, and I'm a private investigator. Mr. Allen asked me to meet you and explain why he couldn't be here in person."

I immediately knew I'd have a hard time erasing the sight of Jacob's crestfallen face from my memory.

"Oh . . . uh . . . you're not . . . uh . . . but I was . . ."

"Here, have a seat," I said. "Let me get you some water."

While I was pouring Jacob some water from the carafe, the door opened and Simon walked in. He took one look at what I was doing and said, "Oh, please sir, let me do that for you."

I went over and sat down at the table and let Simon serve Jacob his water, but when he handed us each a menu and began suggesting a couple of appetizers, I interrupted him. "I'm sorry, Simon, but could you give us a few minutes? We're not ready to order anything yet."

"Of course. I completely understand."

Simon gestured at an electronic pager on the table. "Just use the pager when you're ready to order. I'll be right outside."

After Simon closed the door behind him, I looked across the table at Jacob and said, "I'm sure you've been looking forward to meeting your father today, and I know his absence has to be a big disappointment to you, but let me assure you, he's very eager to make your acquaintance."

Jacob shook his head. "It sure doesn't look that way to me."

"I completely understand why you feel that way, but let me explain some things to you."

"Explain away," he said, taking a sip of water. "I'm not going anywhere."

"First of all, I've read all the emails you and Mr. Allen have exchanged with each other, so I know why you contacted him through the DNAHeritage website."

"What's with the guy? Why is he so suspicious of me that he had to go to the trouble of hiring a private investigator?"

"There's no reason to take it personally, Jacob. My being here has more to do with him than it does with you."

"I'm sorry, but you'll have to explain what you mean by that."

"And that's exactly why I'm here. Before Mr. Allen can meet with you in person, he needs to make you aware of who he is, and how your relationship with him is about to change your life forever. I should probably add, his life will also change and maybe not in a good way."

He nodded. "Okay, Mr. Grey, you have my attention. Tell me about my father."

"Your father, Davis Allen, is *Senator* Davis Allen, the senior senator from Missouri and one of the most powerful men in Congress."

Chapter 17

Jacob Walker sat and stared at me without moving a muscle for maybe twenty seconds, but then the hint of a smile appeared on his face, and all of a sudden, he was grinning from ear to ear.

It was the same expression I saw on his face when he first entered the room and assumed I was his father.

"Amazing! Absolutely amazing. You're saying my father is Senator Davis Allen, the senator from Missouri? That Davis Allen?"

I nodded. "That's what I'm saying. Didn't that possibility ever occur to you?"

He shook his head. "No. No, it never did. For some reason, I just assumed Davis Allen was from Maryland, probably Bakerton, since that's where my mother was living at the time I was conceived."

"And you know this because she kept a diary back then?"

"That's right. It's the only reason I found out about it. I was born in Waterford, and she told me that's where she grew up. I discovered that was a lie when I came across her diary after she passed away." He motioned toward me. "But if you've read my emails to Davis, then you already have that information."

"Yes, I read about your mother's—"

"I suppose I shouldn't call him Davis, should I?" Jacob frowned. "That's what I decided to call him, but maybe that's totally inappropriate now. What do you think?"

"You can discuss that with Senator Allen. At his request, I'll be giving him a call in a few minutes so you can talk to him yourself."

"I'd like that. I'm anxious to hear about his relationship with my mother, and naturally, I'm very curious why he didn't know anything about me." His smile disappeared. "Or maybe he did, and he just didn't want to acknowledge me. Was that it?"

"Why don't we order some lunch, and I'll tell you what I know. After that, you can ask me any questions you like."

"I suppose you probably have some questions for me too."

I smiled at him. "Maybe one or two."

♦ ♦ ♦ ♦

When Simon arrived to take our orders, Jacob and I both had difficulty deciding which entrée to choose. It didn't take a degree in psychology to recognize our indecisiveness was connected to our odd situation.

In the end, the two of us simply followed Simon's recommendations—sausage cannelloni for Jacob and linguine cardinale for me—the two entrées Simon claimed were his favorites, although I noticed they also just happened to be the most expensive selections on the menu.

Even so, after a couple of bites of my linguine cardinale, I decided Mrs. Higbee's recipe for linguine cardinale was much better, and I made a mental note to let her know I considered hers far superior to the one I ate at a five-star restaurant, although I'd wait until she needed a little ego boost to say anything—which might not happen.

I couldn't determine how well Jacob enjoyed his sausage cannelloni because he was concentrating so much on my explanation of Senator Allen's stopover in Bakerton, it was difficult to read his facial expression.

At one point, as I was relating what the senator remembered about the dreams he had during the time he spent at the Roadside Inn, Jacob suddenly stopped eating.

"Did you just say he had a dream about a red wagon?"

"That's right. He said it was the most vivid part of his dream. But when we talked about it yesterday, he said he was wondering if it really was a dream after all. He was asking himself if it could be a hazy recollection of something he actually experienced."

"That's a real possibility," Jacob said, sounding excited. "In my mother's diary, she talks about a red wagon she bought at Christmas one year. I wonder if they're connected."

"I'd be surprised if they weren't." I waited a beat or two, and then I said, "I know Senator Allen asked you in his last email if you would mind bringing her diary with you. Did you do that?"

He nodded and reached inside the pocket of his jacket—which looked brand-new, possibly purchased yesterday—and removed a faded red journal with a rubber band around it. The diary was a little bigger than my hand and appeared to be about an inch thick.

"According to the dates, she started making entries in this journal after she went to work at a drugstore in Bakerton. Evidently, she worked as a pharmacist's assistant, although she never told me she ever had a job like that. After I found the diary, I realized her pharmacy job was probably the reason she moved to Waterford and went to work at AxonTeague, the pharmaceutical company."

"If you don't mind, Jacob, I'd like to take your mother's diary with me so I can go through it later. I'm sure you realize it could be the key to finding out what happened to the senator during the five days he lost in Bakerton, which is basically why the senator hired me. He wants to know why he barely remembers anything that happened to him after he said goodbye to your mother at the diner."

Jacob handed me the diary. "I don't mind letting you take it, but it's not like she wrote in it every day. And, as you'll discover, her writing doesn't always make a lot of sense."

"Does she use her own shorthand?"

"No, that's not it. It's just that I have no way of knowing her circumstances, so it's hard to understand the context of what she's writing about, and then there's the ... uh ... uh ..."

He paused and stared up at the ceiling a moment.

Finally, he shook his head and said, "I guess I might as well tell you about this now. My mother had some mental health issues, but I didn't know anything about it until I was in high school."

Jacob's admission immediately made me wonder if this was the health problem Nina suspected Amanda had, the one that prevented her from getting promoted at AXT.

I laid the diary on the table beside me. "Your mother's health issues could be related to what happened to Senator Allen in Bakerton, so whatever you can tell me about her condition, there's a good chance it could help me with my investigation. That being said, I apologize for having to ask you about something so personal."

"There's no need to apologize. I understand why you think it might be helpful, especially after hearing what happened to him in Bakerton. Believe me. I don't mind telling you what I know."

"I appreciate your understanding."

He pushed his plate aside. "Like I said, I grew up being told a lie, so now I'm willing to do whatever I can to find the truth. It's probably easiest if I just tell you what it was like growing up with my mother."

I listened in silence as Jacob told me about various times in his childhood when his mother acted irrational, was emotionally out of control, experienced crying fits, and became severely depressed.

"She always claimed her behavior was because she had migraine headaches, and that's what she told our neighbor next door who took care of me when my mother was sick. It wasn't until I was a sophomore in high school that I discovered what was going on."

Jacob said one day when he came home from basketball practice after injuring his shoulder, he decided some of the medication his mother used for her migraines might ease his pain. When he found three bottles of prescriptions in her bathroom, he wasn't sure which one was intended for pain, so he looked them up in a drug reference guide his mother kept at the house, and that's when he discovered none of the prescriptions were used for migraines.

"The drugs were prescribed for conditions like anxiety, depression, impulsive behavior, irritability, those sorts of things. Well, to make a long story short, I ended up asking my mother why she had those prescriptions, and that's when she told me she'd been diagnosed with Barringer's Personality Disorder several years ago."

"I've never heard of it."

"She made it sound like BPD wasn't that big a deal, and she told me both the doctor and the therapist she'd been seeing for several years assured her she'd made a lot of progress. I believed her because two of the bottles were still full, and they'd been filled several years ago."

I picked up Amanda's diary. "But you saw indications in here she was having mental health problems when she lived in Bakerton?"

"Yes, I believe so. At least, that's how I interpreted some of the things I read in there."

"Did you drive over to Bakerton to see if you could find out anything about her?"

He nodded. "Oh, yeah. As you can imagine, I was very curious about everything I read in there. In the diary, my mother talks about working at Marston's Drugstore, but naturally, since it was such a long time ago, I couldn't find any place in town by that name. She doesn't say anything about where she lived, although I don't think she lived alone because a couple of times in her diary she writes about being upset at a person named Shelby who forgets to put away the dishes."

"I'm sure I'll learn a lot about your mother from reading her diary, but can you think of anything that would be useful for me to know about her that's not in here?"

He let out a short laugh. "There's a lot about my mother you won't find in—"

Before Jacob could finish replying, Simon entered the room, and after presenting us with a dessert menu, he began removing our dinner plates as we looked over the menus.

"If you're a chocolate lover," Simon said, "I'd suggest either the chocolate panna cotta or the frozen chocolate-chip meringata."

I gestured at Jacob to see if he wanted to order dessert.

"I'm a big fan of chocolate," he said, "but I can skip dessert if you'd rather not have anything."

I was eager for Simon to leave so we could return to our conversation, so I told him we'd take one of each, and when he asked if we'd also like coffee to go with our desserts, we both answered in the affirmative.

The moment he shut the door behind him, I reminded Jacob he was about to tell me some additional information about his mother.

"It's hard to know where to begin." He took a sip of his water and then he reached in his back pocket and removed his wallet.

"I guess I'll start by showing you a picture of her." He removed a photograph and slid it across the table toward me.

The snapshot showed Amanda standing behind a table with a birthday cake in front of her. Unlike the picture Nina downloaded from Amanda's personnel file at AXT—which I wasn't about to mention to Jacob—in this picture, Amanda was smiling and appeared to be having a good time.

"According to what's written on the cake, this was taken on your mother's fiftieth birthday. Would you happen to have a younger picture I could take with me to Bakerton to show people what she looked like when she lived there?"

He pointed at the diary. "If you'll look on the back page of her diary, you'll see she pasted a picture of herself there."

As I began turning to the back of the journal, he continued, "She's wearing a white coat, and I'm sure that's why she put the picture in there. It's a pharmacist's coat with Marston's Drugs embroidered on the pocket. Maybe she was required to wear it for her work, but then again, maybe not. To me, it looks like she's posing in the coat."

"Did she want to be a pharmacist?"

"No, she never told me that, but she *did* talk about wanting to be a pharmaceutical scientist and develop new drugs. That's why I said I wasn't surprised when I found out she worked at a drugstore in Bakerton. I believe if she hadn't had her mental health problems, she would have gone on to college and pursued a degree in chemistry."

"I'm guessing she enjoyed working at AxonTeague then."

"Yes and no. It was more of a love/hate relationship. She wasn't satisfied working in the manufacturing division at AXT. She would have preferred to be in research and development, but the longer she was there, the less she talked about that dream."

Jacob was quiet as I studied the photograph Amanda had pasted at the back of her diary. I agreed with him. The way she was smiling at the camera and striking a pose made it look like she was wearing the coat as a reward or she was wearing it as a joke.

"Your mother was a very attractive young lady," I said. "I can understand why Senator Allen didn't mind sharing a table with her."

"I wish I could tell you why she used the name Shirley with him, but I have no idea what that was about."

"What else should I know about Amanda?"

"It may not have any relevance, but she told me the reason she never dated or ever wanted to get married again was because the man she loved was taken away from her, and it would be too painful for her if she had to go through that again. Of course, I thought she was talking about my fictitious father who she said was in the Air Force and was killed in a training accident."

"Did you ever see any evidence she had actually been married?"

"No, I never saw a marriage license or any photographs, and it wasn't until I was out of college that I realized how strange that was. When I asked her about it, she said it was too painful for her to talk about it, so I dropped the subject."

"Even though she made up the story about who your father was, it's a little difficult to understand why she wasn't interested in dating or getting married."

"I realize that now, and it wasn't a case of guys not being interested in her. My basketball coach was single and he asked her out several times, but she gave him the same story she gave me about not wanting to get hurt again."

"Perhaps that story was true—the part about being hurt—even though whoever hurt her wasn't your father."

Jacob shrugged. "Yes, that's a question I'd like to ask her, but she's gone now, and the answers I need are gone with her."

I was just about to tell him there might be someone who had those answers—someone who knew Amanda in Bakerton—but at that moment, Simon returned with our desserts and our coffee.

After he served us and left the room, Jacob asked, "Will you be placing the call to Senator Allen soon? I don't mean to be pushy, but I'm really anxious to talk to him."

"I'm sure he's anxious to talk to you too. I'll do it as soon as I explain some things to you."

◆ ◆ ◆ ◆

During dessert, I talked to Jacob about the senator's public profile and described how his opponent in the upcoming election, George Houser, was always looking for opportunities to smear him in the media.

"I'm not familiar with Senator Allen's reelection campaign or his opponent," Jacob said. "Even though I've worked in Washington for several years now, there are too many senators and representatives for me to keep up with them all, but believe me, I understand what you're saying about him being a public figure. Any personal thing that happens to him is sure to become a media event."

"Don't get me wrong, Jacob. Senator Allen told me he definitely has plans to make a public announcement and acknowledge you as his son, but he wants to have all the facts in hand before he does that. Hopefully, I'll have some answers for him by the end of the week."

He looked amused at my statement. "I still can't get my head around this. I've seen Senator Allen on television lots of times and I know I've been in at least one meeting with him when I worked for the FCC, but the thought that he's my father is mind-blowing to me."

"I actually think you look a lot like him when he was younger, even more so than his other son."

"How weird is that? When I saw on the ancestry site that Davis Allen had two daughters and a son, I was excited about having a half-brother and sisters, but I expect meeting them could be awkward."

"I'm sure Senator Allen will help you with that."

Jacob pushed his half-finished dessert plate away. "I'm ready to talk to him whenever you're ready."

I pulled my phone out of my pocket. "Let's do it now."

◆ ◆ ◆ ◆

I called the senator's cell phone number, and when he answered on the first ring, it was obvious he was standing by ready to take my call.

"Hi, Senator Allen, this is Mylas. I'm here at Romanos with Jacob, and he's eager to speak with you. You'll be glad to know we've had a very productive conversation, and he's told me several things I think will be helpful in my investigation. If you want, I'll be glad to leave the room now and give the two of you some privacy."

"No, Mylas, that isn't necessary. If you'll put me on speaker, I'll just say a few words to him, and then we can talk privately on Friday. Have you told him about us having dinner together Friday evening?"

"No, I haven't mentioned it. I'm putting you on speaker now."

I put my cell phone down on the table between us, and Jacob leaned in toward it as he spoke. "Hello, Senator Allen, this is Jacob Walker. I'm happy to be speaking with you."

"Well . . . uh . . . yes . . . uh . . . uh . . . me too. It's good to hear your voice. But . . . uh . . . listen Jacob, there's no need for you to call me senator. If you just want to call me Davis, that's fine with me."

Jacob gave a nervous chuckle. "Okay, uh . . . I will. Thank you. That's how I've been thinking about you, but when I found out from Mylas that you were *Senator* Davis Allen, I wasn't sure what to call you."

"I'm sure Mylas explained why I couldn't meet with you in person. I'm sorry if that was a disappointment to you, but I've made arrangements to attend a dinner party at a staff member's house on Friday night, and if you could join me there, we could meet in person."

"I'm sure I can do that, and I'll be looking forward to it."

"I'll do the same. Mylas will give you the details about the time and location. Oh, and Jacob, I hate to ask you to do this, but please don't tell anyone about our relationship until Mylas finishes his investigation. I need to know all the facts of what happened when I met your mother before the word gets out how we're related."

"I completely understand."

After a moment of awkward silence, they both said goodbye, and a few seconds later, Simon returned and asked if we'd like more coffee.

Once I told him no and sent him away with my credit card, I gave Jacob the details about the dinner party at Lockett's house, and as I was doing so, I received a text from Chase Reed.

"Suggest you and the person you're meeting with leave Romanos at different times. I'll explain once you're in your vehicle."

After I texted Reed back that I understood, I told Jacob he could go ahead and leave, and I'd wait for Simon to return with my card.

Jacob shook my hand, said he enjoyed meeting me, and left the room just as Simon returned.

As I was signing the receipt, Simon asked me again if I'd like another cup of coffee.

This time I accepted.

Ten minutes later, I walked out of Romanos.

Chapter 18

While I was sitting in my vehicle waiting for Reed to call me after leaving Romanos, I glanced across the street to see if the blue Ford pickup was still parked there.

I didn't see it anywhere, so I figured Lewis Bond—or whoever was driving—had left the area or perhaps moved to a different location.

Reed must have known I'd be looking for the pickup, because when he called, he said, "The pickup is now parked about halfway down the block at the jewelry store. There's a better view of Romanos' front door there, so the guy moved when a spot became available."

"So you know it's a guy? Describe him for me."

His description sounded exactly like Lewis Bond, so after I told him he was the same guy who followed me yesterday and explained what Nina found out about him, he said, "The reason I told you not to leave the restaurant with anyone is because the guy is taking pictures of anyone who comes out the front door, and he's using a long-range telephoto lens on his camera to make sure he gets a clear shot."

"I'd prefer not to have any photos of me with the person I met for lunch, so thanks for the heads up."

"Sure. No problem."

"Here's the thing, Chase. I'm heading to Bakerton, Maryland, now, and I don't want Lewis following me there, so I'm gonna try to lose him, and I'd like you to make sure that happens."

"I'll stick behind him and let you know when you're clear."

"That'll work. Here's the route I plan to take."

Reed agreed with me that it would be much easier for me to lose Bond if I tried to do it before I got on the freeway, so after speeding up to make it through an intersection on a yellow light, turning down a couple of side streets, and reversing directions twice, I phoned Reed to see if Bond was still on my tail.

"I'm traveling north on Wayfair," I told Reed. "Where's Lewis now?"

"He's on Midland going north. I'm two car lengths behind him. He almost had a wreck at the last intersection you went through. Now, he's pulled into a gas station. As far as I can tell, you're clear."

"That's great. Thanks for your help. I'll be on my way to Bakerton."

"Wait a second, Mylas. My surveillance team is helping Leslie this afternoon, so I know she won't be needing me. How about if I follow you to Bakerton just to make sure you don't pick up another tail?"

Even though I didn't think it was necessary for Reed to shadow me to Bakerton, I could tell he wanted to tag along, so I said, "Sure, better safe than sorry. It shouldn't take us more than an hour to get there, but just so you know, I'll be spending the afternoon asking questions around town, and as long as you're there, you might as well help me."

"Not a problem."

I let Reed know he could find me in the parking lot of a sports apparel store on Wayfair, and he caught up to me four minutes later.

Once we were on the freeway, I phoned him and said, "I might as well use this time to bring you up to speed about the case, and what I hope to accomplish while I'm in Bakerton."

The only comment Reed made after I finished telling him about the Jacob Walker case was, "I'm sure you can't wait to read that diary."

"You got that right. When we get to Bakerton, we'll find a place to sit down and have some coffee while I go through it."

What I didn't tell Reed was that I was counting on discovering something in Amanda's diary—the names of her friends, her favorite hangout, clues to where she lived—anything that would show me where to begin my search of what happened to the senator thirty-seven years ago when he got off the freeway and drove into town.

Otherwise, my trip to Bakerton could be for nothing.

FIVE DAYS LOST: A Mylas Grey Mystery

◆ ◆ ◆ ◆

When we arrived at the town square, I located a coffee shop—the Hot Bean Café—that I remembered from my previous research on Bakerton. It was situated between a quilting shop and an accountant's office, and Reed and I each found parking on the street in front of it.

Reed was wearing his usual jacket, sports shirt, and jeans, which made him blend in with the customers at the Hot Bean Café better than me, although I *did* take off my tie before I got out of the car.

After giving the barista our orders, we found a table away from everyone else—which wasn't that hard since there were only four other customers in the café—and once we sat down, I took Amanda's diary out of my suit coat pocket and flipped over to the back page.

When I showed Reed the picture of Amanda, he took a few minutes to study it, much like I'd done when Jacob showed it to me.

I wasn't surprised by how carefully Reed scrutinized the details of the photograph. When I interviewed him for a job at MGI, he told me he'd been a private investigator in Houston before moving to Washington to become the chief of surveillance at the Bowman Detective Agency.

When I asked him why he preferred running surveillance to conducting an investigation, he said it was a long story, and if I didn't mind, he'd save it for another day.

I told him I didn't mind.

That day hadn't come yet. I wasn't sure it ever would.

"Any thoughts about the picture?" I asked.

"My first thought is that she's a nice-looking girl," he glanced at it again, "and my second thought is that she's smiling like she has a secret. That could just be me, though. I tend to overanalyze things."

"It's not just you. I thought the same thing, like maybe she wasn't supposed to be wearing that coat or she was wearing it as a joke."

When the barista called out our names, I said, "If you'll grab our coffees for us, Chase, I'll start reading this."

"Sure. No problem." He grinned at me as he got up. "I think I'll order me a sandwich too. Unlike someone I know, I didn't get to have a fancy lunch at Romanos, although I doubt if this will make up for it."

I laughed. "You might be surprised, but whatever you get, be sure and put it on your expense report. I'll gladly pay for it."

When Reed returned, I'd read twenty pages of the diary.

Amanda's excellent penmanship made that task easy, and the large flowing letters of her handwriting told me almost as much about her as what I had read.

Although I'd never taken a course in handwriting analysis, I'd been schooled in it when I was defending a client in a murder trial during my lawyering days, and from what I remembered, Amanda's forward-slanted, open letters showed her to be an outgoing type, but the way she crossed her "t's" meant she was impulsive and emotional.

I quickly discovered what Jacob meant about understanding the context of what Amanda wrote. A few days after she recorded that she started working at the drugstore, she wrote, *"Helped D. B. today."*

On another day, she wrote, *"I moved in. I think it's okay."*

After several pages of complete sentences, her writing became disjointed, with repeated words and a lot of exclamation points, as if she were angry or upset about something. *"No! No!!! Not good. So bad!!! Hurts. Won't work."*

At that point, I regretted not knowing more about Barringer's Personality Disorder, so when Reed returned with our coffees and his sandwich, I asked him to call Nina and have her do some research on BPD so I could keep reading.

While he was on the phone with her, I came to a section in the diary where Amanda wrote several paragraphs describing herself as a pharmacist's assistant at Marston's Drugstore. It was written in a narrative style. *"Three months ago, I started working as a pharmacist's assistant at Marston's Drugstore in Bakerton where I grew up. I can't believe I'm getting paid to do this job! Today, Thomas Ingram, the pharmacist, let me help him compound a prescription for an old lady who needs her medication in liquid form. I had to be so careful as I was measuring and mixing the chemicals together, but when I finished, Thomas told me I did a good job. I can't wait to do more of this!"*

Amanda also wrote about her responsibilities at the pharmacy and how much she enjoyed memorizing the drug names and studying the medical conditions they were treating.

On several days, she recorded, *"D. B. came by to see me today."*

Besides D. B., she also mentioned a person named Shelby, but it was usually in connection with household chores. She complained about things like dirty dishes and not cleaning up the kitchen.

"I'm not sure moving in was such a good idea. This may not work out," she wrote six months after her first entry about moving in.

Evidently, the problem resolved itself, because three months later, she wrote, *"Shelby and I went to pick out a Christmas tree at the shopping center today, and when I saw all the kids' toys, I just had to buy a red wagon and a doll. Shelby told me I was crazy for doing it."*

Several pages of the diary were filled with descriptions of how she helped customers by answering their drug allergy questions and recommending over-the-counter medications.

She also wrote about how happy she was when the pharmacist decided to go home for lunch and left her in charge for an hour.

"Thomas said he trusts me to take care of things. How awesome is that? Well, it's pretty awesome if you ask me. Now, I'll have the opportunity to do a little experimenting on my own."

A month after she wrote about Thomas allowing her to run things while he was gone, she wrote, *"I did it! I compounded my own medication today while Thomas was gone. I think it'll help me sleep better, and I'm going to take some home and try it out tonight."*

It was several days later when she wrote, *"I'm sleeping great. I wish I could tell Thomas about my experiments, but I know he wouldn't approve. I could lose my job, and that can't happen."*

Not long after she started messing around with making her own drugs, she had another episode where she wrote down more disconnected words and short angry sentences.

"He didn't!! But he did!! He cheated on me! I'm gone. No more."

Two weeks after that, she wrote, *"I know what I want, I know how I can get it, and if my plan works, I'll be leaving this town for good. D. B. promised to help me."*

As soon as I turned the page and saw the date, June 30, 1985, my heart skipped a beat. Senator Allen was in Bakerton a few days later on July 2, so I figured whatever Amanda wrote would be significant.

It was and it wasn't.

"I have everything ready. I'm ovulating now, and Shelby is leaving town and going to a conference. Perfect timing. Thomas even said I could have next week off. Perfect. So perfect."

When I looked up from reading, I realized Reed had finished his conversation with Nina, his coffee cup was empty, and he'd already eaten his sandwich.

I took a drink of my lukewarm coffee and said, "This is fascinating stuff."

"It must be. You haven't looked up for twenty minutes."

I gestured at the diary. "I only have a few more pages to go, and then I'll tell you what I've learned."

"I don't mind waiting, but be sure and remind me to tell you what Nina found out about the CVM Pharmacy when you get finished."

I nodded and returned to my reading.

There were only ten pages left in the diary, but to my disappointment, there was no mention of Amanda meeting Davis Allen at the Black Bear Diner or what transpired afterward.

The next entry in the journal was six weeks later, and she began by saying, *"I did it! I moved out, and I'm living in Waterford now. I'm pregnant. Yes! Yes! Yes! Since the father is so smart and handsome, I know my baby will be beautiful and super intelligent as well."*

A week later, she wrote that she'd started working at AxonTeague and she planned to save her money so she could get her pharmaceutical degree and eventually work in their research division.

Sadly though, three months later, she filled up two pages of the diary writing about feeling lonely and unloved and declaring she would never trust another man again.

She made the last entry five months after Jacob was conceived. *"My baby kicked today! I finally decided I would tell him (I have a feeling it's a boy, but it's okay if it's a girl) that his father was an Air Force pilot who loved his country, and shortly after I got pregnant, he was killed in a training accident. Yes, I know it's a lie, but I want my son (okay, or daughter) to know his father was an intelligent, patriotic man so it will motivate him to live up to his potential and be successful."*

I turned the page and took one more look at the picture of Amanda in the pharmacist's coat.

I thought I knew why she was wearing it now.

She felt her ability to make her own drugs meant she'd earned it.

♦ ♦ ♦ ♦

Before I told Reed what I discovered about Amanda from the diary, I asked him to tell me what Nina said about the pharmacy on the corner.

"When I told Nina I was in Bakerton with you, she said to let you know she's confirmed CVM Pharmacy bought Marston's Drugstore twenty years ago. However, she said she couldn't access any of their old personnel records because they hadn't been digitized."

"It doesn't surprise me those records aren't available, but I've decided to make the pharmacy my first stop anyway. When CVM purchased Marston's Drugstore, it's possible they asked the pharmacist to stay on and work for them. If so, and he's still there, he might be able to tell us where Amanda lived or who her friends were."

"You know the pharmacist's name?"

"Yes. Amanda talks about him in her diary. His name is Thomas Ingram, and after he taught her some of the basics of compounding medicines, she did some experimenting on her own. Unless I find evidence to the contrary, I believe she concocted some kind of drug and put it in Senator Allen's coffee, and that's the reason he couldn't stay awake when he got to the Roadside Inn that night."

"Are you saying she went to the Black Bear Diner with the intention of drugging a complete stranger?"

I shook my head. "I'm not sure that's what she was thinking, but from what she wrote in her diary, it's obvious she wanted to get pregnant, and she was looking for an opportunity to make that happen. I'm guessing when a handsome young guy walked through the front door of that diner, and she found out he worked on Capitol Hill, she saw it as an opportunity she just couldn't pass up."

"So it's the old story of being at the wrong place at the wrong time?"

"Unfortunately, yes, but I know Senator Allen will want to know more details of what happened when he was at the motel, so I hope we'll be able to talk to the people Amanda mentions in her diary, and anyone else who might know how things actually played out."

Reed looked around him and nodded. "There's probably someone in this town who remembers her. Who else does she mention in there besides the pharmacist?"

"Just two other people—D. B. and Shelby."

"It's odd that she uses names for Thomas and Shelby but only uses initials for D. B. Of course, some people go by their initials, so maybe that's it, but that still leaves us clueless about D. B.'s gender."

I shrugged. "That's also true for Shelby. There are indications Amanda lives with Shelby, and if Shelby is a male, that brings up even more questions. On the other hand, she talks about D. B. coming by the drugstore all the time, and she says this person promises to help her with her plans, which I assume means helping her get pregnant."

"Really? Why would you assume that?"

I handed the diary to Reed. "Why don't you stay here and read the diary for yourself while I walk over to the CVM Pharmacy and see if Thomas Ingram is the pharmacist there. If he's not and no one knows where to find him, then I'm open to your suggestions about where to look for D. B. and Shelby."

I saw Reed glance out the window of the coffee shop in the direction of the pharmacy. "Okay, but if you're not back by the time I finish reading this, I'll mosey on over there myself."

"That works for me, although if you're worried about my safety, I think I'll be fine in the middle of the afternoon at the CVM Pharmacy in Bakerton."

"That's probably true," he gestured toward his right hip, "but just so you know, I always carry, and I assume you do the same, right?"

I smiled as I got up from the table. "That's right."

Chapter 19

The CVM Pharmacy in Bakerton was arranged like most of the other stores in the CVM franchise. The actual pharmacy was at the back of the store and the other merchandise—cosmetics, toiletries, and various other items—was located at the front.

When I walked in, I asked the clerk standing behind the counter where I could find the manager, and she immediately pointed off to her right in the direction of a lipstick display.

"Just knock on the door, and Mr. Anderson will let you in."

Since it wasn't obvious there was a door there—it was painted the same color as the wall and nearly invisible—it took me a minute to see what she meant. The concealed door was a security feature adopted by retail stores with the idea that it would make it harder for potential thieves to know where the store's safe was located, although having a clerk point out the manager's office obviously defeated its purpose.

However, when I walked over and knocked on the door, I also noticed there was a ceiling camera pointed at the spot where I was standing. I assumed the manager didn't think I was a threat because he opened the door almost immediately.

"Hi, there. How can I help you?"

"I'm Mylas Grey with Mylas Grey Investigations, and I'd like to ask you a few questions about someone who worked at this location when it was Marston's Drugstore."

"Sure. Come on in. It's a little cramped, but at least it's private."

He was right. It was cramped.

In fact, there was barely enough room for his desk, a filing cabinet, a large black safe, and a single guest chair in front of his desk.

"I'm not familiar with Mylas Grey Investigations. Are you from around here?" he asked, motioning me toward the chair.

"No, my offices are in Washington, but the case I'm working on for my client occurred in Bakerton thirty-seven years ago. I'm looking for a pharmacist by the name of Thomas Ingram who worked at Marston's Drugstore in 1985. Would he be employed at CVM now?"

"I assume you know CVM bought Marston's twenty years ago. That was when I started working here as a clerk, but as I recall, the pharmacist at Marston's at that time was Scott Donovan, and he retired when CVM took over. I've never heard of Thomas Ingram."

"Do you have any employees here who would be old enough to know the people who worked at Marston's thirty-seven years ago?"

He thought for a minute, and then he shook his head. "No, I'm afraid I don't. Sorry. I don't think I can help you."

"No problem," I said, getting to my feet. "I appreciate your time."

"I imagine it must be frustrating trying to locate people that lived here that long ago. Bakerton has changed a lot since then."

"You're right, and a lot of the places my client remembers no longer exist." As I started to open the door, I turned back around and asked, "Are you familiar with the Black Bear Diner that used to be located here on the square?"

"Sure. It was still in business until about ten years ago when the owner retired and moved to Florida." His face suddenly lit up. "But, hey, if you want to talk to someone who worked there, the lady who was managing the Black Bear Diner when the owner sold the property decided to open a restaurant out by the freeway. Her name is Tootsie Taylor. She's in her sixties now, so I know she would have been living here in Bakerton thirty-seven years ago."

"Thanks. She sounds like someone who might be able to help me. What's the name of the restaurant?"

"Tootsie's Catfish Cabin. Her place is located next to the GasUp Truck Stop. I should warn you. Don't talk politics with her. Tootsie can get pretty worked up about that subject."

"Thanks for the warning."

"Sure thing and good luck."

"To be truthful, I'd rather have information."

◆ ◆ ◆ ◆

When I left the pharmacy, I saw Reed coming out of the coffee shop, and after pointing him toward my car, he met me there.

After quickly summarizing my visit with the manager, I told him I wanted to head over to Tootsie's Catfish Cabin and have a talk with Tootsie Taylor, and I suggested he leave his car parked on the square and ride with me. "That way, we can discuss your thoughts about what you read in Amanda's diary while we're driving over there."

Reed agreed, and once we were on our way, he pulled the diary out of his pocket and flipped over to one of the pages. "I admit I'm curious about the relationship Amanda had with this person named D. B. Do you remember reading what she wrote here?"

He read the passage out loud to me. "*'D. B. follows me around like a puppy dog. I sure wish some cute guys felt that way about me.'*"

"Yeah, I'm curious about that relationship too. If Tootsie tells us she knew Amanda, I'll ask her if she knows anything about D. B. and Shelby. Just so you won't be surprised, I plan to tell her we're running a background investigation on Amanda, but I'm not going to mention Senator Allen. For one thing, the manager at CVM told me not to bring up politics with her, so I assume that also means politicians, but for another, I don't want the senator's name to be associated with Amanda Walker until we have all the facts."

"Gotcha. It's a shame you didn't get to talk to the pharmacist. If Amanda was experimenting with making her own drugs, he might have been able to tell us what kind of drugs they were. I agree with you. It sounds like she mixed up some drugs, gave them to Senator Allen, and then visited him in his motel room when he was out of it."

"Yeah, and now I'm wondering if she gave him too much of the drug, and that's why he can't remember what happened to him."

While we were discussing the possibilities of what occurred, I got a text from Nina asking me if I was available to talk.

I immediately gave her a call.

"Hi, Nina. Chase and I are driving over to Tootsie's Catfish Cabin here in Bakerton. We just found out the owner worked at the Black Bear Diner, so we're hoping she'll be able to give us some information about Amanda. Do you have something for me?"

"Chase said you discovered she was diagnosed with Barringer's Personality Disorder, and you wanted to know more about it, but it doesn't sound like you have time to discuss the research I've done."

"You're right, we're almost to the restaurant. Can you just give me the bullet points and send me the details in an email?"

Whenever Nina did research on an unknown subject, she wasn't enthusiastic about condensing it into a capsulized format, but I figured since she knew Reed was listening to our conversation, and he didn't know her that well yet, she wouldn't give me any pushback.

I was only partially right.

She voiced her disapproval, but she kept it to a minimum.

"There are a lot of facets to this disease, so it's gonna be hard to give you bullet points, but BPD manifests itself in sporadic irrational behavior and emotional outbursts. The person doesn't always use good judgment and tends to perceive things differently than most people, although they can continue to function in a way that seems normal to others. Most patients with BPD experience sleep disorders, depression, and anxiety, and there are several other minor symptoms, but since you don't have much time, I can put the rest of my research in an email to you. I'd still like to talk to you about it later, though."

"That'll be great, Nina. Thanks a lot. This really helps."

"I figured it would. We'll talk later."

After I disconnected the call, I looked over at Reed and said, "Here's a tip when you're working with Nina. There's nothing she likes better than analyzing data, researching complicated subjects, and accessing hard-to-get information, but she also likes for you to recognize it took a lot of effort on her part to drill down and mine the data."

"Thanks for the tip. I actually thought that might be the case. Did anything she say about BPD change your mind about Amanda?"

I shook my head as I drove in the parking lot of the restaurant. "No, if anything, what she told me only reinforces the picture I'm beginning to see of Amanda as a troubled young woman."

He waved his hand at the restaurant, which resembled a log cabin. "Maybe Tootsie can color in that picture a little more."

"Let's go find out."

♦ ♦ ♦ ♦

The smell of fried catfish greeted us even before we opened the door and stepped across the threshold. It was intermingled with the odor of fried hush puppies, fried chicken, fried okra, fried everything.

It was midafternoon when Reed and I walked in, and since the lunch crowd had left already, there was no one behind the hostess counter to greet us.

As we waited for someone to show up, we took in the ambience of Tootsie's Catfish Cabin. Besides the loud rock music, it consisted of dozens of open-mouthed catfish mounted on the wall, wooden plaques with sayings about the joys of fishing, and a bunch of colored photographs labeled "great catches."

A few seconds later, an older woman with faded blond hair came through the swinging door of the kitchen carrying a tray of glasses. As soon as she deposited them in an alcove, she walked over to the hostess counter and picked up a couple of menus.

"Good afternoon, Gentlemen. Are there just two of you today?"

"That's right," I said, "but we're not here to eat. We'd like to speak to the owner. Is Tootsie around?"

She laid the menus down on the counter and grinned at us. "You're looking at her. I'm Tootsie. What can I do for you? Or maybe I should just tell you up front I don't want what you're selling."

I shook my head. "We're not selling anything. We'd just like to get some information. I understand you used to work at the Black Bear Diner several years ago. Is that right?"

She put her hands on her hips and glared at me. "Are you a cop? This isn't about Carl, is it? I've already told a couple of snoopy detectives everything I know about him, so you're wasting your time."

I gave her what I hoped was my most winsome smile. "No and no. We're not cops, and this isn't about Carl. We don't know anyone named Carl in Bakerton."

"Okay, so if you're not cops and you're not salesmen, who are you?"

I gestured at one of the tables. "Would you mind sitting down and talking to us for a few minutes? I promise we won't take up more than a few minutes of your time."

"In case you haven't noticed, this is a restaurant. Those tables are reserved for paying customers."

I continued smiling at her. "What if we ordered some coffee?"

She scowled at me.

"And some dessert?"

She responded with a deep-throated chuckle and crooked her finger to indicate we should follow her. "Right this way, Gentlemen."

We followed Tootsie over to a table by the window, and once Reed and I sat down, she recited the dessert menu. Not surprisingly, it consisted of three kinds of fried pies—apricot, peach, and apple.

Tootsie disappeared into the kitchen and a couple of minutes later, she brought us our order—apple for me and peach for Reed. After telling us to dive in, she grabbed some mugs from a nearby beverage station, along with a pot of coffee, and returned to the table where she poured us each a cup of black coffee, including one for herself.

Once she sat down, she nodded her head at me. "Okay, Buster, now that you're a paying customer, I'll answer your questions, but you gotta tell me who you are first."

"Sure. My name is Mylas Grey, and this is Chase Reed. We're private investigators looking into the background of a young woman who grew up in Bakerton. The problem is she left here thirty-seven years ago so we're having a hard time finding out anything about her. We know she frequented the Black Bear Diner, and the manager at the CVM Pharmacy told us you used to work there, so we're hoping you'll be able to help us fill in some blanks."

"Are you gonna tell me her name?"

"Amanda Walker."

Tootsie shook her head as she looked down at the table. "The name sounds familiar, but I can't place her. That was a long time ago, you know."

I pulled Amanda's diary out of my jacket pocket and flipped over to the last page, turning the journal around so it was facing Tootsie.

As soon as she laid eyes on the photograph, she bounced her head up and down a couple of times. "Oh yeah, Amanda Walker. Now I remember her. She worked at Marston's Drugstore."

"That's right."

I didn't say anything while I waited to see what she would say next, which I figured would be what she remembered most about her.

"Amanda was one mixed-up young lady. One day she'd be all happy and eager to talk to me, and then a few days later, she'd be so down in the dumps I could hardly get a word out of her."

"But you remember talking to her?"

"Oh, yeah. She was a regular customer at the diner after she started working at Marston's, so I got to know her pretty well." She paused a second. "Now that I think about it, I always wondered what happened to her after she quit her job at Marston's."

"Did she ever eat at the diner with any of her friends?"

She shook her head. "No, I don't remember Amanda having that many friends. The only person she ever hung out with was Dexter Bodine, and I think that was only because she felt sorry for him."

Reed spoke up. "Do you know if she called Dexter by his initials?"

"Ummm. I can't remember, but some people called him D. B., so maybe she called him that too."

I asked, "Why did Amanda feel sorry for him?"

She winced a little. "I'm not exactly sure what was wrong with Dexter, but let's just say he was mentally challenged. It wasn't that he couldn't function; he just had a hard time learning, plus he was socially inept so people made fun of him. When I met him, he was living in a group home, but he hung around Amanda a lot. She didn't seem to mind. In fact, she was always helping him with stuff."

"What kind of stuff? Give us an example."

"I can give you a couple of them. For one thing, one of my customers told me Amanda helped him make the high school football team. Dexter was a great big guy, and he always wanted to play football, but he had a hard time understanding the plays, so according to my customer, Amanda taught him the plays, and then she convinced the coach to let him be part of the team. I remember she also helped him get a job when he got out of high school."

"How'd she do that?"

"From what she told me, it sounded like she blackmailed the owner when he came in the drugstore to get . . . uh . . . let's just say a rather personal prescription."

"What kind of job was it?"

Tootsie motioned toward the window. "He was the night clerk at a motel that used to be on the other side of the freeway. They tore it down several years ago, and now there's a hardware store there."

"What was the name of the motel?"

"The Roadside Inn."

◆ ◆ ◆ ◆

Even though I suspected Reed and I were each thinking the same thing, I was glad to see we both managed to keep our composure when we heard there was a connection between Amanda, Dexter, and the Roadside Inn.

I figured if we had shown any reaction to the news, Tootsie would have started questioning us about our interest in the Roadside Inn, or she might have suspected we weren't being straight with her and refused to answer any more questions from a couple of out-of-town strangers about past citizens of Bakerton.

I was glad that didn't happen.

I still had a lot of questions I wanted to ask her.

First though, I told her how delicious my fried apple pie was.

Reed got the hint and did the same, and she responded to our flattery by insisting on refilling our coffee mugs. Once she topped them off, I said, "We understand Amanda lived with someone named Shelby. Would you happen to know anything about that?"

"I only know what she told me. To be truthful, I advised her not to move in with him. Shelby was a playboy, and a lot older than she was."

"How much older?" Reed asked.

She shrugged. "I don't remember, but he owned his own house, which I know she found appealing. Amanda didn't have any family after her grandmother died, and she told me she wanted to have lots of kids. She said she wanted to fill that house up with them."

I asked, "Would you happen to know Shelby's last name, and if he still lives here in Bakerton? It sounds like he'd be a good source of information about Amanda."

She looked out the window. "It was something like Conway or Conner, or maybe it was Crawford. He was some kind of salesman."

"What about where he lived?"

"I don't know the address, but I know it was one of the older homes near the square."

"What about Dexter? Does he still live in Bakerton?"

"I have no idea. Once Amanda stopped coming around, I never saw him again."

She looked puzzled for a second. "When you say you're doing a background check on Amanda, it's not for some government job in Washington, is it? Don't tell me that's where Amanda went after she left here."

"I'm sorry. We're not at liberty to tell you why we're doing the background check on her."

Tootsie looked annoyed. "Well then, that just tells me it's definitely a job in Washington. I can't believe she'd take a job with those pencil pushers who expect us working stiffs to support them and their champagne tastes."

I figured any further discussion with Tootsie wouldn't get us anywhere, so I pulled out my wallet and laid a fifty-dollar bill on the table. "Thanks, Tootsie. We've enjoyed the fried pies and coffee, and we've also appreciated your taking the time to talk to us."

She eyed the fifty-dollar bill.

For a moment, I thought she was about to ask if I wanted change.

Instead, she picked it up and said, "Sure. Come back when you want some great catfish and not just some answers."

I decided not to tell her I wasn't a fan of catfish.

Chapter 20

The moment we got back in the car, before I even said a word to Reed about what Tootsie told us, I got Nina on the phone.

"Hi, Nina. I need you to look up something for me ASAP."

"Sounds like you had a productive meeting with Tootsie. What is it and why is it so urgent?"

"In her diary, Amanda talks about someone named Shelby, and we just found out this person is a guy, and Amanda was living with him in an older home near the square in Bakerton. I need an address for him so Chase and I can see if he's still around. Tootsie wasn't sure of his last name, but she gave us three possibilities—Conway, Conner, or Crawford—but it's possible none of those names are the right ones."

"I'll get right on it. It should be easy enough for me to find an address in the county assessor's records. I'll text you when I locate it. Anything else I can do for you?"

"After you find an address for Shelby, see what you can dig up on Dexter Bodine. Amanda also mentioned him in her diary, or rather she used his initials. Dexter was, and maybe still is, a resident of Bakerton. He and Amanda went to high school together, and when he graduated, he worked at the Roadside Inn. That's all I've got on him."

Once I got off the phone with Nina, I looked over at Reed and asked, "So now that we know Dexter worked at the Roadside Inn, and Amanda wrote in her diary that she was counting on him to help her with her plan, how do you see the situation at the Black Bear Diner playing out when Senator Allen showed up?"

He ran his hand over his chin several times. "I don't know, Mylas. Shouldn't you be telling me what *you* think? I'm just a surveillance guy."

"No, Chase, you're not. You're a lot more than that. It's obvious you know how to conduct an investigation, interrogate a witness, analyze the facts, and come to a conclusion. I don't doubt that for a minute, and I have a feeling you're very good at it too."

He stared straight ahead without saying anything. "Yeah, I was good at it once, but then I made a big mistake and someone got killed. That's when I realized I wasn't as good at it as I thought I was."

"So you decided to stick to surveillance?"

He gave me a smile. "Yeah, pretty much."

"Well, today, you're not a surveillance guy. You're helping me investigate this case, and I'd like to hear what you think happened when Davis Allen entered the Black Bear Diner that evening."

"Okay, I'll tell you what I think. I believe Amanda had some kind of drug with her when she went to the diner, and she planned to give it to a guy she thought would be a good candidate to be the father of her child. Her intention was for this to happen at the Roadside Inn. She must have either phoned Dexter to be on the lookout for the guy she was sending to spend the night at the motel, or she made some other arrangement with him so he would know how—"

"Wait a second, Chase. I just realized that's probably why Amanda told Senator Allen her name was Shirley. The last thing she said to him was that he should tell the clerk at the Roadside Inn, 'Shirley sent me.' That must have been a secret phrase between her and Dexter."

He nodded. "That makes sense."

I shrugged. "It makes sense, but it's still speculation. That's why we need to find Dexter and see if he's able to tell us what happened after the senator got to his room. It's hard to believe Amanda carried out her plan without his help."

"Yeah, I figure Dexter let Amanda in the room, and then he helped her drug the senator to keep him there. Evidently, Dexter was a big guy, so he could have handled it."

I agreed with Chase, but his statement triggered something I'd read in Amanda's diary that got my attention.

I said, "There's a paragraph in Amanda's diary that I found interesting. It's where she talks about having everything ready, and then she says the timing is perfect because Shelby will be out of town. I'm wondering why she'd care if Shelby was gone since she'd be spending that time at the Roadside Inn."

"I suppose if Shelby was home, he'd notice her absence. If he was gone, he wouldn't question where she was."

"That's true, but what if—"

Before I could finish my sentence, Nina called me back.

"What have you got?" I asked.

"I've got Shelby Conway who owns a house at 209 Foster Avenue. That's two blocks from the courthouse on the south side of the square. I'm sending you a picture of a man named Shelby Conway I found on an insurance website. It looks like Shelby is an insurance salesman."

"Okay, so his last name is Conway, he's an insurance guy, and you're telling me he still lives at this house near the square?"

"I'm telling you according to the assessor's office, Shelby still *owns* the house. Whether he still lives there is something you'll have to find out for yourself."

"We're on our way."

♦ ♦ ♦ ♦

Since I was anxious to check out Shelby's address, I asked Reed if it was okay if we headed over to Foster Avenue without stopping by the square to pick up his car.

"Sure, no problem. We'll get it later."

I handed him my phone. "Take a look at this photograph Nina sent me of Shelby. I don't know how old the picture is, but if you ask me, he's in great shape for an older guy."

He studied it a minute. "He sure is, especially for a guy in his early sixties. But you know what they say; if a guy works out and eats healthy, he can easily look ten years younger than his real age."

I pointed at myself. "I'm sure that's why I only look thirty-five."

He chuckled. "Yeah, right. But keep in mind, we're the same age, and I don't work out or eat healthy, and I look younger than you."

I shook my head. "No way you look younger than me."

Reed looked down at Shelby's picture again. "I'm betting he looks older than this photograph, but he just didn't want to change the picture." After giving me my phone back, he asked, "What explanation will you give Shelby for why you're asking questions about Amanda?"

I turned off Main Street onto Foster Avenue. "I was just thinking about that, and I decided if he's married and has a family, it might be embarrassing for two guys to show up and start asking questions about his old girlfriend."

"Yeah, he might even refuse to talk to us."

"On the other hand, people don't usually mind answering questions if they think there might be money involved, even questions about an old girlfriend, so here's what I think I'll do. I'll tell him Amanda recently passed away, and we're here to tie up some loose ends about her estate."

"So you'll imply Amanda left something for him in her will?"

"Yeah. What do you think about that approach?"

"Works for me."

◆ ◆ ◆ ◆

Shelby Conway's house at 209 Foster Avenue was a large, white clapboard, two-story structure with a detached garage, one of several historical-looking homes on the street.

The architecture was typical of residences built in the early 1900s with a turret at the top capped off with a dome that included some decorative gable trim. The same kind of intricate woodwork could be seen along the roof line and on the outside columns.

Like many homes of that era, there was a wraparound porch with plenty of room for rocking chairs, a swing, and kids' toys, although on Shelby's porch, there were only a couple of wicker chairs and some empty flowerpots.

When I slowly drove by the house without stopping, Reed never asked me what I was doing.

I figured he knew what I was doing—making sure I knew as much as possible about the property before I pulled up in the driveway.

"The place looks occupied to me," I said, as I turned the corner. "There's some furniture on the porch. The shades are open, and I didn't see any flyers stuffed in the front door. What do you think?"

"It sure looks like someone's living there, but with such a big house, I'm surprised there aren't any cars in the driveway. Of course, I suppose they could be parked in the garage."

"Yeah, and maybe no one's living there but Shelby."

"I can see why Amanda decided to move in with him. That house must have seemed like a mansion to her."

After making a circuit around the block, I pulled in the driveway at 209 Foster Avenue, and Reed and I got out of the car and walked up the sidewalk to the front porch.

The porch creaked as I leaned over and rang the doorbell.

After standing there for maybe thirty seconds, I started to ring the bell again when I heard the lock on the door disengage.

When it swung open, several questions we'd been asking ourselves about Shelby were immediately answered.

Shelby Conway was still living at the house, and he looked exactly like the picture Nina sent us.

Whether that meant he worked out and ate healthy, I wasn't sure.

All I knew was that he looked younger than his sixty-plus years.

◆ ◆ ◆ ◆

As soon as Shelby opened the door, I purposely took a step back, hoping he wouldn't perceive us as a threat.

I did so because Shelby was eyeing us suspiciously.

"What can I do for you?" he asked.

"I'm Mylas Grey and this is Chase Reed. We're private investigators who've been hired by the family of Amanda Walker. She recently passed away, and her estate hasn't been settled yet, so we're here in Bakerton trying to locate Shelby Conway. Would that be you, sir?"

His eyes narrowed as he took in this information.

"Uh . . . yeah, that's me. Did you say Amanda Walker?"

"That's right. I wonder if you'd mind if we came inside so we could talk to you for a few minutes?"

At first, I thought he was about to say no and ask us to leave, but then his demeanor changed from suspicion to curiosity, and he reached over and unlocked the storm door.

"I guess I can spare a few minutes."

"Thank you," I said, following Shelby into the living room. "We appreciate your time."

It was obvious he'd been reading in his recliner when I rang the doorbell, and as he motioned for us to take a seat on the couch, he picked up the book he'd left on his chair, put it in the magazine rack next to the recliner, and resumed his seat.

"I'm interested in what you have to say, Mr. Grey, but I can't give you much of my time. My wife will be home in a few minutes. She's gone to pick up our grandkids, and when they get to the house, I guarantee you things will get a little chaotic."

I gave him a smile. "Sure, I understand. So the name Amanda Walker *is* familiar to you?"

"Well, I knew a girl named Amanda Walker, but that was a long time ago, and I haven't seen or heard from her for years. I have no idea why someone would be looking for me in connection with her estate."

"How well did you know Amanda?"

He frowned. "How well did I know her?" He shrugged. "Pretty well, but what does that have to do with her estate?"

Suddenly, I started getting a little worried about the tactic I'd chosen to get information out of Shelby, especially when I realized he'd tensed up and was looking agitated.

When I hesitated as I was trying to decide whether to change tactics, Reed spoke up. "We're just verifying the facts we were given, Mr. Conway. It's important for us to know we've got the right person."

All of a sudden, without any warning whatsoever, Shelby rose to his feet, reached behind his back, withdrew a handgun, and pointed it at us. "I don't know what you're trying to pull, but you need to leave now. I don't believe a word you're saying, and I want you out of my house before my family gets back."

"Hold on," I said, raising my hands in the air. "You can put your gun away. We'll be glad to leave. Believe me, we're not here to harm you or cause you any trouble."

"You expect me to believe that when you're sitting here in my own living room lying to my face?"

Out of the corner of my eye, I saw Reed shift his weight away from his right side and suddenly, I realized, unlike me, he didn't have his hands raised. Although I couldn't believe he'd actually go for his gun in these circumstances, I'd never worked with him before, so I didn't know that for sure.

What I knew was that I had to do something.

And I had to do it now.

◆ ◆ ◆ ◆

I could think of only one way to diffuse the situation. It wasn't something I wanted to do, but it seemed to be my only option.

"You're right, Shelby," I said. "We've been lying to you about why we're here."

He tilted his head slightly to the right, looking surprised and a little skeptical by my admission.

"Okay, so tell me what you're doing here."

"I promise I'll do that as soon as you put your gun away."

"Why should I believe anything you say?"

I gestured over at the magazine rack beside his recliner. "Because you believe what's in that Bible in the magazine rack there underneath the book you were reading, don't you?"

He quickly glanced over at the magazine rack where I'd noticed a well-worn leather Bible with some papers sticking out of it.

"Uh . . . of course I do. I'm a Christian. I read the Bible every day, but what does that have to do with why I should believe you?"

"You can believe me because I'm telling you I was wrong to lie to you, and I'm sorry I did it. It wasn't the right thing to do, and I'm not trying to excuse myself, but I'm new to this Christianity thing. I've only been a believer for a few months, and I admit I'm still struggling with letting go of some things I used to do, like lying all the time."

A smile crept across his face, and a few seconds later, he lowered his gun. "Okay, I believe you. But you'll need to tell me what you're really doing here, and why you lied to me."

"First of all, we really are private investigators. My agency, Mylas Grey Investigations, was hired by Senator Davis Allen, the senior senator from Missouri, to look into an incident that happened to him in Bakerton thirty-seven years ago. That's what we're doing here."

As I was talking, Shelby returned his gun to his holster and sat down in his recliner again, although he remained poised on the edge of his seat as he listened to my explanation.

"At the time of this incident, the senator was doing a summer internship on Capitol Hill, and he was traveling to New York City to celebrate the Fourth of July with some of his fellow interns. When he got off the freeway and drove into Bakerton to get something to eat, he met a young woman at the Black Bear Diner. She called herself Shirley, but when he saw a picture of Amanda recently, he realized she'd given him a phony name, and he'd actually eaten dinner with Amanda. After the two of them had dinner together, he said—"

"Did this happen on the Fourth of July or was it a few days before?"

"Senator Allen stopped in Bakerton on July 2, 1985."

If I interpreted the look on Shelby's face correctly, the date struck a chord with him, but he didn't say anything, so I decided to finish my story before asking him about it.

He nodded. "Okay, go on."

"After Davis and Amanda had dinner together, he said he felt too drowsy to get on the road again, and she suggested he get a room at the Roadside Inn. Once he got there, he fell asleep immediately. He's not clear what happened after that. All he remembers is having a series of dreams, which he admits could have been experiences he was actually having, but he was too out of it to realize what he was doing. When he woke up, he had a terrible headache, and when he went to check out of the motel, he discovered he hadn't just spent one night there. He'd actually been in his motel room for five days."

"What?" Shelby shook his head. "That doesn't make sense. How could that have happened?"

"That's what the two of us are trying to figure out," I said, gesturing over at Reed, who appeared more relaxed now that a gun wasn't pointed at him, although he was definitely keeping an eye on Shelby.

"How did Senator Allen explain it?" Shelby asked.

"He thought he must have been really sick, maybe had the flu or a high fever. That's the story he told his friends, and according to him, he mostly forgot about the whole thing. Now, he realizes Amanda must have put something in his coffee or drugged him some other way."

"So why did he decide to have you investigate this incident after all these years?"

"A few weeks ago, he received an email from an ancestry website called DNAHeritage. Are you familiar with it?"

"Not that one, but yeah, I know what you're talking about."

"The email he received informed him he had a thirty-six-year-old son named Jacob Walker."

Chapter 21

Shelby looked stunned by this revelation, but then a few seconds later, as I began describing the lunch I had with Jacob and what he told me about his mother, his facial expression changed from surprise to frustration.

By the time I finished telling him what I'd learned from reading Amanda's diary, he was shaking his head.

"I don't know what to say. I wasn't aware of any of this, and I certainly didn't know Amanda was pregnant when she left here."

I took Amanda's diary out of my pocket. "I don't doubt that, Shelby, but I suspect you'll still be able to help me decipher some confusing entries in Amanda's diary that don't make a lot of sense to me. I believe they could be related to your relationship with Amanda."

He looked down at his feet. "I want you to know I'm a very different person today than I was back then. When I turned thirty, my life changed when I met my wife. Julia is a very committed Christian, and she eventually led me to make my own commitment of faith. Now, I'm really embarrassed by all the bad choices I made back in my twenties."

Before I could tell him I understood where he was coming from, Reed said, "We've all made our share of mistakes, Shelby."

He nodded. "Instead of asking me questions, why don't I tell you how I met Amanda, and what happened between us before she left me a note telling me she was leaving Bakerton for good." He pointed at the diary. "It might explain whatever she wrote in there about me."

"Sure, go ahead," I said.

He fidgeted in his chair for a few seconds before telling us about going to work at his father's insurance agency after getting out of college when he was twenty-three. He said he'd only been working there a year when both his parents were killed in a car accident.

"My dad's insurance agency was very successful, and even though I was only twenty-four, I suddenly found myself in charge of it. Since I was an only child, I also received a substantial inheritance, which included this house that my grandparents purchased when they were first married."

Shelby went on to describe how he suddenly became the town's most eligible bachelor and started spending every weekend going to wild parties and entertaining young ladies at his house.

"I'd been living that way for at least a couple of years when I met Amanda. She came by to see me to purchase some car insurance shortly after her grandmother passed away. I think we connected because we both had suffered a loss, but I also enjoyed the way she mothered me. She even scolded me about picking up after myself."

"In her diary, Amanda doesn't say anything about when she met you," I said, "but she does write about moving in with someone."

"That would be me." He swept his hand around the room. "The first time she was here, she couldn't stop talking about what a big house this was, and how perfect it would be for raising a family."

"How would you describe your relationship?"

"We got along okay, but there were times when she'd get upset at me for no reason. When that happened, she'd be depressed for several days, and I'd just try to stay out of her way until she got over it."

"She writes about someone cheating on her. Was that you?"

He hung his head again. "Uh-huh. It was after she started talking about us getting married and having kids. For Christmas, she even bought a doll and a wagon for our future kids. After that, I wanted to get out of the relationship. I just couldn't deal with her emotional problems. So yeah, I cheated on her, and she found out about it."

"But she didn't move out of the house?" I asked.

"No, and I didn't ask her to move out. Actually, I was afraid of what she might do. But during the summer of '85, I decided I'd talk to her when I got back from an insurance convention in Philadelphia."

"Was that where you went in July of 1985 when Senator Allen was here in Bakerton?"

He nodded. "That's right, and when I got back from the convention, Amanda had moved out of the house. The note she left me said something like, 'I don't need you in my life anymore. I'm making my own family and leaving Bakerton for good.' "

"Did you try to find out where she went?"

He made a futile gesture. "Well, I didn't try very hard, that's for sure. I went by Marston's Drugstore and the pharmacist said she'd written him a note thanking him for everything he'd taught her, but he had no idea where she went. I also tried to talk to this weird kid she hung out with named Dexter Bodine. I actually suspected he'd been at the house here and helped her move out while I was gone."

"Why did you suspect that?"

"Back then, I used to work out every day, so I drank a lot of protein shakes, and whenever Dexter showed up at the house, he always wanted one of my shakes. When I got back from Philadelphia, there was only one protein shake left in the pantry, and I knew I'd stocked up before I left. Amanda couldn't stand them, so I figured Dexter drank them all. There were several other signs he'd been here too."

"Like what?"

"Well, for one thing, he drove an old beat up Dodge van that leaked oil, and there was a big oil leak in my driveway. Another reason I knew he'd been here is that some furniture in the basement had been moved around. I figured that was because he helped Amanda haul away some of her grandmother's things. When she moved in, I let her store some of her furniture in the basement. She also took that red wagon she put down there, along with the toys she bought for what she called her future family."

"What did you mean when you said you *tried* to talk to Dexter?"

"Dexter lived in a group home—I believe he had some kind of mental disability—and when I went over there and asked if I could speak to him, he refused to come out of his room. When I went to the director and asked if I could speak to him, she told me Dexter was in a bad place right now, and I should leave and not bother him, so after that, I gave up trying to find Amanda."

"Do you know if Dexter still lives in Bakerton?"

"No, he passed away about ten years after Amanda left. When I saw an obituary in the paper about it, I wondered if he and Amanda had stayed in touch, but I didn't give it a lot of thought. By then, I was married to Julia and had two kids, plus I was a deacon in our church, so I just wanted to put that part of my life behind me."

"I appreciate your willingness to be so open with us, Shelby," I said. "I wasn't expecting it, and I certainly didn't deserve it by trying to deceive you when you invited us into your home."

He cringed a little. "I apologize for pulling my gun on you, but I'd do anything to protect my family."

"That's understandable, and now, I'd like to ask you to do something for me, but if you don't want to do it, or you feel there's not enough time to do it before your wife gets home, then that's okay too."

He glanced down at his watch. "I still have a little time before she gets back. What is it you want me to do?"

"Would you mind showing us your basement?"

♦♦♦♦

Shelby said he didn't mind, but he was curious why I wanted to see it, so I explained about the dreams Senator Allen had and his vivid recollection of seeing a red wagon in them.

He looked puzzled. "So are you thinking he was here at my house and not at the Roadside Inn the whole time?"

"I think that's a possibility. I don't believe it would have been that difficult for Dexter and Amanda to transport him over here from the motel, especially since you said Dexter had a van."

"That's true, and Dexter could have easily carried a man. I've seen him play football, and he was a powerhouse on the field."

"If you'll show us your basement, I'll take some pictures with my phone, and see if anything looks familiar to Senator Allen."

As Shelby stood to his feet, he said, "It's not a finished basement. We mainly just use it for storage, but if you'll follow me, I'll be glad to show it to you. It's really not that scary, but when my grandkids play down there, they call it the dungeon."

We followed him through the kitchen and into a laundry room, where a set of stairs led down to the basement.

Once we were down there, he showed us where he'd added some shelving against one of the walls and set up a ping-pong table for the grandkids, but other than that, he said he hadn't made any changes in the basement since Amanda lived in the house.

"Would you mind showing us where the furniture was stored that belonged to Amanda?"

"It was over here in this section," he said, walking across the cement floor to where there were several pieces of antique furniture—a rocking chair, an end table, a rolltop desk—along with a treadle sewing machine and an old bicycle.

All the items were shoved up against the exposed brick of one of the basement walls. The furniture was dusty, but it appeared to be in good shape, and I didn't see any signs of mold, even though it was humid.

"I know it might be difficult for you to remember, but do you recall how this area looked when you came down here after you got back from your trip and discovered Amanda had moved out?"

He glanced around the area for a second.

"Since my parents were always reluctant to throw anything away, there was a lot more furniture down here then. I'm talking about a sofa, an old desk, a couple of mattresses, and probably a bunch of other stuff I can't remember. Ordinarily, most of the stuff was pushed up against the wall, and what I noticed when I got home was that some of the furniture was moved out in this open space. I just thought it was because Amanda had moved everything around trying to get to her grandmother's belongings."

"What kind of furniture was out here in the open?"

He walked over to an area where there were some boxes labeled Christmas decorations.

"This is where I found the two mattresses," he said. "They were here next to this wall stacked one on top of the other."

He pointed to his right. "The sofa was over there, and next to it was a cabinet my grandmother used for her sewing supplies. I believe the rocking chair was somewhere in this area."

Reed pointed over to another section of the basement and asked, "Do you have a toilet down here?"

Shelby nodded. "Yes, there's a half-bath over there next to where the heating unit is. My grandparents had it put in when they were thinking about making this into a fallout shelter during the Cold War."

I said, "One of the things the senator remembers from his dream is that he had a hard time breathing. He said it was like the air was heavy. I figure if he was down here where the air is damp, and he was fighting the drugs in his system, that might be the reason."

Shelby nodded. "Yeah, it's always been musty down here, so that might be the reason he described it like that."

"One last question," I said. "Where was the red wagon Amanda bought for her future family?"

"If I remember, Amanda had it here against the wall opposite where the mattresses were."

I walked over to where Shelby said the mattresses were stacked, and when I looked back at where he said the red wagon had been, I said, "If this was where Davis was sleeping off the drugs Amanda was giving him, the wagon would have been directly in his line of sight when he was trying to wake up, so maybe that's why he remembers it so distinctly."

"Didn't Senator Allen tell you he couldn't feel his legs?" Reed asked. "Maybe that's because Amanda had him restrained in some way."

Shelby rubbed his forehead. "It's so hard for me to imagine what you're describing actually happened down here. And to think Amanda did such a horrible thing to a future senator is just mind-blowing."

I said, "I know I've asked a lot of you already, Shelby, but until you hear from me, I'd rather you didn't tell anyone what we've just been discussing. I realize you might want to tell your wife but—"

"No. No, I won't do that," he said, shaking his head. "Believe me. I won't say anything to Julia or anyone else about any of this."

He glanced down at his watch. "Speaking of my wife, maybe we need to wrap this up now."

I pulled my phone out of my pocket and took several shots of the basement from various angles, and then we went back upstairs, where we exchanged phone numbers.

"You should be hearing from me in a few days, Shelby. I'm not exactly sure how Senator Allen is going to handle his announcement about Jacob being his son, but I wouldn't be surprised if he decides not to mention Bakerton, especially when I give him the details of what I believe must have happened in this house."

"Of course, I'd be grateful if he wouldn't say anything about where Amanda was living at the time. Several people in this town probably remember Amanda and I were living together back then, so there might be a reporter knocking on my door if he did that."

Reed shook his head. "I guarantee you there'd be more than just one reporter knocking on your door. There'd be dozens, and they'd be camped out on your street for weeks. It might not just be reporters either. There are a lot of crazies out there these days."

Shelby smiled. "Why do you think I carry a gun?"

Reed said, "Same reason I carry one." He gestured over at me. "If Mylas hadn't convinced you to put away your weapon, you might have seen it."

Shelby extended his hand toward me. "Again, I apologize for pulling my gun on you."

"Not a problem, Shelby," I said, shaking his hand, "and thanks for your help. I'll be in touch."

After Reed and I said goodbye to Shelby, and we were walking out to my car, he said, "Were you being straight with Shelby when you gave him that story about becoming a believer, or was that just something you came up with to get him to put his gun away? I mean, it doesn't make any difference to me. I'm just curious."

"I was being straight with him."

He nodded. "That's interesting."

"Someday when we have time to sit down and talk, I'll be glad to tell you what caused me to make that decision. Right now, though, I need to call my housekeeper and tell her I'm gonna be a few minutes late for dinner. If I don't, I'll regret it."

As soon as we pulled out of Shelby's driveway, I called Mrs. Higbee and told her it would be close to seven before I made it back to the house. She didn't sound too upset, but then I realized Whitney was in the kitchen with her, so that might have tempered her response.

"Tell Whitney I'll call her when I get on the freeway," I said. "I want to hear how her day went."

"By the smile on her face, I think it went pretty well, but I'll let her tell you about it."

A few seconds after I disconnected the call, I pulled into a parking space next to Reed's Honda Odyssey, and just before he got out, he asked, "What's your next move with the senator's case?"

"If he's available tomorrow, I'll make an appointment to speak with him in person and give him the details of what we found out today. Even though some of it is conjecture, he'll have Amanda's diary and Shelby's recollection of events, so I hope he'll be satisfied with my findings."

"And what about the guy who was following you? Will you tell the senator about Lewis Bond too?"

"No, I don't think I will. I know of no reason why Bond would be interested in the Jacob Walker case."

"Maybe not, but Bond is definitely interested in you."

"Yeah, and it's beginning to irritate me."

When Reed opened the car door, he looked back at me. "Let me know if you need help getting rid of that irritation."

I told Reed thanks, and I'd see him tomorrow.

However, I intended to take care of Bond myself.

And I intended to do it tomorrow.

PART FOUR

Chapter 22

Thursday, January 13

Unlike the previous morning, everything went smoothly when Whitney left the house with Joe to finish up her photography assignment for the church brochure.

Before she left, I told her I planned to take her out for a celebratory dinner when she was finished, and she said it could be a celebration for both of us since from what I told her last night, it sounded like I would be wrapping up the Jacob Walker case soon.

Last night during dinner—a dinner Mrs. Higbee only had to delay by ten minutes—I had Whitney give me the highlights of her photography sessions first, and then I told her about my lunch with Jacob and my subsequent trip to Bakerton.

When we finished, we both agreed we'd each had a successful day, and then she told me about a parent who wanted to make an appointment with her to take pictures of their whole family.

"It was really hard to tell her I was only in the area for a few days, and I wouldn't be able to do it," Whitney said.

"Maybe that means you need to open a branch office of WEE Photography here in Washington."

She laughed. "I'm not sure I would ever get used to the traffic in this town. By the way, Mylas, thank you for having Joe drive me around. It made everything a lot easier."

"He'd probably be willing to work for you for free if you decided you wanted to relocate here."

She shook her head. "It's taken me years to build up my clientele in Columbia. Starting over would be really difficult."

At that moment, Mrs. Higbee came in the dining room to serve us dessert—coconut cake with vanilla ice cream—so I decided to wait a few more days before bringing up the possibility of her moving to Washington. However, I couldn't help but notice Whitney didn't dismiss the idea of moving to Washington entirely.

Or was I being too optimistic?

◆◆◆◆

When I got to the office, I made two phone calls. The first one was to Lockett. Once I updated him on the case, he set up an appointment with Senator Allen for two o'clock. After that, I called Nina.

As soon as I told her I was ready to hear about the research she'd done on Barringer's Personality Disorder, she said she'd be down to my office in ten minutes.

"I need ten minutes because I just found out something about the Trudy Phelps Investigation Agency, and I need to verify it first. It's something I'm sure you'll be interested in."

"Take all the time you need. I'll be here all morning."

When Nina tapped on the door, I'd just gotten off the phone with Leslie after giving her an update on my findings in Bakerton.

Nina gave me a quick greeting before she walked over to the conference table and opened up her laptop. "I've got several things to tell you, but I'll start with what I learned about Barringer's Personality Disorder. It's usually referred to as BPD and . . ."

Even though I sat down at the table and listened to her research—nodding at the appropriate times—I felt sure I knew enough about BPD to know the role it played in Amanda's behavior at the diner and in the early years of Jacob's life. Now, I was ready to move on.

However, when Nina wrapped things up, I suggested she give me a printout of her materials, and I would take them with me when I saw Senator Allen at two o'clock.

"Oh yes, I'll be glad to do that. I'm sure he'll be interested in it. The next thing I have for you is what I found out about Dexter Bodine. Since you didn't call me about him last night, I bet you already know this, but I found an obituary on him in the *Bakerton Gazette* in 1997. I haven't found the cause of his death yet, but I hope he wasn't that relevant to your case since you won't be able to interview him."

"In reality, Dexter was pretty relevant to what happened to Senator Allen in Bakerton, but Shelby Conway was able to fill in most of the blanks for me. Shelby's the one who told me Dexter passed away."

"So tell me what you learned about Amanda and what happened after the senator stopped off in Bakerton to spend the night."

I briefly went through the case with her, but she was content at only hearing the highlights, so it didn't take me that long.

When I finished, she said, "It's still a shame you didn't get to interview Dexter. To me, he's a missing piece of the puzzle."

"You're right, but I'm confident I have the overall picture of what happened, and I'll be surprised if it's not enough to satisfy Senator Allen. If you don't mind, though, I'd like to change the subject from Jacob Walker and talk about Trudy Phelps now."

She frowned. "You didn't want me to do research on Trudy Phelps, did you? I just thought you wanted more information on her client list."

"That's right. I don't care about Trudy. I just want to know why one of her detectives is running surveillance on me, and I assume he's doing it for one of the clients at her agency."

"In that case," Nina said, turning her laptop around so I could see the screen, "take your pick from Trudy's clients."

Nina had a list of a dozen clients who'd signed up for Trudy's executive services with her detective agency, and as I went down the list, only one name popped out at me.

Fiona Burkhart, the journalist.

Once I saw the name, I got up from the table and walked over to my desk to retrieve the business card Fiona gave me.

"Well, are you gonna tell me what you're thinking, or do I have to guess?" Nina asked.

"If I made you guess, which one of those names would you pick?"

"Ummm. I'd go for Fiona Burkhart. She's the journalist who wrote that article about Senator Allen last Sunday, and I seem to remember you had some kind of run-in with her several years ago."

"I also saw her last Monday when I was leaving the senator's office. She immediately jumped to the conclusion he must have hired me to find evidence to refute the accusations she'd made against him in that article."

"So you think Fiona Burkhart contacted the Phelps Agency to have someone follow you?"

I punched some numbers in on my phone.

"I'm about to find out."

◆ ◆ ◆ ◆

But I didn't find out immediately. Fiona's phone went to voice mail, and I had to leave a message asking her to call me back.

After I thanked Nina for her help, she left and went back down to her office to put together the materials on BPD so I could take the packet to my meeting with Senator Allen.

Meanwhile, I transferred the pictures I'd taken of Shelby's basement to a flash drive to give to the senator, and then I started writing my final report on the Jacob Walker case for my files.

I was about halfway through by the time Fiona called me back.

"Hi, Mylas. I wondered if I might be hearing from you soon."

"Why would you wonder that?"

"Call it a reporter's instinct."

"I doubt if it has anything to do with your instincts. I'm guessing the agency you're using to gather information for your stories informed you their detective got burned by me on two separate occasions, and you knew I'd eventually trace him back to you. By the way, his name is Lewis Bond, and I know he works for Trudy Phelps."

She let out a low chuckle. "I'm impressed, Mylas. Not because you spotted someone following you, but because you connected the dots so quickly. That was fast work."

"I can't take all the credit. I have an incredible staff working for me, but even so, I have a lot of questions for *you*."

"What a coincidence. I have a lot of questions for you too. Perhaps we should get together so we can come up with some answers."

"I'm not sure that's necessary. You can probably answer this question right now. What did you hope to accomplish by having me followed?"

She gave an exaggerated sigh. "Oh, Mylas. That is such a complicated question, and as I'm sure you know, complicated questions don't have simple answers."

"On the contrary, it seems like a fairly simple question to me."

"Yes, but what may seem like a simple question can quickly lead to something more complicated. Like for instance, I was curious where you might start looking to refute the claims I'd made against Senator Allen in my article, so I had you followed to answer that simple question. But then, that's where things got complicated."

"You had no basis to even ask that question in the first place, Fiona. The accusations you made against Senator Allen were so ridiculous, there was no reason for him to hire me to refute them, so I have no idea how things could have gotten complicated when you had me followed."

"Things got complicated when I learned you made a trip to EnViron Industries in Waterford on Tuesday, but all you did was sit in the parking lot for twenty minutes."

"Perhaps I parked there because I realized I was being followed, and I wanted to figure out why."

"Yes, I actually thought that might be the reason, so I was prepared to forget the whole thing, but then I received some new information yesterday after you had lunch with someone at Romanos."

"What kind of new information?"

"When Trudy's staff did an analysis of the photographs taken by her detective at Romanos, they discovered one of the men having lunch at Romanos yesterday—and I have reason to believe he was your lunch date—is employed at EnViron Industries. His name is Jacob Walker. Does that name ring a bell with you?"

"Even if it did, there'd be no reason for me to discuss him with you. He may or may not be a client of mine, and as you well know, I don't discuss my clients with reporters."

"Actually, I think I have a very *good* reason for you to discuss Jacob Walker with me."

Whether it was the serious tone in her voice, or the way she emphasized "good," I suddenly had a sinking feeling in the pit of my stomach. "I can't imagine what that would be."

"The reason I think you should discuss Jacob Walker with me is that I have it on good authority that Jacob Walker had a phone conversation with Senator Allen during that lunch, and in that call, the senator talked about keeping their relationship a secret. At one point, I understand he referred to how he met Jacob's mother. Now obviously, I don't have all the facts about this situation or about their relationship, which is something I would certainly want to do before I wrote anything about it. That's why I suggested the two of us should get together and share some answers with each other."

Since I couldn't believe Jacob was the source of Fiona's information, I could only think of one other person—Simon the waiter—whose wallet was probably a little fatter after divulging what he overheard in that conversation.

Unfortunately, I had no choice what to do next.

"I commend you for wanting to get your facts straight, Fiona, and I'll be more than happy to get together with you so I can clarify whatever your source told you. My schedule is pretty tight today. Would tomorrow morning be soon enough?"

"Sure. Where would you like to meet?"

"Why don't we meet here at the Greystone Center?"

"That's perfect. Shall we say ten o'clock?"

"That works for me. I'll let my receptionist know you have an appointment. She'll show you to my office."

"I think we'll both find the meeting beneficial, Mylas."

Interesting?

No doubt about it.

Beneficial?

To be determined.

♦ ♦ ♦ ♦

By the time I arrived at Senator Allen's office suite in the Russell Building, I hadn't made up my mind at what point during our meeting I should tell him about my conversation with Fiona Burkhart.

There was no doubt I'd have to tell him.

Before leaving my office, I tried to call Lockett to get his advice about when he thought I should discuss my conversation with Fiona but I didn't get a chance to talk to Lockett because my call immediately went to voice mail.

In the end, I did something I should have done when I was trying to make my decision, and as I was walking down the hall toward the senator's office, I breathed a short prayer and asked for guidance.

I was glad to hear the senator sounded upbeat when I knocked on the door. "Come on in. It's open."

As expected, I also found Lockett inside.

He was sitting on the couch, and the senator was standing behind his desk, looking as if he might have just hung up his phone.

While he was greeting me, he also motioned me over toward the chair I'd occupied when I'd been in his office on Monday.

I nodded at Lockett as I sat down, and he gave me a big smile. It was the kind of smile I'd seen on his face when I was head of the R & I Group and he knew I was about to give the senator some good news.

"Nathan told me you've completed your investigation, and you have some answers for me," the senator said, sitting down next to Lockett. "I can't tell you how happy I am to hear that. I'm not sure what's been harder on me—keeping this secret from my wife and kids, or not being able to see the son I never knew I had."

"I assure you, Jacob is just as anxious to meet you in person as you are to meet him. Have you spoken to him on the phone since you talked to him at Romanos yesterday?"

"Yes, I talked to him last night and again this morning. He seems to fully grasp the importance of not saying anything to anyone until I call a press conference and make a formal announcement of our relationship."

"Personally, I'm glad to hear that," Lockett said. "I have no doubt he knows he could call up some tabloid reporter right now and get some big bucks for the kind of information he has."

"I don't believe Jacob is the kind of person who'd do something like that," I said. "His motivation seems to be to get to know Davis Allen and to have a relationship with him and his family."

"That's the feeling I get from him too," the senator said.

"Even so, Senator, I think you should know Nina's research on Jacob yielded more information about his financial situation than I had the other day, and while he's not underwater yet, he's headed in that direction. Nina can give you that information if you want it."

The senator pursed his lips and looked away from me for a moment. "Ummm. Let's hold off on that for now. I'd rather be able to tell Jacob I'm not aware of his finances, and perhaps offer him assistance by providing him with housing or something along those lines. You know I've got that townhouse in Georgetown my relatives use when they come to visit us in Washington. I was actually thinking about suggesting he move in there, rent free of course."

"That's very generous of you," Lockett said.

He waved his hand dismissively. "It's the least I can do. Once I tell my wife about Jacob, I'm sure she'll want to do even more."

The senator gestured at me. "Well, what did you find out, Mylas? I trust I'll be able to tell my family, as well as my constituents, I wasn't a willing participant in Amanda becoming pregnant with Jacob."

I nodded. "Yes, I believe I've been able to determine that, although I'm sure the evidence I have will not be as convincing to some as it will be to others."

"Oh, I assure you," the senator said, "when I make my announcement, there'll be plenty of people out there who'll insist I've been keeping Jacob a secret, and there will even be some who believe I have other children I've refused to claim, or that I'm an outright scoundrel, morally unfit to hold public office."

"I believe if we handle the announcement correctly," Lockett said, "we'll keep those voices to a minimum. However, it's imperative we control the narrative from the very beginning. As soon as we hear from Mylas, we'll need to start planning how we can do that."

I pointed over at the senator's laptop on his desk. "Before I get started, do you mind if I grab your laptop so I can show you some pictures I took while I was in Bakerton?"

FIVE DAYS LOST: A Mylas Grey Mystery

"No, of course not. Go ahead."

"In the meantime," I said, opening my briefcase and removing Amanda's diary, "I'm sure you'll be interested in seeing this."

The senator took the diary from me with both hands, staring down at its faded cover as if he might be having second thoughts about opening it and reading what was inside.

However, by the time I returned to my seat with his laptop, he'd opened it to the first page.

"Would you prefer to take a few moments to go through the diary before I tell you what I discovered in Bakerton?" I asked.

He closed the cover. "No. I want to hear what you have to say first."

"Then I'd like to suggest you flip over to the back page of Amanda's diary and take a look at the photograph she pasted there."

He did as I suggested, and a few seconds later, when he saw the photograph of Amanda in her white pharmacist's coat, he nodded.

"Yes, that's Shirley, all right. That's exactly how she looked when I was introduced to her in the diner in Bakerton, except of course, she wasn't wearing that coat from Marston's Pharmacy, and she wasn't calling herself Amanda."

"Well, Senator, that's where the story of how you lost five days in Bakerton actually begins. It begins at Marston's Pharmacy."

Chapter 23

It took me thirty minutes to explain to Senator Allen what my investigation uncovered regarding what happened to him from the moment he walked in the Black Bear Diner to when he checked out of the Roadside Inn five days later.

I began by showing him the passages in Amanda's diary where she talked about compounding her own sleep medication and the entry where she said she was making plans to become pregnant.

After I turned to the section in her diary where she wrote about counting on someone named D. B. to help her carry out her plans, I told the senator I was able to locate a former employee of the Black Bear Diner named Tootsie Taylor who said those initials belonged to Dexter Bodine. I also described her recollection of Dexter, and what she remembered about Amanda's unstable personality.

Tootsie's description of Amanda seemed to surprise the senator, but then I went over what Jacob told me about his mother's mental issues, and as it turned out, the senator said he'd heard of Barringer's Personality Disorder.

He said one of his legislative assistants had recently prepared some materials on mental health issues for him so he could talk about them during a senate committee hearing. When he told me that, I decided there wasn't any need to show him Nina's research on BPD.

After we discussed Amanda's condition, I told him when he met Amanda at the diner that evening in 1985, she was living with a man named Shelby Conway.

"I went to see Shelby," I said. "He's in his sixties now, but he still lives in the same house where he and Amanda were living together."

The senator sat up a little straighter. "You spoke to him? Was he involved in Amanda's scheme?"

After assuring him Shelby was out of town at the time and was definitely not involved in what happened to him, I told him about Amanda purchasing a red wagon for her future child and storing it in the basement at Shelby's house.

"Oh, really? So do you think that means I was also there?"

"Well, Senator, there's no way of knowing that for sure. Amanda and Dexter are both dead now, and they're the only ones who could have answered that question with any certainty."

"Not necessarily. I was there. Or at least it sounds like I was there, and then there's that DNA evidence that proves Amanda and I had a child together."

"You're right, of course, so in a nutshell, here's what I think happened to you when you came into the crowded diner that night, and the hostess asked you if you'd mind sharing a table with someone."

The senator leaned back against the sofa cushions and listened without comment while I went through the sequence of events.

"I believe Amanda was at the Black Bear Diner that evening hoping to have an encounter with someone and become pregnant. Of course, her thinking was skewed by her mental condition and the betrayal she felt when she found out Shelby cheated on her. I think she realized he wasn't interested in marrying her and giving her the family she craved, so she intended to get pregnant and leave Bakerton for good.

"Dexter was her willing accomplice in this scheme, but I have no way of knowing if he was incapable of recognizing her sickness, or if he just didn't fully comprehend what she intended to do. You said Amanda wanted you to talk about yourself during dinner, and I suspect once she realized you were a smart guy with a bright future, she recognized you were the perfect candidate to father her child. To make sure you were compliant, she may have given you too much of the drug she had mixed up at the pharmacy, and that's why you barely made it to the motel room before falling asleep.

"There's no way to know what made her decide to move you out of that motel room and over to Shelby's house. Maybe that was her intention from the beginning, or perhaps she panicked when she realized she'd given you too much of the drug, and to keep you alive, she needed to move you somewhere so she could keep you hydrated until the drugs wore off or she figured out an antidote.

"At some point during those five days, I believe she and Dexter loaded you into his van and drove you over to Shelby's house, where they put you in the basement. Amanda writes in her diary that she didn't have to work the week Shelby was out of town, and according to Shelby, he saw evidence Dexter was at the house during that time."

I held up the flash drive containing the photographs I'd taken in the basement of Shelby's house. "Shelby allowed me to take these pictures of his basement, and I'd like you to take a look at them. I think it's possible the dreams you had were actually recollections of the time you spent sleeping off the drugs in a corner of his basement."

I placed the laptop on the coffee table in front of the couch, and Lockett and the senator both leaned toward it as I scrolled through the different images.

When I got to the one I'd taken of the basement wall where Shelby thought the red wagon had been stored, the senator held up his hand.

"Wait a second, Mylas. None of those other scenes look familiar, but that one . . ." he paused and pointed at the image, "yes . . . that one, well uh . . . it gives me a really funny feeling."

He continued staring at it for a moment, and then he looked up from the laptop and said, "Do you recall what I told you about my dream? I said I remembered someone saying, 'Wagons should be filled with kids. They shouldn't be gathering dust.' Well, that immediately popped in my mind as soon as I saw that basement wall."

I shook my head. "I'm sorry, Senator, but I'd forgotten you told me that. Yes, that makes sense now, and from what I've found out about Amanda, I believe it's something she would say."

I went through a few more things in the diary, plus I explained my theory of why Amanda called herself Shirley—although I pointed out it was pure speculation on my part that Amanda used Shirley as a code word to send a signal to Dexter—and then I closed the laptop.

"Well, Senator, I don't know about you, but I'm satisfied with the scenario I've put together of what happened to you that night in Bakerton. To me it's the only explanation that makes sense with the facts we've been given, and I also believe it explains why you don't remember much of it."

"I agree," he said, nodding his head. "Naturally, I wish I knew what drug Amanda gave me, or maybe I should say, what combination of drugs she gave me, but yes, I'm satisfied with your investigation."

"It rings true to me too," Lockett said, "but now the hard part comes. How much of this do you want to make public?"

"That's the hard part, all right," the senator said.

"While that's a decision for you to make, Senator," I said, "I'd like for you to keep in mind that Shelby Conway and his family still live in that house in Bakerton, and if you disclose that location, you'll make his life miserable for several months, maybe even longer."

Senator Allen rubbed his forehead. "Yes, you're right, and no, we can't do that to him or his family."

"Not to worry," Lockett said. "We'll figure something out. The main thing—like I said before—is for us to control the narrative. Personally, I'd like to suggest a two-prong approach. Besides having a press conference where you'll read a statement and introduce Jacob—if he's agreeable to doing that—then I'd also like to set up an exclusive interview with one of the cable news networks or print journalists, someone who'll let you tell your story, but who won't be seen as particularly sympathetic to you."

As soon as Lockett mentioned journalists, I figured it was time for me to deliver my bad news about Fiona Burkhart, but then it suddenly occurred to me how it might not be such bad news after all.

"I guess this is as good a time as any to tell you about an unfortunate phone call I had to make today."

◆ ◆ ◆ ◆

Both men looked concerned when I told them I was followed when I drove over to Waterford to check out EnViron Industries, and also when I met Jacob at Romanos for lunch.

"At the time, I didn't think whoever was running surveillance on me had anything to do with Jacob, but when I found out the guy who was following me worked for the Trudy Phelps Agency, I asked Nina to get me her client list, and that's when I discovered Fiona Burkhart uses Trudy's agency to run investigations for her."

Senator Allen didn't just look concerned now, he was visibly shaken by this news.

I motioned toward him. "I figured Fiona was still under the impression you hired me to dispute the ridiculous claims she made against you in her article, so I called her before I came over here this afternoon. My intention was to tell her there was no point in having me followed, but that's when she dropped a bombshell on me."

The senator shook his head. "I don't think I wanna hear this."

After I relayed the gist of the conversation I had with Fiona, I said, "I believe someone at the Phelps agency bribed the waiter who served Jacob and me at Romanos, and he's the source of Fiona's information. Whether the room was bugged, or if he was able to overhear your conversation with Jacob, I'm not sure, but in the end, Fiona's journalistic antenna is on full alert for a story."

"You mean a scandal, don't you?" Lockett asked.

"That too. Naturally, I had to agree to have a meeting with her to discuss what she thought she knew, so she's coming to my office tomorrow morning at ten o'clock. I figured that would give us enough time to come up with a plan of how to handle her questions."

"I'm sure she's already drawn her own conclusions," the senator said.

"You could be right, but I was thinking it might be advantageous to both you and Fiona if I could offer her an exclusive interview with you after you made the announcement claiming Jacob as your son."

"What? Are you kidding me? Why would I do that?"

Lockett held up his hand. "No, wait a minute, Senator. I think Mylas has a good point there. Fiona already suspects something is going on between you and Jacob, and we don't want her coming up with the wrong story or disputing the facts you'll be presenting at your press conference, so offering her an exclusive interview with you will probably keep her from doing that."

"Yes, but if I sit down with her and give her permission to ask me questions, that's bound to give her legitimacy with my constituents, as well as the public."

"She'll also be aware of that," I said. "When we spoke the other day, she was bragging about how far she'd come in her career, so if she doesn't recognize the opportunity you're giving her, I'll be sure and remind her of it."

Lockett said, "It could be a win-win for both of you, and after she wrote that derogatory article about you, no one can say you chose a reporter who was already in your corner."

Senator Allen shrugged his shoulders. "Okay, I'll do it. I trust your judgment on this, Nathan, but I want to do it before I have the press conference, which we're doing on Saturday, aren't we?"

"Yes, so why don't we have Mylas arrange for Fiona to show up at my house tomorrow night around nine o'clock, and you can do the interview after you've had a chance to visit with Jacob. You said you were planning to tell Nelda and your kids about Jacob tonight, so the timing shouldn't be a problem."

"No, the timing shouldn't be a problem, but I want us to start working on my statement right away, so that when I meet with Fiona tomorrow night, I'll have the script clearly in my head."

Lockett immediately pulled out his phone and said he would have Claudia Dyer, the senator's press secretary, join them so they could get started on the statement, and as soon as he got off the phone with her, I told him I knew he didn't need for me to be present for that, so I'd be on my way.

As I was about to close my briefcase, I saw the documents on Barringer's Personality Disorder that Nina had prepared, so I handed them to Lockett. "You might need Nina's research to explain Amanda's behavior when you're preparing him for the press conference."

He smiled as he took the papers from me. "Let me guess, Mylas. You'd prefer not to take these documents back to your office and have Nina find out you didn't give them to Senator Allen."

I raised my hands. "You caught me."

♦ ♦ ♦ ♦

As I was driving home after leaving Capitol Hill, I was congratulating myself on the way I handled the Fiona Burkhart situation with Senator Allen when I suddenly realized the idea of having her do the interview with the senator wasn't my idea at all.

It was God's way of answering my prayer for help.

I almost took credit for my idea again when I took Whitney to dinner at Fletcher's Steak House for our celebratory dinner, and she asked me how my meeting with Senator Allen went.

After telling her about Fiona Burkhart, and how I'd suggested to Senator Allen that she be the journalist to interview him about Jacob, she complimented me on coming up with the idea.

"Well, to be truthful, Whitney, even though I came up with the idea, I know I didn't think of it on my own. Just moments before I went into my meeting with Senator Allen, I asked God to help me know what to do about Fiona, so I have to give him all the credit for the idea popping in my head."

She nodded her head. "Well, I'm glad you recognize that. I've known people who've been Christians since they were children, and they seldom acknowledge their achievements are God's way of blessing them, or even that he's the one giving them their next breath."

"To be truthful, my first instinct isn't for me to think about God guiding me in what I do. It's just not natural for me. What's natural is for me to scheme, deceive, and figure out stuff on my own."

She laughed. "You and everyone else in the world."

She reached over and squeezed my hand. "Is that why you arranged for me to be the photographer for the church's brochure? Was this a scheme you and Nathan came up with to convince me I ought to move to Washington?"

I put her fingers up to my lips and kissed them. "Well, kinda sorta. It was Nathan's idea, but I was eager to go along with it. So did it work? Would you consider relocating here?"

"I would only do it for one reason."

"Hmmm. What would that be?"

"To be near you, of course."

"Sounds like a good enough reason to me."

Chapter 24

Friday, January 14

Even though I offered to have Joe drive Whitney anywhere she wanted to go or even to give her the keys to the Mercedes and let her do some exploring on her own, she told me she was content to spend the morning reading in the Library while I was at the office.

The Library was what Mrs. Higbee called my upstairs living room.

It made perfect sense because it was lined on both sides with built-in bookshelves packed with books.

I stopped in there to tell Whitney goodbye before I left for the Greystone Center, and when I did, I found her curled up on the sofa reading a whodunit with Babe sprawled on the floor at her feet.

"Are you still okay about going to dinner at Nathan and Diana's house tonight?" I asked.

"Yes, I'm fine with it, although I admit I'm still a little nervous about having dinner with Senator Allen." She tucked a strand of her hair behind her ear. "Do you think his wife will also be there?"

"I really don't know. He was supposed to tell his family about Jacob last night, so I can't believe Nelda—that's his wife's name—wouldn't be there so she could meet Jacob in person."

"How well do you know her?"

"Not that well, but she's always been very nice to me. Unlike a lot of politicians' wives, she doesn't enjoy the limelight. In fact, she refuses to campaign with him, and Diana told me she said she'd be happy if her children didn't follow in their father's footsteps."

Whitney shook her head. "I can't help but wonder what her reaction was last night when her husband told her he had another child. That must have come as quite a shock."

"I can't even begin to guess, but I have a feeling she'll handle it just fine. She's not nearly as concerned about public opinion as her husband is, and from the short amount of time I've spent with Jacob, I'll be surprised if she doesn't find him to be a likable guy."

"You can probably guess I'm also looking forward to meeting Jacob."

I leaned down and gave her a kiss. "I'm sure everyone will find *you* extremely likable."

My actions caused Babe to immediately jump to his feet and demand equal attention.

I gave him attention but not a kiss.

◆ ◆ ◆ ◆

When I arrived at the Greystone Center at nine-thirty, I came in through the back entrance and bypassed the lobby, but as soon as I got to my office, I phoned downstairs and told Kendall I was expecting Fiona Burkhart for a ten o'clock appointment.

Even though I didn't ask Kendall to do it for all my appointments, this time, I asked her to escort Ms. Burkhart up to my office personally.

"Ms. Burkhart is a reporter, Kendall, so don't be surprised if she asks you a dozen questions and is curious about everything going on here at the Greystone Center. I'd prefer that you only give her general answers and don't volunteer anything personal."

"Gotcha. I know who she is, Mr. Grey, so I'll be on the alert for her tactics."

"Good enough."

I spent the next fifteen minutes preparing some materials for Fiona's visit, and when Kendall knocked on the door, I slipped everything inside a manila folder and left it on my desk.

After inviting Fiona inside, I thanked Kendall for escorting her upstairs, and once she made sure Fiona's back was turned, she gave me an eyeroll before heading back over to the elevators.

I wasn't exactly sure what that look meant.

"Well, Mylas," Fiona said as she walked in, "if your intention was to show potential clients you run a first-class operation, then you've succeeded. I have to say you've got a beautiful building here, and whoever decorated it did an excellent job."

"Thanks, Fiona. My decorator was Inez Flora."

"Yep. First-class all the way."

I motioned her toward the seating area. "Have a seat. Could I offer you a cold drink or perhaps some coffee?"

She nodded as she sat down on the couch. "I'll take some bottled water if you have it."

I brought two bottles of cold water over to the seating area, and after handing her one, I twisted the cap off the second one and sat down in a purple wingback chair across from her.

She motioned toward the painting above my head. "I'm no art connoisseur, but I'm betting that piece set you back a pretty penny."

Whether Fiona was just making small talk before getting down to the matter at hand, or her intention was to ferret out information so she could add some detail to an article she might write on me later, I wasn't sure, but I decided to respond as if it were the former.

"Yes, the price tag on it was substantial, but I was told it was from an up-and-coming young artist, and it would keep its value for years to come. However, I'm not an art connoisseur either."

"Maybe not, but you're a top-notch investigator, and even though I mistakenly thought Senator Allen hired you to get information to dispute what I wrote about him, I still believe I was right about him hiring you to run an investigation for him."

"Yes, Fiona, you *were* right about that."

Her eyes widened at my admission. "You're confirming that?" She grabbed her iPad out of her handbag. "Did I hear that right?"

"Yes, I'm confirming it."

She opened the tablet and touched an icon. "Does that mean you're prepared to tell me about this investigation?"

"Possibly. It depends on whether you're interested in having a one-on-one exclusive interview with Senator Allen before he calls a press conference tomorrow to make a big announcement."

I could almost see the wheels in Fiona's head begin to spin.

"I'm sure you already know the answer to that. Of course, I am."

"Yes, I thought you might be open to speaking exclusively to the senator. You should know that one of the conditions for the interview is that you—"

"I don't do interviews that have restrictions or pre-conditions."

"This isn't exactly a pre-condition, and there are no restrictions, but the interview has to take place this evening, and the other condition is that you can't publish it until after Senator Allen holds his press conference tomorrow."

"You want to do the interview tonight? Uh . . . okay, that'll work. Can I assume the senator will answer any questions I have about Jacob Walker, and he'll also be willing to discuss anything else my source at Romanos told me?"

"That's correct. Can Senator Allen assume you'll agree not to publish the interview in any medium—TV, print, online—until after his press conference tomorrow?"

She nodded. "Yes, you have my word the interview won't be released until after his press conference."

"In that case, if you're interested, I'm willing to give you some background information to help you prepare your questions for the interview tonight."

She looked up from her iPad where she was making a notation. "You mean strictly background information? You're not talking about questions you want me to ask him?"

"Strictly background. No questions. From our conversation the other day, I suspect you'd rather be known as a serious journalist instead of some scandal sheet reporter. If that's true, then this interview will go a long way toward helping you achieve that objective. That is, if you treat the senator fairly and without bias. In other words, if you follow the advice you gave me."

She let out a low chuckle. "You mean my advice about laying aside any preconceived ideas you have about the senator?"

"Yes. If the snippets of information you gave me yesterday are any indication, I'm guessing you have some preconceived ideas about what's going on with Senator Allen."

"Well, yeah. Who wouldn't?"

"I urge you to lay those aside. I'm confident Senator Allen will be fully transparent with you."

"I'm sure it doesn't surprise you I'm not in agreement with Senator Allen's policies on certain issues."

"No, it doesn't surprise me, but if you want to be the type of journalist who's respected for rising above politics and presenting the news without bias, then this interview is your chance to prove that."

"You wouldn't be trying to work a little psychology on me there, would you, Mylas?"

I gave her a smile. "Maybe a little."

"Let's get to it then. What kind of background information do you have for me?"

◆ ◆ ◆ ◆

I went over to my desk and grabbed the manila folder, which contained some materials on ancestry websites, their popularity, and what kind of results to expect.

Although DNAHeritage was one of the sites listed, I didn't single it out when I told her she might want to read about the various services they offered before her interview with Senator Allen tonight.

"Very interesting, " she said, "but you're not going to tell me why you want me to read this information?"

"No, but I guarantee you'll find it beneficial when you sit down with the senator. Something else you might want to look into before tonight is Barringer's Personality Disorder; that is, unless you already know about it."

"No, I've never heard of it," she said, typing on her iPad. "Is there anything else?"

"That's it."

"So where am I gonna do this interview? At the senator's office?"

"No. Senator Allen will be at his chief of staff's house for a dinner party this evening. It should be winding down around nine o'clock, so if you show up then, he'll be ready to speak with you. I went ahead and put Nathan Lockett's address there in the folder."

"Yes, I've got it here. I don't suppose it would be okay if I showed up earlier so I could attend the dinner party."

"Only if you want to have this exclusive interview with Senator Allen cancelled. If so, then by all means, show up at seven. Otherwise, be there at nine."

She slipped her iPad back in her handbag. "I'll be there on the dot at nine o'clock."

As I was walking her over to the door, she said, "You know, Mylas, I have a feeling the two of us could work together pretty well. My contract with the Phelps Agency is over in a couple of months. I might give you a call then and see what my options are."

"Sure, Fiona, give me a call. I'll assign my associate, Leslie Irving, to handle your contract personally."

She looked a little disappointed when she walked out the door.

◆ ◆ ◆ ◆

When Whitney and I arrived at Lockett's residence on Berryhill Road, there were already four cars in his driveway, but there weren't any news vans on the street or other obvious signs the media had been alerted to anything newsworthy taking place.

All the vehicles looked familiar to me.

Three of them belonged to members of Senator Allen's staff—Claudia, his press secretary, Donovan, one of his legislative aides, and Toni, Lockett's secretary.

The fourth vehicle, a black Cadillac Escalade, belonged to Senator Allen.

There was no sign of Jacob Walker's white Honda SUV.

Diana greeted us at the door and after she gave Whitney a hug, she pointed us toward the living room.

"Everyone's in there having appetizers while we wait for Jacob to arrive. I'll join you as soon as I finish checking on things in the kitchen."

When Whitney and I walked in the living room, Lockett rushed over to greet us, and then he went around introducing Whitney to everyone, even Senator Allen, whom she met on her last visit.

After the senator told her it was nice to see her again, he introduced his wife Nelda, who was gracious to Whitney, although her smile didn't look quite as bright as it usually did.

Moments later, the senator walked over to where I was standing by the entryway. "How did you think your meeting with Fiona Burkhart went this morning? Nathan told me she agreed to do the interview."

"I could be wrong, Senator, but I really think she'll treat you fairly and if she—"

I stopped in midsentence when the doorbell rang.

Neither of us made a move.

"I think you should be the one to answer it, Senator."

"Yes, you're right, Mylas. I should answer it."

He walked over and turned the knob, and father and son saw each other for the very first time.

Chapter 25

To say Diana's dinner party was a success wouldn't do it justice. The food was excellent—standing rib roast with oven-roasted potatoes, creamed spinach au gratin, and homemade rolls—plus the guests were entertaining, and there was a surprise at the end.

The surprise at the end was the arrival of Fiona Burkhart.

No one on the Senator's staff knew she was coming except for Claudia, and when the doorbell rang at precisely nine o'clock, I noticed Claudia immediately retreated to a far corner of the living room as if she couldn't stand the thought of being in the same room with Fiona.

Her actions were understandable.

As Senator Allen's press secretary, she was responsible for fielding questions about the derogatory article Fiona had written about the senator, and from what Nathan told me, she wasn't in agreement with the decision the senator made to allow her to interview him about Jacob.

When Fiona arrived, Senator Allen, Nelda, and Jacob were still sequestered in Lockett's study, and since I was responsible for making the arrangements for the interview, Lockett suggested I answer the doorbell.

"Good evening, Fiona," I said, "you're right on time."

"Of course, I am. That doesn't surprise you, does it?"

"Not at all. Why would you turn down an opportunity like this?"

"If someone else had offered it, I might have turned it down, but I believe you're someone who delivers on his promises."

"That's always my intention, but like most people, there are times when I don't live up to my intentions, even the best of them."

"Well, Mylas," she said, touching me lightly on the shoulder, "I'll let you know if this interview doesn't deliver on what you promised."

Lockett was standing in the doorway of the living room as Fiona and I entered the foyer, and after I introduced him, he offered to take her back to his study, where he told her Senator Allen was waiting.

Before they left, I motioned for Whitney to join me, and when she came over, I put my arm around her and said, "Fiona, I'd like for you to meet a very special friend of mine, Whitney Engel. She's here visiting me from Columbia, Missouri."

Fiona appeared flustered for a moment, but then she offered Whitney her hand and told her how pleased she was to meet her.

I didn't believe her for a second.

◆ ◆ ◆ ◆

After they disappeared down the hallway, I asked Whitney if she was ready to leave, and when she indicated she was, we thanked Diana for her hospitality, told everyone else good night, and headed for the front door.

Before we got there, Claudia asked Whitney to wait a second, and while the two of them were having a brief conversation, Diana took the opportunity to pull me aside. "How are things going between you and Whitney?" she asked. "Do you think she's enjoying herself?"

"Things are going great, and yeah, I think she's having a good time."

"She seemed very comfortable here tonight."

"That's what I thought too."

At that moment, Whitney walked up, so we told Diana goodnight once again and headed out to my car.

Once I pulled out of the driveway, I asked Whitney, "Well, how did you enjoy your first dinner party in Washington?"

"It was a lot of fun. What surprised me was how down-to-earth everyone was, especially Nelda. I knew she had to be dealing with a lot of emotions, but she still seemed interested in my photography business, and she even wanted to know where I lived in Columbia."

"What was your impression of Jacob?"

She laughed, "If there was anyone at the party who seemed more nervous about being there than I was, it had to be him. I have a feeling he's still in shock about what's happened to him."

"That's exactly how I felt, but he seemed to loosen up when the senator began asking him questions about his responsibilities as the Government Affairs Director at EnViron."

"Yes, now that you mentioned it, he did seem more relaxed after that. He still looked overwhelmed, though. The only person I saw talking to him besides you and Senator Allen was Nelda."

"I can tell Nelda's a little tentative about him, but I think the two of them will become friends eventually." I glanced over at her and smiled. "Speaking of friends, you and Claudia seemed to have struck up a friendship."

"Yes, I enjoyed meeting her. She grew up in St. Louis, and even though we didn't go to the same high school, we discovered we were both photographers for our high school yearbooks."

"It looked like she was giving you her business card as we were leaving."

She chuckled a little. "Yes, Mr. Private-Investigator-who-doesn't-miss-anything, that's what she was doing. I was planning to tell you about that, but then I got sidetracked talking about Jacob. The reason she gave me her card might surprise you."

"Okay, I'm prepared to be surprised."

"She told me if I ever wanted to get a job in Washington, I should let her know because she has a lot of contacts with public affairs people who are always needing a photographer."

I gestured at her. "I hope you're not thinking I put Claudia up to talking to you about that. I haven't said a word to her about you. In fact, I seldom have an occasion to talk to her about anything."

She was quiet for a moment.

"Well then," she finally said, "when we get back to your house, I think we need to talk."

Oh, no.

Whenever a woman said we needed to talk, I got worried.

♦ ♦ ♦ ♦

It took several minutes after Whitney and I got back to my house before we sat down in the Library to have our talk.

That's because we had to answer Mrs. Higbee's questions about the dinner party and assure her we didn't need anything to eat.

And besides that, we had to let Babe welcome us back home as if we'd been gone for several weeks during our four-hour absence.

When I joined Whitney on the couch in the Library, she smiled and said, "There's no need to have that serious look on your face, Mylas. I think you're gonna like this talk."

"Okay, that sounds promising."

"Do you remember when I told you a couple of days ago that when I prayed about coming to see you in Washington I felt like I was supposed to do that and that while I was here, God would work everything out for my good?"

"Sure, I remember. You said that was the house you were living in."

"Well, since I've been here, I've had a big photography assignment that I've thoroughly enjoyed, I've been able to meet lots of interesting people, and tonight, I found out there would be plenty of photography assignments for me if I lived in Washington. And to make that even better, the person who told me about that possibility didn't even know I was considering moving here."

"Wait. Did I hear that right? Are you considering moving here?"

"Why do you look so surprised? Haven't you been dropping hints about me moving here from the moment I arrived?"

"Those weren't hints. I thought I made myself perfectly clear. I'd love for you to be here so we could see each other as often as possible."

She reached out and touched my face. "I want that too, Mylas, so when I get back to Columbia, I plan to call a realtor about putting my house up for sale, and once I finish up the appointments I have on my schedule, I won't be booking any new ones." She shook her head. "I know you realize this, Mylas, but this will be a really big move for me."

I leaned over and gave her a kiss. "Of course I do, Whitney, but you won't need to worry about a thing. I can arrange everything for you. I'll rent you a studio, and then I can use my contacts to—"

"Whoa. Hold on a minute, Mylas," she said, putting one hand on top of the other to form a T. "Time out. If I'm going to do this, I need to do it on my own. Besides, I won't need a studio when I first move here. I can work out of my house, or my apartment or wherever I'm living. I'm not saying you can't make some calls for me, but I'd rather do as much as I can for myself."

"Oh sure, I get that."

"I know finding a place in Washington is probably difficult, and since you know the city so well, I'll need your help with that for sure."

"Consider it done."

I wrapped my arms around her and pulled her close to me. "I can't tell you how excited I am for you. And yes, for me too. I love you, Whitney, and I believe we have a future together."

"I love you too, Mylas, and I also think we have a future together, but we really don't know each other all that well yet, and that's why I'm willing to move halfway across the country. I want us to be sure this is God's will for our lives before we commit ourselves to each other."

"The sooner you get moved here, the sooner we can work on that. So would you like to start looking for a place to live tomorrow? You'll be here another week, won't you? We could spend that time finding the perfect location for you."

She laughed. "Okay, that's fine. But didn't you say you had new cases to work on next week?"

"Yes, but I'm sure I can do both."

And I did.

Never The End, Always A Beginning

ACKNOWLEDGEMENTS

Although many people have given me support and encouragement in the process of writing *Five Days Lost*, first and foremost, I wish to thank my husband, James, and my daughter, Karis, who have never failed to uplift me with their prayers, strengthen me with their love, and bolster me with their confidence. Next to my Lord Jesus Christ, there is no one I love more.

I also wish to thank everyone who's given me advice, made suggestions, offered comments, and answered questions about ancestry sites, DNA results, and compounding drugs.

A special word of gratitude goes to Lenda Selph and Kim Kemery, my incredible editor/proofers, and to all my beta readers, whose eye for detail continues to provide me with invaluable insight. You're the best!

Last, but not least, I want to thank you, my faithful readers, who never stop asking me, "When is your next book coming out?" You are my inspiration, and the reason I stay up writing past midnight.

A NOTE TO MY READERS

Dear Reader,

Thank you for reading *Five Days Lost,* Book V in the Mylas Grey Mystery Series. If you enjoyed it, you might also like the other books in the series, *One Day Gone, Two Days Taken*, *Three Days Clueless*, and *Four Days Famous,* plus my other two series, The Titus Ray Thriller Series, featuring CIA intelligence officer, Titus Ray, and the Silas McKay Suspense Series, featuring Silas McKay, operations officer for Discreet Corporate Security Systems in Dallas, Texas.

You'll find an excerpt from *One Night in Tehran*, Book I in the Titus Ray Thriller Series, on the pages that follow. All my books are available in print, eBook, and audiobook exclusively on Amazon.

The next book in the Mylas Grey Mystery Series, *Six Days Spent,* is due for release at the end of 2023.

Would you do me a favor and post a review of *Five Days Lost* on Amazon? Since word-of-mouth testimonies and written reviews are usually the deciding factor in helping a reader pick out a book, they are an author's best friend and much appreciated!

Would you also consider signing up for my newsletter? You'll find a signup form on my website, **LuanaEhrlich.com**, where you'll be offered a FREE book in the Titus Ray Thriller Series just for signing up for my newsletter.

One of my greatest blessings comes from receiving email from my readers. My email address is **author@luanaehrlich.com.** I'd love to hear from you!

Excerpt from

One Night in Tehran

Book I in the
Titus Ray Thriller Series

PROLOGUE

In far northwest Iran, a few minutes after clearing the city limits of Tabriz, Rahim maneuvered his vehicle onto a rutted side road.

When he popped open the trunk of the car to let me out, I saw the car was hidden from the main highway by a small grove of trees. In spite of our seclusion, Rahim said he was still anxious about being seen by a military convoy from the nearby Tabriz missile base.

For the first time in several hours, I uncurled from my fetal position and climbed out of the vehicle, grateful to breathe some fresh air and feel the sunshine on my face. As my feet landed on the rocky terrain, Rahim handed me a black wooden cane. I wanted to wave it off, but, regrettably, I still needed some help getting around on my bum leg.

Rahim slammed the trunk lid down hard.

"You can stretch for a few minutes," he said, "but then we must get back on the road immediately. Our timing must be perfect at the border."

Rahim and I were headed for the Iranian/Turkish border, specifically the border crossing at Bazargan, Iran. He was absolutely confident he could get me out of Iran without any problems.

However, during the last twenty years, I'd had a couple of incidents at other border crossings—Pakistan and Syria to be precise—so I wasn't as optimistic.

While Rahim was tinkering with the car's engine, I exercised my legs and worked out the stiffness in my arms. As usual, I was running through several "what ifs" in my mind. What if the border guards searched the trunk? What if the car broke down? What if we were driving right into a trap?

I might have felt better about any of these scenarios had either of us been armed. However, Rahim had refused to bring along a weapon.

Carrying a gun in Iran without a special permit meant certain imprisonment. Imprisonment in Iran meant certain torture, so I *certainly* understood his reasons for leaving the weaponry back in Tehran.

Still, a gun might have helped my nerves.

I was surprised to hear Rahim say I could ride in the front passenger seat for the next hour. He explained the road ahead was usually deserted, except for a farm truck or two, so it seemed the perfect time to give me a brief respite from my cramped quarters.

I didn't argue with him.

However, I thought Rahim was being overly cautious having me ride in the trunk in the first place—at least until we got nearer the Turkish border.

I'd been passing myself off as an Iranian of mixed ancestry back in Tehran, and now, having grown out my beard, I didn't believe a passing motorist would give me a second look.

When I climbed in the front seat, the cloying smell of ripe apples emanating from the back seat of Rahim's vehicle was especially pungent. Flat boxes of golden apples were piled almost as high as the back window, and the sweet-smelling fruit permeated the stuffy interior of the car. On the floorboard, there were several packages wrapped in colorful wedding paper. I was sure they reeked of ripe apples.

We had been back on the road for about twenty minutes when Rahim said, "Hand me one of those apples and take one for yourself, Hammid."

Although Rahim knew my true identity, he continued to address me by the name on my Swiss passport, Hammid Salimi, the passport I'd used to enter Iran two years ago.

Unfortunately, it was now a name quite familiar to VEVAK, the Iranian secret police, who had already prepared a cell for me at Evin Prison in northwest Tehran.

After we had both devoured the apples, Rahim rolled down his window and threw the cores down a steep embankment.

"When you get back inside the trunk," he said, "you'll have to share your space with some of those." He gestured toward the apple boxes in the backseat.

I glanced over at him to see if he was joking, but, as usual, his brown, weather-beaten face remained impassive. Although I'd spent the last three months living with Rahim's nephew, Javad, and learning to discern Javad's emotional temperature simply by the set of his mouth or the squint of his eyes, I'd barely spent any time with Rahim. During the last two days together, he'd never made any attempt at humor, and it didn't appear he was about to start now.

I protested. "There's barely enough room for me back there."

"It will be snug with the boxes, but you will fit," he said. "If the guards open the trunk, I want them to see apples."

I felt a sudden flash of anger. "Before we left Tehran, you told me they wouldn't open the trunk at the border. You said they wouldn't even search the car."

My voice sounded harsh and loud in the small confines of the car.

However, Rahim calmly replied, "They will not search the car, Hammid. They have never searched inside. They have never searched the trunk. It is only a precaution."

He turned and looked directly at me, his penetrating black eyes willing me to trust him. It was a look I instantly recognized. I had used that same look on any number of assets, urging them to ferret out some significant nugget of intel and pass it on to me, even though I knew the odds of their being caught were high.

He returned his eyes to the road. "Surely you're acquainted with making minor changes as a plan evolves."

I took a deep breath. "You're right, of course." I suddenly felt foolish at my amateur reaction. "Planning for the unexpected is always smart. The more precautions you want to take, the better it will be for both of us. I'm sorry for questioning you."

For the first time, I saw a brief smile on his face. "There's no need to apologize," he said quietly. "The last three months have been difficult for you. Your paranoia is understandable."

Rahim shifted into a lower gear as we approached a steep incline. When we finally rounded a curve on the mountainous road, our attention was immediately drawn to two military vehicles parked on the opposite side of the road about one-half mile ahead of us. Several men were standing beside two trucks. They were smoking cigarettes and looking bored.

"It's not a roadblock," I said.

"No, we're fine."

Suddenly a man in uniform, leaning against the front bumper of the lead truck, noticed our approach and quickly took a couple of steps onto the highway. He signaled for us to pull over.

"Say nothing unless they speak to you first," Rahim said. "My papers are inside the glove box. Do not open it unless I say, 'Show them our papers.'"

"I have no papers, Rahim."

He eased the car onto the side of the road. "I put them inside the glove box," he said, "but don't open it unless I tell you to do so."

As the military officer crossed over the highway toward our car, I watched the reaction of the men standing outside the two vehicles. Although the insignia on the officer's uniform indicated he was a captain in the Iranian Revolutionary Guard Corps (IRGC), the men traveling with him were not in uniform. However, that didn't mean they weren't soldiers.

In fact, as I studied them, I knew they had to be affiliated with some aspect of Iran's vast military organization. They wore nearly identical Western clothing, had short military haircuts, and all their beards were regulation trim.

No longer bored, the men appeared alert now as their captain approached our car.

To my surprise, Rahim was opening the door and getting out of the car before the captain spoke one word to him. His behavior went against one of my favorite tenets of tradecraft: never draw attention to yourself.

The soft-spoken man I had been traveling with for two days suddenly disappeared. Instead, a loud, fast-talking stranger took his place.

"Captain," Rahim asked, "how may I assist you today? Did you have a breakdown? What a lonely stretch of road on which to be stranded."

Within seconds of greeting the captain, Rahim threw his arm around his shoulders and walked him away from our car and back across the road. There, Rahim engaged in conversation with some of the men, and at one point, they all broke into laughter at something he said.

After a minute or two, I saw the captain draw Rahim away from the group and speak to him privately.

Although I could hear none of their conversation, I tensed up when the captain gestured across the highway toward me. As Rahim continued an animated conversation with him, they began walking back across the road together.

Arriving at the car, Rahim opened the back door and pulled out two boxes of the apples we were transporting.

"Here you are, Captain. Take two of these. I'll bring two more for your men. You will not find finer apples in all of Iran."

As the captain leaned down to take the apples from Rahim, he glanced inside the interior of the car, quickly taking note of the apples, the wedding presents, and the black cane I'd placed between my legs. Lastly, his scrutiny fell on my face.

I smiled and deferentially lowered my head toward him, greeting him in Farsi. He didn't respond, but Rahim was speaking to him at the same time, so I wasn't sure he'd heard me.

The captain was already walking back to the transport trucks when Rahim stuck his head back inside the car and removed two other boxes.

Our eyes met.

He nodded at me. I nodded back.

Everything was fine.

While Rahim was distributing the apples among the men, I took the opportunity to look inside the glove box. I found three items: Rahim's passport, his travel documentation, and a small handgun.

Presumably, the handgun was my documentation had the captain demanded it.

There was something about having a fighting chance that did wonders for my morale, and I found myself smiling.

I shut the glove box before Rahim returned.

I decided not to say anything to him about my discovery.

Without a word, Rahim got back inside the car and started the engine. As we drove past the captain and his men, several of them raised their apples to us in a goodbye salute.

"That was quite a performance, Rahim."

He continued to glance at his rear-view mirror until the group disappeared from sight.

Finally, he said, "The captain only wanted information on road conditions. He said he'd heard there were some rockslides in the area. One of the drivers was complaining about his brakes, and he was worried about the safety of his men as they made the descent."

"Who were those men? What unit did they belong to?"

"The captain didn't say, but their cigarettes came from Azerbaijan. That should tell you something."

Azerbaijan bordered Iran and was about six hours north of our location. Although it had once been a part of the Soviet Union, it was now an independent republic with close ties to Iran. Like most Iranians, the majority of the people were Shia Muslims. Tehran wanted to keep it that way. I'd heard rumors there was a unit of Iran's military specifically assigned to make sure the Sunni minority in Azerbaijan remained the minority. The unit in charge of such an operation was the al Quds force.

"Members of al Quds, then?"

"That's my guess. We've been hearing reports the Sunnis are growing in popularity. Tehran won't sit still while that happens. But that's good. Mossad likes it when Tehran is distracted."

"Why wasn't the captain interested in me?"

"I told him you were my father, plus you look harmless, Hammid."

It was true. I'd lost weight during my three-month ordeal, and since I'd spent the time indoors, my skin had taken on an unhealthy pallor. However, I doubted I looked old enough to be his father.

"I also told him you'd fallen in the orchard and injured your leg. He wasn't surprised at your reluctance to get out of the car, if that's what you're thinking."

I remembered the way the captain had inspected the contents of our car and his lingering look at my cane. He may have believed Rahim, but he had checked out his story anyway.

"You said you were on your way to your cousin's wedding in

Dogubayazit?"

"Yes, and if I hadn't given him the apples, he might have inquired further about the gifts."

He flicked his hand toward the wedding presents on the backseat floorboard. "Then, I would have insisted he take one or two of those gifts for his sister."

As in most Middle Eastern countries, bribes and "gifts" were a way of life among the people, especially with military and government officials. Nothing got done without them. If you made inquiries or requested help from any bureaucrat, they expected something in return.

"You were very generous with the apples back there. Will you have enough for your friends at the border now?"

I tried not to sound worried, but whenever I found myself involved in someone else's operation, I got nervous.

He was dismissive. "Yes, there will be plenty. Now help me find the turnoff road. It leads over to a lake, but the sign is hard to see. We'll make the switch there."

He slowed down, and we both concentrated on the passing landscape. The trees were dense, and the late afternoon shadows made finding the lake road difficult.

"I think it's coming up," Rahim said.

I pointed off to my right. "There it is."

He made a sharp right turn onto a dirt road leading through a canopy of trees. One-half mile down the road, a secondary road branched off, and Rahim was able to make a U-turn at the fork in the road. Then, he pointed the car back toward the main highway.

Rahim killed the engine, and after glancing down at his watch, he looked over at me. At that point, I knew I was about to be given The Speech, a last-minute review an operations officer usually gave to a subordinate before a critical phase commenced.

Technically, I wasn't a subordinate of Rahim's organization.

Still, I listened carefully.

"Remember the traffic at the border will move very slowly, and once I'm pulled over, I expect there will be a long wait. At times, you will hear loud voices. That's not a cause for worry. If you hear angry voices, especially my angry voice, you should start to worry."

He paused for a long moment. Then, he opened the glove box and removed the handgun I'd seen earlier.

He handed it over to me with an understanding smile. "I'm assuming you found this already."

I checked the chamber.

It was loaded.

"Thanks, Rahim."

"Any questions?"

"No. I'm confident you've thought of everything."

We both got out of the car, and I helped him remove some of the apple boxes so he could stack them in the trunk after I was inside.

Before climbing in, I said, "Rahim, please hear me when I say I'm grateful for everything you and Javad have done for me. Perhaps, someday, I can repay you."

Rahim placed his hands on my shoulders and looked into my eyes. "That will never be necessary, Hammid," he said. "It has been God's will for us to help you."

As I tucked myself into the trunk again, I found myself hoping it was also God's will for me to make it out of Iran alive.

PART ONE

Chapter 1

Bill Lerner looked like a worried grandfather when he patted me on my knee in the backseat of the Lincoln Town Car and asked, "What's your state of mind, son?"

Our driver, Jamerson, gave me a quick glance in the rearview mirror.

I knew Jamerson had probably heard Lerner ask other intelligence officers that same question whenever he escorted them from Andrews AFB to one of the Agency safe houses in the quiet residential neighborhoods around McLean, Virginia.

I could hear the uncertainty in my voice as I responded, "I'm not sure, Bill, but it's good to be home."

Lerner ran his hand over his military-style haircut and shot back enthusiastically. "You bet. We'll get you debriefed, fix you up with some good grub, and then you'll be ready for some R & R."

Lerner's conversations never varied much.

His job consisted of making sure I felt safe—both he and the driver were armed—providing a listening ear if I needed to talk, and being the first in a long line of people who would bring me, a Level 1 covert operative, back to some sense of normalcy.

Lerner gestured toward my left leg, which I'd been massaging as we drove along. "That giving you trouble?"

"Yeah, a bit."

Once again, Jamerson stole a glance at me in the mirror. What was up with this guy? Was it just curiosity or something else?

I tried to dismiss my paranoia as nerves, pure and simple.

For the past several months, I'd been living on the edge in Tehran. However, three days ago, with Rahim's help, I'd made my escape from Iran, crossing the border into Turkey without incident.

Nevertheless, because I couldn't just turn my instincts on and off like a water faucet, I continued to mull over Jamerson's interest in me.

Lerner pointed to a large house at the top of a winding lane. "Well, in these new digs," he said, "you'll have some state-of-the-art rehab equipment for that leg. Support purchased this little *casa* for a song during the housing bust." He laughed. "It's been remodeled to our specifications, of course."

I didn't laugh.

I was too numb.

We pulled in front of the "*casa*," which was at least a 10,000-square-foot house. It was surrounded by gigantic oak trees, and in the distance, at the back of the house, I spotted a large lake with a boat dock. As we pulled into the circle drive, I half-expected to see a butler and several uniformed maids appear at the front door to welcome the master of the castle home.

The house was well situated on several acres of forested land and located within a gated neighborhood of similar residences. I imagined most of the well-to-do owners had their own security systems. We had entered the safe house property through a remote-controlled sliding gate, and I suspected security cameras had been tracking us ever since.

"This one is called The Gray," Lerner said.

The name made sense. Instead of addresses or numbers, the Agency used color-coded names for their safe houses, and while the exterior of the house was blindingly white, the window shutters and the front door were painted a muted shade of bluish gray.

Previously, I had been debriefed in The Red. It was at least half the size of this one and had a red-tiled roof. There was no butler, just a slightly plump Italian cook named Angelina who had helped me gain back the weight I'd lost on a mission into Pakistan. The neighbors thought I was her son. The complexion I'd inherited from my father made it easy for me to pass myself off as an Italian, or even an Iranian of mixed ancestry.

Lerner got out of the car and headed for the front door. "Jamerson, get his kit from the trunk and meet us inside."

I took my time getting out of the car.

I paused to zip up the jacket of the tracksuit I'd been issued at the air base in Turkey, and then I leaned back inside the car and picked up the cane from the back seat.

All the while, I was keeping an eye on Jamerson. He grabbed the duffel bag given to me on the flight over from Turkey, and when he closed the trunk, our eyes met.

He motioned toward the front entrance with a slight nod of his head. "After you, sir."

I was almost six feet tall, and he was about my height, but, unlike me, he had a beefy body. I wondered how many hours he spent in the gym each day.

I hadn't seen the inside of a gym for years.

I hobbled toward the door, thankful Jamerson hadn't offered to help me.

In fact, if he had, I might have marshaled whatever strength I had left and slugged him.

Pride was a great energizer for me.

Lerner was already standing inside the giant foyer of the mansion, having keyed in the front door's security code beyond the range of my prying eyes. He was speaking in hushed tones to a middle-aged couple. I presumed they were the homeowners—at least to the other residents in the neighborhood.

After Jamerson had deposited my duffel bag on the floor, I asked him, "Ex-Marine?"

"Yes, sir."

"You served at the American Embassy in Iraq in 2008?"

There was no mistaking the pride in his voice. "Yes, sir. I'm surprised you even remembered me. You weren't in very good shape that day."

"How could I forget—?"

"Greg and Martha," Lerner said, interrupting our conversation, "let me introduce you to your newest houseguest."

As Lerner steered them in my direction, Jamerson gave me an understanding nod, and I turned my attention to the couple in charge of the safe house.

Greg was in his late fifties with a slight paunch around his middle and close-cropped gray hair. He smiled at me with a lopsided grin. His wife was petite, had short black hair and piercing blue eyes.

I shook their outstretched hands.

"Titus Ray," I said.

Martha's smile was warm. "Welcome home, Titus."

♦ ♦ ♦ ♦

Martha immediately took me on a "tour" of the house. It lasted almost thirty minutes.

On the first floor, besides the huge eat-in kitchen, dining room, living room, and den, there was also a study, a library, and a media room.

I was sure the basement level was like no other house in the area. Three rooms made up a mini-hospital with an operating table, x-ray apparatus, laboratory facilities, and a pharmacy. There were also fully equipped physical therapy rooms and a soundproof conference room, wired with state-of-the-art audio and video equipment.

Upstairs, along with the master suite occupied by Greg and Martha, there were six bedrooms. Security officers were in two of the bedrooms, but I was the only guest of The Gray at the moment.

As Martha escorted me to my room, she casually mentioned other facilities, so I suspected there had to be a safe room somewhere, plus a room for all the security and communications equipment. Those rooms were either located on the basement level, or in a part of the house I would have to discover for myself.

My bedroom was at the end of the upstairs hallway, the furthest from the master suite and next door to one of the security officers' rooms. As soon as Martha left me alone, I opened the wooden shutters and spent a few minutes appreciating the view.

ONE NIGHT IN TEHRAN

The manicured landscape included a large boulder waterfall with a cobblestone path running alongside it. I assumed the path led down to the lake. I suspected there might even be a tunnel from the basement right down to the dock and boathouse. Most safe houses remodeled by Support had secret exits somewhere.

Within an hour of my arrival, Greg appeared at my bedroom door. He informed me I was scheduled to see Dr. Terry Howard in the basement "hospital" for a physical.

It would not be my first encounter with Terry Howard.

Howard and I had met when I was recruited by the CIA in 1980 in the middle of the Iran hostage crisis. My time at The Farm, the CIA's training facility at Camp Peary in Williamsburg, Virginia, had been full of surprises, one of which had been a case of appendicitis.

About two hours into a three-day training exercise, I had noticed a slight pain in my right side. Howard, who had just completed his residency at Massachusetts General Hospital in emergency medicine, was a member of our four-person squad, and when I popped a couple of aspirin, he started to suspect something was wrong with me.

However, our team had come in last in our previous exercise, and as the team leader, I was determined it wasn't going to happen again, so I kept ignoring my discomfort.

The task took place in and around Raleigh, North Carolina, and involved locating a human target, eliminating the hostiles—another squad of trainees—and delivering the target across a "border." The border in this case was the Virginia state line.

By midnight of the first night, as my team and I were meeting together in a cheap motel on the outskirts of Raleigh, I started vomiting.

After one such trip to the bathroom, Howard ignored my feeble objections and pushed on my belly. He ended his exam by asking me some ridiculous questions. Finally, he announced I was having an appendicitis attack and wanted me to check into a hospital.

I angrily disagreed and insisted on completing the task first, so Howard backed off for a couple of hours. However, after the four of us determined the location of our target, my pain became noticeably more intense.

At that point, Howard started hammering me with the facts of a burst appendix.

His lecture convinced me to work out a compromise with him.

Without informing anyone at The Farm, Howard took me to the ER at Duke Raleigh Hospital and made arrangements with a surgeon to remove my diseased organ. From my hospital bed the next day, I continued to direct our mission, using one of the team members as my messenger.

On the third day, our target was secured, so the team picked me up from the hospital, and we made our run for the border.

Unfortunately, we came in second.

However, none of our trainers ever found out about my emergency appendectomy. The only time they questioned me was before my initial overseas assignment. Then, the examining physician noticed my scar and remarked that someone had failed to enter my appendectomy on my medical records. At that point, I backdated the operation's date, and that was the end of it.

After our training, Dr. Terry Howard had been assigned to the Middle Eastern desk. I'd seen him a few times since then, twice for debrief exams and once in Kuwait when he was called in to examine some high-value targets before we started interrogating them. Now, since he was the attending physician at The Gray, I assumed he was assigned to Support Services permanently.

After Greg escorted me to the elevator, I told him I could make it the rest of the way on my own. Even though Greg's assignment included keeping an eye on me, he didn't voice any real objection to my small gesture of rebellion. However, as the elevator doors began to close, I noticed he hadn't moved. To reassure him, I gave him a small wave goodbye before the doors completely shut.

When I entered the exam room, Terry Howard was fussing over a set of empty vials used to draw blood; his head was bent low, trying to read the labels with a pair of bifocals perched precariously over his nose.

"Hey, Doc, how are—"

He juggled two of the vials, almost dropping one of them. "Aaagh! Titus, you startled me."

ONE NIGHT IN TEHRAN

"Sorry. I thought you heard me." I waved my cane in his direction. "This thing makes a lot of noise."

"No, it doesn't," he grumbled. "And don't bother apologizing. I remember how you used to like sneaking up on people."

Terry Howard had reached his late fifties with a full head of hair, no wrinkles—except for a few lines across his forehead—and he still had the slim physique he'd had when I first met him.

His grumpy demeanor remained unchanged also.

"You don't look good at all," he groused, wrapping the blood pressure cuff around my arm.

"Well, I need a haircut."

He grunted and continued taking my vitals, making meticulous notes as he probed and prodded. Lastly, he examined what had been my busted left leg.

"It was bad, huh?"

"They said I shattered my femur and tore all the knee ligaments. It wasn't pretty."

He shook his head. "With that much damage, you were either in a car accident or playing in the NFL."

"I jumped off a very high roof. Forgot to tuck and roll."

"That would do it."

Even though he had the security clearance to do so, Howard didn't question me about the particulars of my injury—that would be the job of my debriefers. He inquired relentlessly, however, about the functioning of every part of my body.

Finally, he put his hand on my knee and gave it a twist. "Did that hurt?"

The pain was excruciating.

"Ouch. Yeah!"

"Good. Maybe the surgery didn't damage your nerves too badly."

I tried massaging the pain away. "What kind of test was that?"

He ignored me and pointed to my cane. "You'll need a few weeks of rehab to get rid of your little crutch there," he said. "After that, I can't guarantee you won't continue to have some pain, but, as I recall, pain was never a big deal to you anyway."

He reached over and touched my appendix scar.

"I'll never forget how infuriated you were with me during that training run in Raleigh when I told you your appendix was about to burst. I've never seen anyone so enraged before."

Before I could protest his recollection of events, he asked me, "Have you learned to control that temper of yours yet?"

I wanted to give him a flippant answer, but in light of the decision I'd made one night in a tiny living room in Tehran, I decided to reply with the truth.

"I'm really trying, Doc, really trying."

Chapter 2

They left me alone for three days. At first, I figured it was because I'd arrived on Friday, and all my debriefers wanted to have a long weekend.

Later, I found out it was because Gordan Bolton—the Agency's chief of station in Turkey and the first person to greet me when Rahim released me from the trunk of his car in Dogubayazit—had suggested my bosses give me a few days off to decompress before starting my debrief.

I did nothing on Saturday except eat, sleep, and become familiar with the house. Every time I showed up in the kitchen, Martha fixed me a huge meal.

For his part, Greg stayed as close to me as possible, moseying with me through the kitchen, the media room, the library, just keeping an eye on me, but willing to engage in conversation if I felt like talking.

I didn't.

I met Jim and Alex, the security officers.

Jim was an outgoing type of guy, and like me, he was in his late forties, although his thick brown hair was already turning gray. The left side of Jim's face was disfigured by a two-inch scar running from his eye socket to his ear. However, he exuded self-confidence.

His attitude reassured me because I felt shrouded in a blanket of uncertainty.

Alex, who appeared to be in his early thirties, had curly blond hair, an acne-scarred face, and deep-set blue eyes. He barely spoke to me when we were introduced, and I had the distinct impression my presence made him nervous.

His reaction was understandable.

Covert operatives coming in from a failed mission tended to make Agency people skittish.

◆◆◆◆

After waking up on Sunday morning, I took my mug of thick black coffee outside, stared at the pool and gardens, and finally started asking myself some serious questions about my future.

Did I want to stay covert? Would I even be allowed to do so? After what happened in Tehran, were they going to offer me a desk job—analyst or such?

I thought about that for several minutes.

I decided I'd go crazy if I wasn't allowed out in the field.

The night before I'd left Tehran, Javad had asked me a question. I had answered him truthfully. However, what did that mean for my career now?

I was surprised by my feelings of helplessness and insecurity.

My emotional tenor reminded me of a time, ages ago, when Laura had left me for another man. I'd felt just as vulnerable then. Our divorce was one of the driving forces behind my accepting an offer to come to work for the CIA in the first place.

Did my life need to take a different turn now? Was it time to leave the Agency?

Praying about these questions felt like something I ought to do.

I bowed my head.

Nothing came.

Prayer wasn't a familiar practice in my life.

◆◆◆◆

By midmorning, I was getting antsy, and even though I was officially quarantined at The Gray until my debrief was over, I briefly considered leaving the house for a couple of hours.

I knew that the Agency's quarantine restrictions—no outside communication, television, or internet—were in place to preserve the integrity of the debrief. However, as much as I agreed with this concept in principle, trying to obey such rules always proved to be an entirely different matter altogether.

Despite my restlessness, though, I discarded my escape plans.

Instead, I wandered into the library, where I found a variety of reading choices on the shelves. There were the classics, lots of "how to" books—so I could learn about installing a toilet or making a PowerPoint presentation—and some contemporary fiction. I also found a whole shelf of religious books and different versions of the Bible.

I finally selected *A Tale of Two Cities*, *The Cambridge Guide to Astronomical Discovery*, and a Bible.

Then, I slipped off to my room.

Greg knocked on my door around one o'clock and asked me if I wanted some lunch. I followed him downstairs and into the kitchen where Martha was slicing up some roast beef.

When she saw me, she immediately picked up a remote control and turned off the flat-screen TV mounted on the wall in the breakfast nook.

Fox News Sunday was playing.

After putting down the remote, she looked over at Greg and silently mouthed an apology, "Sorry."

He waved her off.

He must have thought I hadn't heard anything.

Chris Wallace had been asking someone about Iran's nuclear program.

Alex was perched on a stool at the kitchen island wolfing down a sandwich. He gave me the once-over, nodded his head, and left the room.

Greg grabbed the vacant stool, and I sat down next to him.

Martha placed a big roast beef sandwich in front of me, along with a small bowl of potato salad. "Thanks. This looks great."

She acknowledged my compliment with a smile. "You want lemonade again?"

My mouth was full, so I just nodded. A few minutes later, she placed a large icy glass in front of me.

"Greg, can I get you something?" she asked her husband.

"I'll take a cup of coffee."

After she handed him a mug, a knowing look passed between them, and seconds later, she made an excuse and left the room.

A few minutes after she left, Greg removed a sheet of paper from his shirt pocket. "Here's the schedule for your debrief tomorrow," he said. "It looks pretty straightforward. I know you've been through this drill several times."

I took the schedule and stuffed it inside my jeans pocket without looking at it.

"You like working for the Agency, Greg?"

I wasn't sure whether it was my question or the fact I was beginning to talk, but Greg smiled when he gave me his answer. "Yes, yes, I do."

He took a sip of his coffee then gestured at his surroundings. "Obviously, this is a pretty cushy job."

"Did you ever go operational, work in the field?"

His eyes shifted slightly to the left, and he hesitated a moment before answering. I had no doubt he was weighing whether it was more important to keep me talking or follow Agency rules. He decided on the former.

However, he sounded apologetic when he answered me. "Only Level 4 action, but Martha was Level 2. We met at an Agency in-house party and got married six months later."

"So you had to transfer to Support services after you were married?"

"Yeah. There were some options, but . . ." he looked over at me, then up at a camera mounted in the ceiling, "you know how difficult it would have been to live any kind of normal life, much less see each other, if either of us had stayed in Operations."

I agreed. "It wouldn't have worked."

He nodded his head, drained the last of his coffee, and walked over to the sink, carefully rinsing out his cup.

"Did Martha have a hard time adjusting?"

Looking perplexed, he asked, "Adjusting?"

"You know. Did she miss . . ." I struggled to find the right words, "her sense of purpose about what she was doing?"

He thought about my question for a moment. "I don't think she missed the ops at first. We couldn't really talk about it, of course, but I suspected her last assignment had gotten a bit ugly. I'm sure that made the change easier." He shifted uncomfortably. "Look, Titus, you know we aren't supposed to—"

"Did she stop believing?"

There was no mistaking the anger in his voice. "Believing? You mean did she stop believing her actions were helping her country?"

"No, of course not. I'm talking about that inner calling that—"

An alarm went off—a steady *beep, beep, beep*.

Suddenly, at that moment, Jim burst through a door off the kitchen. I had just assumed the door led to the pantry.

Assumptions can get you killed.

Beep. Beep. Beep.

Jim motioned toward me. "Follow me."

Beep. Beep. Beep.

As I headed in his direction, Martha and Alex rushed into the room.

Beep. Beep. Beep

Alex quickly walked over to a wall console and entered some numbers on a keypad.

The beeping stopped.

Seconds later, the intercom from the security gate squawked. Greg started to answer it, but Jim motioned for Martha to take it.

She took a deep breath and pressed the button.

Calmly she said, "Yes."

The female voice on the other end was high-pitched and had a Boston accent. "Oh, Martha, it's me, Teresa. I just need to drive up and have you sign this petition. It won't take a minute. I hope I'm not bothering you and Greg."

Before hearing Martha's reply, Jim ushered me past the pantry door, through a false wall at the back of the pantry and into a large room. It contained a wall of security monitors, computers, and several different kinds of communications equipment.

On one of the monitors, I saw a very thin woman dressed in a pair of black slacks and a yellow blouse. She was standing outside the security gate speaking into the intercom. As I watched, she got back inside her Mercedes and waited for the gate to slide open.

Jim was watching the other video feeds from around the grounds, while also keeping an eye on a nearby computer screen as it rapidly scanned through thousands of images using the Agency's facial recognition software. As soon as a match for Teresa came up on the computer screen, he hit the button for the gate to open.

Speaking into his wrist mike, he said, "We have benign contact. Repeat. Benign contact."

Alex keyed back, "Copy. Benign contact."

Jim looked over at me. "She's just a neighbor. She called Martha earlier in the week to see if she would sign a petition to keep the city from cutting down a tree on the right-of-way. It's creating a traffic hazard." He shook his head. "Teresa's a champion of lost causes."

I took the chance to look around.

I felt sure the door on the opposite wall led to a safe room. Once a person was inside, the room could not be breached—at least not easily.

Jim glanced up at me. "Yeah, that's the safe room, but we're good right here. Martha knows how to deal with this situation."

We watched as Martha opened the front door and invited Teresa inside the foyer. They were smiling and chatting like actors in a silent movie.

Everything seemed fine, but I found myself wishing I were armed.

Along with Jim, I scanned the monitors showing the video from the grounds.

"Where's the feed from the pool house?" I asked, nervously.

He pointed to a split screen. "It's this one. It's shared with the feed from the garage."

We went back to watching the action on the screen, and I asked him to turn the audio on.

Martha and Teresa moved into the living room where Greg joined them. He was carrying a book, trying to look as if Teresa's arrival had interrupted his reading.

He and Martha sat down on the sofa, and using Greg's book for a hard surface, they signed Teresa's petition.

As they played out their deceptive scenario, I could see the differences in their operational styles firsthand.

Greg's face was stiff, devoid of any expression; his hand movements were jerky and nervous, and his voice was just a bit too loud.

However, Martha appeared relaxed, even comfortable, as if she were enjoying herself. Her body posture mirrored Teresa's movements, and she stayed in sync with Teresa's conversational pattern.

After a few minutes, Jim and I watched as the three of them walked toward the front door together.

"She's consistently good," Jim said. "Greg's always twitchy, though."

My nerves eased up, and I turned away from the security console and walked around the room, poking my nose into a wall cabinet, running my hand over some books on a bookshelf.

"The gun safe is downstairs."

I turned and smiled at him. "I'm that obvious, huh?"

"I've been in your shoes, that's all."

He opened the door to a cabinet and took out a pistol.

"I keep an extra firearm in here. It would have been yours if our security had been breached."

"Good to know."

He quickly put the gun back in its hiding place.

"You didn't hear it from me, though." He made a sweeping motion with his hand. "Of course, no one hears anything in here."

I made a mental note of that information. Since everything was being monitored throughout the safe house, at least the communications room was one place I could have a frank conversation without fear of blowback.

I turned my attention back to the monitors and watched Teresa pull her car into the street. When the gates closed behind her, Jim gave Alex the all clear.

I looked around the room one last time.

I said, "Well, I guess I'd better get back out there."

Jim flipped a switch to unlock the door leading through the pantry to the kitchen.

As I walked past him, he put his hand out to stop me.

"Look, Titus, I know I'm not supposed to know as much about you as I do, but there's always talk, you know that. Well . . . I want you to know, I'm here if you need anything or if you'd just like to talk to someone."

"Thanks, Jim."

I started toward the door, but then I turned back and said, "Could I ask you a question?"

"Of course."

"What's the most important thing in the world to you?"

At first, he seemed taken aback by my question.

Then, he quickly recovered and said, "I'd have to say it's my family. My wife and two kids mean everything to me."

I nodded.

"Why would you ask me that?"

"An asset asked me that question just before he was murdered."

He gave me a look of understanding.

"So, how did you answer him?"

"I never got the chance."

Chapter 3

On Monday morning, I awoke with a sense of relief mingled with trepidation—similar to the way I usually felt when I was about to embark on a new mission.

However, unlike most of my operations, my Agency debriefing should only take a couple of days—depending on who was on the debriefing team and how they were interpreting my narrative.

When I thought about who might be assigned to my debriefing team, I decided it was time to shave off my beard.

I also decided, after studying my face in the bathroom mirror, that Terry Howard was wrong; I didn't look that bad. Granted, I wasn't George Clooney handsome, but who was?

Years ago, someone had told me I was a pretty good-looking guy. Since then, no one had told me otherwise.

My trainers at The Farm had described my face as one that "blended." They considered that a good thing. Put me in a restaurant, a bus station, a mosque, and I blended right in. I didn't draw attention.

Only, as it turned out in Tehran, one time I did.

After taking a quick shower, I put on the clothing supplied for me by Support Services—a pair of dark slacks and a blue oxford shirt. My debriefers would be in very formal business attire, but I knew if I looked halfway decent and appeared to be in my right mind, that's all they expected of me.

Unlike Bud Thorsen—who had a nervous breakdown after a two-year stint in Yemen and had arrived at his debriefing sessions in his pajamas—I did not want a transfer to a desk job.

At least, I didn't think so.

After I got dressed, I tried praying again. Javad and his wife, Darya, had told me it was easy, just like talking to someone. They had often prayed for me while I was living with them in Tehran, and I suspected they continued to pray for me even now.

I bowed my head and told God I wasn't looking forward to spilling my guts at the debrief. I admitted I was uncertain about my future, and it was eating away at me, and I also asked him to help me control my temper. When I finished, I decided Javad was right—praying wasn't really that hard.

Because I had no desire to stand around and make small talk with any Agency personnel, I skipped Martha's breakfast and remained in my room until Greg knocked on my door.

Then, I headed down to the festivities.

◆ ◆ ◆ ◆

I arrived at the lower level conference room just as Martha was coming out the door.

She gave me a fleeting smile and whispered, "I left you some cinnamon rolls. Make sure you get some." As I held the door open for her, she added, "There's also a carafe of lemonade for you."

I whispered back. "Thanks."

Although the conference table in the room could easily seat ten people, only four chairs were occupied. Douglas Carlton, my official handler and the operations officer for my mission, was seated on the right side of the table all alone.

He would be in charge of the debrief.

He was reading from a stack of papers, and I knew he was probably studying the overnight cables. Carlton was someone who prided himself on being a "detail person," and he would inform everyone of this organizational attribute at least twice in every meeting.

Carlton was bald-headed with enormous brown eyes that grew larger whenever he disagreed with something being said. He was a meticulous dresser. Today he wore a gray, pinstriped suit, long-sleeved white shirt—with the hint of a cuff showing—and a pastel-colored tie adorned with tiny, silver geometric designs.

He looked like a Wall Street banker.

Ours was a love/hate relationship.

He caught a glimpse of me out of the corner of his eye and quickly got up from his chair and started toward me.

I met him halfway. He grabbed my outstretched hand and put his other hand on my shoulder, squeezing hard.

Speaking each word as if it were a sentence all by itself, he said, "So. Good. To. See. You." He pumped my hand for several seconds. "You look . . ." he paused and looked me over from head to toe, "amazingly well after all you've been through."

"I've gotten some rest," I said, "and I've been eating like a horse since I got here."

"Good." He pointed toward a credenza where an assortment of snacks and drinks were laid out. "Why don't you get yourself something to eat, and we'll get started."

As I turned to go, he patted me on the back. "I understand you didn't have any breakfast this morning."

Carlton always wanted you to know he knew more about you than you thought he did.

This personality trait accounted for the hate part of our relationship.

I grabbed a cinnamon roll and a cup of coffee and took my assigned seat at the head of the table.

Carlton was seated to my left. He was distributing stacks of documents to the other three debriefers who were seated across the table from him and to my right. They had not been speaking to each other when I entered the room, and they remained focused on other tasks as I sat down.

The farthest person from me was Katherine Broward, the Agency's chief strategic analyst. She was intent on texting or entering some information on her iPhone, and she had not turned her head or met my gaze since I'd entered the room.

Katherine was also dressed in a gray business suit, but, unlike Carlton, she wore a frilly red blouse underneath her jacket.

Since she had been with the Agency for less than 10 years, I put her age at around thirty-five, but discerning a woman's age was difficult for me. Discerning beauty, however, was an entirely different matter, and I knew Katherine was a very beautiful woman. She had long, honey-blond hair, green eyes, and a rather prominent chin.

At one time, Katherine and I had tried to have a relationship.

However, I'd only managed one lunch, followed by dinner a week later. Then, I was off to Afghanistan. I don't remember the excuse Katherine gave me when I asked her out upon my return, but I do remember thinking it was a very believable lie.

"Sorry, I'm late."

Every head turned as Robert Ira entered the conference room.

As I observed the look on Carlton's face, I realized he, like everyone else, seemed surprised to see the Deputy Director of Operations show up in person for the debriefing of a covert intelligence officer.

Carlton quickly got up from his chair. "Deputy Ira, this is a pleasant surprise. I didn't realize the Director was sending someone over for the debrief."

Ira placed a large black briefcase on the conference table. "I hope this isn't an inconvenience."

"No. No. Not at all," Carlton said. "Here, take this seat. I'll move over."

Ira eased his large bulky body into the chair just vacated by Carlton. Then, he opened his briefcase and rummaged around inside it a moment, finally removing a laptop computer.

The Deputy's pudgy face, combined with his stringy gray hair and bulbous red nose, made him appear more like a cartoon character than a high-ranking intelligence administrator.

However, I'd always suspected his looks were a bit of cunning camouflage for his devious but brilliant mind. In his position, an unappealing appearance went hand-in-hand with an unappealing job.

Robert Ira was the point man for the CIA's Director of Operations. He was sent out to look for operational and political minefields that could blow up in the Agency's face.

To that end, he was tasked with assessing the successes and failures of an operation and of evaluating its financial gains and losses.

His bottom-line reports to the Director were both feared and cheered. They could bring either curses or blessings on the agent involved.

I had been the recipient of both.

However, Ira seldom left Agency headquarters, preferring instead to sit in his office gathering data from operational officers, reading reports, making phone calls, and holding endless meetings. His presence at my debrief signaled someone was definitely worried about some aspect of Operation Torchlight.

Those worries were well founded.

Carlton cleared his throat and addressed the room. "First, I'd like to begin by making some introductions, then, I'll take care of the preliminaries, and finally," Carlton paused and glanced over at me, "we'll hear from Titus."

That was partly true. They would indeed hear from me, but I, in turn, would hear from them. That's the way an operational debrief worked: I would tell my story; they would ask me questions. Some of those questions would be intended to show how much they knew, and how little I really knew.

I didn't mind that.

I've never minded finding out what others thought I didn't know.

Carlton began his introductions.

"Titus, I believe you're already acquainted with Katherine." Carlton gave her a nod. She, in turn, gave me just the briefest hint of a smile. "You're also acquainted with Mr. Haddadi, who's here to help us with any language and cultural issues we might encounter today."

Komeil Haddadi had been a high-ranking scientist in Iran's nuclear program until five years ago when he had walked into the American Embassy in London and defected—much to everyone's surprise and delight. Carlton was a member of the team who had spent several weeks interrogating him, and I'd never heard Carlton call him anything but Mr. Haddadi. However, since the two of us had spent considerable time together two years ago, while prepping for my assignment in Iran, I'd always called him Komeil.

Komeil reached across the table and clasped my hand in both of his. "So good to have you back."

As Komeil gave me a broad smile, I was reminded of pictures I'd seen of the Shah of Iran. He resembled the Shah enough to have been his brother.

Carlton finished up his introductions. "Sitting next to Mr. Haddadi is Tony Fowler. He's our outside observer for this debriefing session."

Fowler was an African-American with square, wire-rimmed glasses and a short, neat haircut. I noticed he kept fiddling with his iPad, even while Carlton was introducing everyone.

I wasn't acquainted with Tony Fowler, but we exchanged perfunctory nods.

Because Fowler was the outside observer for my debrief, it didn't surprise me we'd never met before. In fact, had we known each other, he could not have been the outside observer.

All operational debriefing sessions were assigned a person from another division, someone who had not been involved in the mission itself and who did not know the covert intelligence officer being debriefed. The reasoning behind this rule was that an outside observer brought a new perspective and provided insights not otherwise apparent to the operational team. The Director had instituted this regulation at the urging of a congressional oversight committee ten years ago, but the responsibility for choosing the outside observer had been turned over to the DDO, Robert Ira.

In my opinion, outside observers asked far too many questions during a debrief. This slowed down the whole process and interfered with the intelligence officer's flow of thought in narrating the events of an operation. Such irrelevant interrogations primarily occurred because a debrief was an invaluable opportunity for an observer to delve into operations beyond his or her intelligence scope, giving that person a treasure trove of information. Such knowledge was highly coveted and served as a powerful commodity within the walls of the Agency.

Carlton turned to his left and addressed Ira. "Once again, let me say how privileged we are to have you in the room today, Deputy Ira. I believe you've met everyone here before?"

He smiled at Katherine and glanced briefly at the rest of us. "Yes, I have."

"I'll begin with the formalities," Carlton said, "and let me remind everyone that these sessions are being recorded."

Carlton cleared his throat yet again. When he spoke, his voice was slightly stilted.

"Session One. This is Operations Officer, Douglas Carlton, in the intelligence debrief of Titus Alan Ray, Level 1 covert operative for Operation Torchlight."

He pointed a finger in my direction. "Begin the narrative."

"Two years ago, I entered Iran on a Swiss passport. My cover name was Hammid Salimi, the son of an Iranian watchmaker and a Swiss businesswoman. My legend was solid. I was in Tehran to open up a market for my parent's line of luxury watches and jewelry. The contacts I made among the elite in the Iranian regime were to serve as the prime recruiting ground for a cadre of assets Operations hoped would help fund the Iranian opposition and topple the government."

Not surprisingly, Fowler was the first committee member to break into my narrative. However, his eyes barely left his iPad as he threw out his questions.

"Aren't most wealthy Iranians in lock-step with the regime?" he asked. "How was such an operation even feasible?"

Carlton responded immediately. "Yes, Tony, that's an excellent question, and it's one I'll be happy to answer."

Carlton picked up a set of documents on the table, although he didn't refer to them immediately.

"All our data pointed to a great disaffection among the upper echelon of Iranian society. We heard from a variety of sources," he gestured toward Komeil, "including Mr. Haddadi, who indicated that the elite in Iran might be willing to help the opposition, despite continually receiving incentives from the government."

Mr. Haddadi shifted in his chair and opened his mouth, but before he could utter a word, Carlton began reading from the set of papers he was holding. He'd chosen several sections describing the mind-numbing psychological details about the thinking of Iran's upper class.

As his voice droned on, I knew I wasn't the only person in the room feeling sleepy.

Finally, when I couldn't stand it any longer, I interrupted him. "I recruited four assets within six months and two more the next year."

Fowler looked up from his iPad.

I added defiantly, "It was obviously a workable operation."

Fowler peered at me over the tops of his glasses, studying me for a few seconds. Then, he said, "Duly noted."

Perhaps trying to lower the testosterone in the room, Katherine spoke up.

"Our product from these recruits was extremely beneficial," she said. "Not only was Titus able to penetrate this closed community, he was also able to gain access into—"

"Well, let's not get ahead of ourselves," Carlton said, obviously trying to regain control of the meeting. "Titus, continue the narrative."

I spent almost an hour explaining how I went about identifying my targets by developing business relationships, cultivating ties in banking circles, and socializing with the affluent in Iranian society. When I got into some of the more specific details of the money I was spending to live such a lavish lifestyle, Deputy Ira started rapidly typing on his laptop.

I did not take that as a good sign.

Katherine, probably thinking the same thing, asked a question that prodded me on to a different topic. "Titus, wasn't the purchase of your apartment the reason you were able to develop a friendship with Amir Madani?"

At the mention of Amir's name, Fowler's head shot up and Ira suddenly stopped typing.

I was puzzled at their sudden interest.

"Correct," I said. "I was sitting at an outdoor café with Farid, one of my recruits, when an acquaintance of his stopped by our table. Farid introduced his friend to me as Amir."

As I described my chance encounter with Amir, I noticed a slight tic had developed below Fowler's left eye.

"I immediately recognized the man as Amir Madani," I said, "one of Iran's nuclear scientists, so I decided to use Farid to see if I could get closer to him."

"How?" Fowler asked.

"Pardon me?"

"How were you able to recognize him?"

"Well, because . . ." I hesitated for only a split second, but it was just enough time for him to hit me with a barrage of other questions before I could finish answering his first one.

"Since your operational mandate was to cultivate assets to finance the opposition, what was your interest in this Amir?" he asked. "Your warrant didn't include targeting Iran's scientists, did it?"

I suddenly found myself extremely curious about Tony Fowler.

Because he was the outside observer on the committee, the position he held in the Agency was unknown to me. He could be employed in any section of Operations. Of course, everyone else in the room, except possibly Komeil, knew the name of his division.

For my part, I was beginning to suspect which door his key card might open. However, if I were guessing correctly, it meant someone at the Agency had deliberately sabotaged my mission in Tehran.

Carlton immediately spoke up. "Of course, I authorized it."

Fowler seemed stunned. "You did?"

For several seconds, Fowler seemed to be grappling for another question. Finally, he asked, "When?"

Carlton's eyes grew wider. "When? You mean you want the actual date?" A puzzled look passed over Carlton's face. Moments later, he looked over at Ira, as if hoping the DDO might be able to clear up his confusion.

However, the deputy immediately turned his attention to his laptop, ignoring Carlton's bewildered stare.

Fowler was adamant when he answered Carlton. "No, I don't want a date. I want a timeline."

Carlton shuffled through his notes. While I had no idea what was bothering him about Fowler's question, I could tell he was simply stalling for time.

Fowler continued questioning Carlton. "Did you authorize contact before or after Titus recognized him? I want to understand how it was that Titus knew this man in the first place. There are thousands of people walking the streets of Iran. It seems odd that he would be able to—"

"I showed him pictures," Komeil said, barging into the exchange.

Fowler looked surprised. "Why would you do that?"

"Look, Tony," I said, before Komeil could answer him, "Perhaps I should have explained how I went about preparing for this mission. My oversight may have caused you some misunderstanding, and I take full responsibility for that. Let me back up and tell you about my preparation for Operation Torchlight."

I noticed a smile flicker across Katherine's face, and I wondered if she knew I was simply trying to buy Carlton time to resolve his confusion.

Fowler removed his glasses and began massaging his temples. "Sure, why don't you do that?"

I launched into a myriad of details explaining how Legends—the branch of Support Services responsible for creating identities—had prepared my background, my credentials, and my entry into Iran. Then, I inundated Fowler with the kind of research I undertook prior to a mission. Finally, I described how Komeil and I had worked together to enable me a quick integration into Iranian society.

"I met with Komeil three times a week for two months," I said. "We only spoke Farsi when we were together. When we—"

"Why are you so fluent in Farsi?" Fowler asked. He sounded surprisingly accusatory. "Were you ever in Iran before this assignment?"

I turned to Carlton for approval. He gave me a dismissive wave of his hand. "Go ahead," he said, while continuing to look through his stack of documents.

"No, I had never been to Iran before this mission. And the language? It's just a gift. It doesn't take me long to acquire fluency in any language."

I started to elaborate about how many languages I spoke, but Fowler had no real need to know. An operational debriefing was not so much about the operative as it was about the operation. Tony Fowler was not cleared in this setting to know more about me than Carlton wanted him to know.

"Komeil briefed me on some prominent people I should get to know in Tehran," I said. "As I was studying the photographs of these people, I came across several group shots he had taken with some of his scientific colleagues while they were attending a conference together. We talked about their backgrounds, and that's how I recognized Amir Madani when I saw him that day."

I twisted open a bottle of water sitting in front of me and took a very long drink.

As I drank, Fowler appeared impatient, anxious for me to continue my narrative. I knew he wanted an explanation of why I'd decided to seek authorization to start courting Amir when my mission's objective didn't include contact with one of Iran's nuclear scientists. For some reason, such information appeared to be extremely important to him.

However, I placed the empty bottle of water back on the table and remained silent.

I waited for Fowler to ask me the question again. I needed to hear his exact words and sentence structure, to catch the nuance, and to watch his facial expression.

As the silence grew, Carlton made an elaborate show of checking his watch. "Titus," he said, "let's break for lunch and resume in two hours."

Carlton watched as Tony Fowler hurriedly left the room. Then, when the door slammed shut, he turned to Ira. "Deputy, could we have lunch together?"

I had no idea where the two of them were going for lunch, but wherever it was, I knew Carlton wasn't leaving there until Deputy Ira had served him up some satisfactory answers. When it came to getting answers, Carlton was like a kid bugging his mom for a new toy—he would never give up until he got what he wanted.

This personality trait accounted for the love part of our relationship.

Chapter 4

Since I wasn't allowed to leave the grounds until clearing my debrief, I took the plate of food Martha had prepared for me and escaped onto the patio, sitting at a table beside the Olympic-size swimming pool. It was a beautiful sunny day in April, and although the wind was chilly, I wanted the freedom of being outdoors too much to care about the temperature.

As I ate my chicken salad sandwich, I decided not to think about the dynamics occurring inside my debrief. Instead, I watched two groundskeepers cleaning out a flowerbed.

They appeared to be enjoying each other's company, laughing and talking together as they worked. However, the longer I watched them, the more I realized I wasn't just showing them passing curiosity.

On a professional level, I was assessing them, scrutinizing their movements, trying to determine if they presented any real danger to me. Since The Gray was encased in a secured environment, my obsessive exercise made me wonder if I'd been living the clandestine life too long.

Was it mentally healthy to be so suspicious? Was my wariness a sure indicator I needed to get out? Should I take the initiative and ask to be transferred to a desk job?

Yet, being a covert intelligence operative was the only thing I knew how to do, and I did it very well. I knew that.

As a kid growing up in Flint, Michigan, I thought I wanted to be a police officer or maybe an FBI agent.

My parents never discouraged me, nor, for that matter, did they encourage me to pursue law enforcement. In fact, my dad, Gerald, who worked on the assembly line at GM, didn't pay much attention to me at all.

In some ways, he was the typical alcoholic dad. He worked on the line all day, and then he drank himself to sleep every night. He wasn't mean, and he didn't mistreat my mom or my sister. He was simply emotionally absent from our family.

My mother, Sharon, who was a high school science teacher, relied on empirical evidence to explain her husband's behavior.

"When Gerald came home from Vietnam, he was a broken man," she often told people. "He saw way too many horrible things over there, and it's haunted him ever since."

Perhaps my father experienced the most horrifying aspects of that war, but he was never willing to talk to me about any of them, and I certainly tried often enough. As a young boy, I asked him endless questions about the Army. What was it like to be shot at? How did it feel to see someone die? However, his answers were always vague or monosyllabic. As a teenager, his attitude infuriated me, and we exchanged heated words on a regular basis. By the time I left for college, we were barely speaking.

As expected, my relationship with my father was a topic the Agency psychiatrists discussed with me when I applied for the CIA. At the end of those intense sessions, I finally realized my failure to bond with my father was the motivation behind my willingness to embrace Laura Hudson and her family.

Laura and I had met during my first month at the University of Michigan. Within a few weeks of being introduced, we were spending all of our time together, and during one weekend in November, she invited me home to meet her parents.

Roman and Cynthia Hudson were welcoming, gracious people. I was immediately drawn to them, especially Roman, who owned a hardware store in a strip mall in Ann Arbor and started calling me "son" as soon as we were introduced.

Instead of returning home for Christmas during my freshman year, I spent my entire two-week break with Laura's family in Ann Arbor. It was then I learned Roman had also been in Vietnam, but there was a big difference between him and my father—he was more than willing to talk about what he'd done over there.

The first time Roman had mentioned Southeast Asia was when Laura and I had stopped by the hardware store on Christmas Eve to see if we could help with the holiday rush. Laura's mother, Cynthia, was working as a cashier, so Laura had opened up another cash register, while I went to find Roman. I located him at the back of the store in the sporting goods section where he was showing a gun to a customer.

Because I'd never been around firearms before, I watched in awe at how easily he handled the weapon, stripping it down, explaining its features, and then putting the whole thing back together in the blink of an eye. Roman noticed my fascination at his expertise, and when the customer left, he immediately began telling me stories of his time in Vietnam working for the CIA.

Laughing at himself, he said, "They called us spooks back then."

For Christmas, he gave me my first weapon, a .22 revolver, and I spent the rest of the week at the gun range. The following year, during my Spring break, two important things occurred: I asked Laura to marry me and Roman gave me a Smith & Wesson .357 magnum.

I married Laura the following June.

For a wedding present, her parents gave us the down payment on a small house near the campus. However, between both of us going to school full time and working at our part-time jobs, I barely remembered living there. Besides that, I chose to spend most of my free time with Roman.

Roman not only continued teaching me everything he knew about weaponry, he also tutored me in the rudiments of the tradecraft he was taught during his brief time working for the Agency. I hadn't made a conscious decision to join the CIA yet, but before starting my junior year of college, I switched my major from business to international relations with a minor in languages.

By our second year of marriage, Laura was growing increasingly unhappy about my relationship with her dad. Even though I knew Laura hated all the time I was spending with Roman, I refused to change at all. When we would argue—which was often—I'd lose my temper and say incredibly cruel things to her.

Eventually, Laura found someone else.

The day she asked me for a divorce, she said, "You didn't fall in love with me, Titus; you fell in love with my dad."

She was right, of course.

At first, I blamed the failure of my marriage on my disappointing family life. Later, I realized when Laura and I had met, I'd been sinking in a sea of uncertainty. Then, out of the fog, Roman had appeared to me as a lighthouse, and I'd been drawn to him as my only means of rescue.

Perhaps not surprisingly, a week after signing the final divorce papers, I was talking to a CIA recruiter.

◆ ◆ ◆ ◆

After finishing up my sandwich, I went back inside and put my dishes in the kitchen sink. The room was empty, so I faced the ceiling camera, raised my arm, and made a circling motion with my forefinger. Within a few seconds, Jim came through the pantry door.

"Got a problem?" he asked.

"Just a question."

He gestured for me to follow him, and we went back to his lair in the communications room. As soon as he sat down in front of the security monitors, I saw him glance up at the feed coming from the kitchen video. He noted the time on a yellow pad.

Then he pointed toward a chair. "Have a seat."

The chair he indicated faced a wall of wide-screen monitors displaying video from several different news agencies. The headlines scrolling across the screens indicated something newsworthy was happening in North Korea, and I was sorely tempted to feast my eyes on every word and satisfy my curiosity.

However, I resisted. I knew I was about to break one of the house rules, and one broken rule a day was my self-imposed quota.

Jim looked amused when I repositioned the chair so I was facing him instead of the screens. "What's your question?"

"Before I ask it, I want you to know I'm assuming several things, which will be obvious to you when I ask the question. If I'm assuming incorrectly, and you don't want to answer the question, then know for certain I won't think less of you."

He considered my statement for a couple of seconds, and then he nodded. "Okay."

"Tony Fowler."

Jim blinked his eyes several times.

I continued with my question. "Have I been playing around in his backyard?"

This time Jim's reaction was to stare at me without blinking. He did this for what seemed like a long time, but it was probably only twenty seconds or so.

I knew he'd been monitoring the feed from the video in the debriefing room during the morning session. That was his job. He could also lose his job if he revealed the identity of the outside observer to me.

However, if Jim had truly "been in my shoes," as he'd indicated to me on Sunday, then he also knew the position I was in with Tony Fowler. He understood how valuable this little bit of information was to me as I continued my narrative in the afternoon session.

He continued to hold my gaze.

I waited.

"Yes," he finally said.

I suddenly realized I'd been holding my breath. "Thanks."

"No problem."

He pointed toward the security feed from the kitchen. "When you go back out there, I'll run this back and erase it when you move away from the kitchen sink."

"That should do it."

◆ ◆ ◆ ◆

I still had some time before my debrief was scheduled to resume, so I slipped upstairs to my bedroom. I needed a few minutes alone to get my head around what I'd discovered.

The information Jim had just confirmed for me was that Tony Fowler was head of the Nuclear Security Division (NSD). Now, it made sense why he had reacted so strongly when I'd mentioned meeting the Iranian nuclear scientist, Amir Madani.

Fowler's portfolio at NSD included running agents in any country seeking nuclear weapons, and he should have been well acquainted—at least by name—with all of Iran's nuclear personnel. Fowler's division had a number of covert operatives in Iran responsible for developing assets in their nuclear program. Perhaps one of them had even tried to recruit Amir.

Of course, from a geographic standpoint, having such a broad scope to his job description meant Fowler was required to co-ordinate his operations with other regional divisions. Otherwise, an operative from the Middle East Division and an operative from NSD might be targeting the same asset.

For example, imagine that Carlton had a covert intelligence officer in place in Tehran. Now imagine this officer had accidently met a nuclear scientist at a café and decided to develop him as an asset. In such a scenario, the correct Agency procedure called for Carlton to inform NSD of said encounter. However, Carlton could not just walk across the hall to the NSD and discuss the matter with Tony Fowler in person. No, the Agency would never allow such a direct communication between divisions. Instead, protocol called for Carlton to inform Robert Ira. Ira, in turn, was responsible for notifying Fowler and the NSD that an agent wished to pursue contact with a nuclear scientist.

If Fowler had no objection—such as he was pursuing the asset himself or had some information on him that precluded contact—Ira would then relay the message to Carlton, who would authorize his intelligence officer to develop the asset.

Now, the picture was becoming clearer.

Either Carlton had never notified Robert Ira of my request to pursue Amir—which was unlikely because Carlton had emphatically affirmed in the morning session that he'd authorized my contact—or Ira had never informed Fowler that a Middle Eastern operative was asking permission to target a nuclear scientist.

Thinking back on Fowler's behavior in the morning session, I came to the conclusion Fowler had not known about my pursuit of Amir as a CIA asset until I'd mentioned it. Was that the reason Robert Ira was at my debriefing? Had he failed to inform Fowler I was pursuing Amir Madani?

If so, why didn't the DDO follow the correct procedure and coordinate with Fowler's office on such a critical issue? For the whole field of operations to work smoothly, there had to be cooperation among the different divisions. Otherwise, operatives and assets would overlap, and it would be chaotic and dangerous for everyone, especially in a hostile environment like Iran.

Iran was one of the most difficult countries in the world in which to gather intelligence. Civilians and military personnel were taught—by the propaganda arm of Iran's elite Revolutionary Guards Corps—to be constantly on the alert for "infiltrators" and "enemies" who wanted to penetrate all aspects of society so they could exploit Iran's "secrets." In such an atmosphere, human intelligence gathering, especially in regard to Iran's nuclear program, was abysmal—so sparse as to be non-existent. Government agencies were forced to rely on satellite surveillance or the occasional defector, like Komeil Haddadi, to obtain even an inkling of what was going on inside Iran's nuclear community.

Such a shortage of intelligence had been foremost on my mind when I'd originally contacted Carlton about checking out Amir and possibly targeting him as a source. Since the NSD had done such a lousy job of finding and developing assets, now I wondered if Robert Ira had taken things a step further and simply cut the NSD division out of the loop entirely, never even informing Fowler that an intelligence officer—namely, me—had requested permission to pursue an Iranian scientist as a potential asset.

If my suspicions were correct and Ira had given Carlton the green light without informing Tony Fowler, then he'd blatantly disregarded crucial inter-division communication and had jeopardized my life. Far more importantly, his decision had contributed to—if not caused—the murder of my assets.

Now, I had a big decision to make.

ONE NIGHT IN TEHRAN

End of Chapter 4

To continue reading *One Night in Tehran*, you can visit the author's website, **www.LuanaEhrlich.com** and click on the link to purchase the book through Amazon or go directly to the Amazon website and enter the name of the book followed by the author's name.

Luana loves to hear from her readers. Contact her through her email: **author@luanaehrlich.com**.

Printed in Great Britain
by Amazon